SHIPROCK BABY

I0591406

R. Bruce Logan

Black Rose Writing | Texas

ISBN: 978-1-68433-938-9
PUBLISHED BY BLACK ROSE WRITING
www.blackrosewriting.com

Printed in the United States of America
Suggested Retail Price (SRP) $19.95

Shiprock Baby is printed in Gentium Book Basic

*As a planet-friendly publisher, Black Rose Writing does its best to eliminate unnecessary waste to reduce paper usage and energy costs, while never compromising the reading experience. As a result, the final word count vs. page count may not meet common expectations.

Cover Image: Blood Moon Over Shiprock, with permission from Matt Payne Photography https://www.mattpaynephotography.com/

For the missing and murdered indigenous women
and girls of North America

SHIPROCK
BABY

PREFACE

Who am I to write this story? How would I know what it feels like to be a seventeen-year-old rape victim, or the mother of one?

I confess. As a white male, living in an affluent community, I have not been immersed in the ideas, values, norms, practices, traditions or beliefs of the Navajo people, and despite months of research, I have likely missed some nuances, big and small, about life on a reservation.

I am, however, deeply moved and profoundly outraged at the scourge of murdered and missing Indigenous women and girls (MMIW). By attempting to shine a light on this social problem through the medium of fiction, it is my hope that readers will become more aware of an egregious injustice in North America.

R. Bruce Logan
Salt Spring Island, British Columbia

Asdzáá Naadleehi, Changing Woman, was the first deity, who created us. We are all her children. She led our people in a life full of prosperity with songs and prayers. When it became known that she had reached puberty and experienced her first menses, the holy people came together, each bringing a white shell they held precious. They dressed her up in a white buckskin, adding the shells onto her dress. She stood there glowing in such beauty and they gave her the name Yoogail Asdzáá, White Shell Woman. The gathering and tying of Changing Woman's hair with buckskin signifies the importance of gathering one's own thoughts, determination and focus. Changing Woman represents transformation and rebalancing of the male and female energies in the universe.

From The Story of Changing Woman (website).

PROLOGUE

Shiprock Peak, New Mexico,
August 3, 1994

Although only ten, Rebecca was clearly the leader of the three. It had been her idea to sneak their bikes off Indian Service Road 13 and onto the dirt trail leading to Shiprock Peak, the igneous formation known to the Navajo elders as *Tsé Bit'a'í.* Willie and Ronald, both aged eleven, went along with the plan, neither having ever been right up to the edge of the volcanic structure, which towered 1,500 feet above the surrounding high desert floor.

Just as they arrived, a faded blue pickup truck raced away from the base of the peak. The three youth caught a fleeting glimpse of a slender young woman behind the wheel.

It had also been Rebecca's idea to bring along a pack of Marlboros, pilfered from the shelves of City Market, in the town of Shiprock, 15 miles to the northeast. Again, Willie and Ronald had bought into this plan, both having only recently discovered the kicks of smoking cigarettes.

They dumped their bikes on their sides next to the house-sized rocks of the talus slope. Rebecca flipped back the red top of the Marlboro box, displaying a small tattoo of an owl on the back of her hand. A light wind out of the north whistled around the great rock formation. The sky was ominously dark as black clouds congregated around the sloping and jagged peak.

"Kinda spooky here today." Ronald's brave snicker belied his fear.

"Ah, it ain't nothing," Rebecca said. "Me and my uncle climbed up into the rocks on a day like this. We're not supposed to, cuz it's sacred. Nothing happened though." She passed the box around and the boys each fumbled out a cigarette and awaited a light from Rebecca's Dad's Zippo, snitched from his trousers pocket as he slumbered.

Their first drags produced a spate of coughing on Willie's part, and then he said, "That noise. Hear it?" His voice had gone squeaky with fear. "Like ghosts or something." He flicked his cigarette into the sand and lifted his bike off its side. "I'm outta here."

"I don't hear nothing but a little wind." Rebecca kicked at a couple of loose pebbles.

"I hear it too." Ronald's voice trembled. "Definitely like a ghost. Or worse. It's moaning or something."

"You're just wimps. There ain't no ghosts on this mountain." But Rebecca said it without conviction as she too heard a faint mewling in the fibrillating air around the mountain.

A distant rumble of thunder sounded as raindrops the size of pennies dappled the sand.

"Yeah. Let's get out of here." Ronald picked up his bike and threw his leg over the saddle.

"Wait." Rebecca scrambled over smaller rocks at the base to get to a boulder the size of a garage several feet up into the talus skirt. "That sounds like a puppy. I'm gonna check."

"No, it's forbidden to go onto the mountain without a medicine woman."

"Just wait. I'm getting closer. I can hear something crying."

Furious and blinding, a jagged streak of lightning struck the top of the mountain. Less than a second later a deafening crash of thunder shook the earth. Still astride their bikes, the two boys clasped onto each other and let out a primal scream in tandem, their eyes tightly closed.

Rebecca emerged from behind the huge rock and climbed down through the lower boulder train carrying a faded blue and white Adidas gym bag, from which the wails could be heard.

Now curious, their fears temporarily allayed by Rebecca's bravado, the boys dismounted their bikes and stood watching, oblivious to the surrounding thunderstorm. Rebecca stepped from the lowest of the rocks onto the level desert floor. "Now, let's see what we have." She placed the bag on the ground and unzipped it as the boys hovered over her shoulder.

The three of them stared down at a pink-faced, whimpering baby wrapped in the fragment of an old brown army blanket.

CHAPTER ONE

Gallup, New Mexico / Window Rock, Arizona,
November 15, 2020

By the time she turned off Interstate 40 and headed north on Route 491, she had been driving for just over three hours. With her fuel gauge reading under a quarter of a tank and her bladder sending signals of mild urgency, she needed a pit stop, but the recent resurgence of Covid-19 cases in and around Gallup impelled her to keep driving to her destination – Window Rock, Arizona, about 27 miles to go.

Through Gallup, it took her another fifteen minutes to reach the turnoff onto Route 264 at the hamlet of Ya Ta Hey. The navigation system in her Toyota Highlander told her she was still 25 minutes from her destination, and the pressure on her bladder had become more insistent. On the west side of Ya Ta Hey, she found a wide spot on the shoulder, where a cluster of creosote bushes would offer some concealment.

After, as she stood fastening her pants, a dome shaped object partially buried in the sand caught her attention. Brownish-red and about five inches in diameter, she at first thought it might be a tortoise shell, and she tapped it with the toe of her running shoe. It seemed firmly planted. Again, with her toe, she scraped away some of the sand around its base. The dry sand moved easily and she revealed more of the object, vertically too long to be the shell of a turtle.

As she continued to excavate sand with her feet, two empty eye sockets appeared. She screamed and jumped back. She had partially unearthed a human skull.

Too terrified to move, she stood quaking until she could breathe again, and then she picked her way carefully back to her vehicle, wary of any other bones that might be in the vicinity. Her fingers trembling, she punched 9-1-1 into her cell phone and reported what she had found to the dispatcher.

"Okay, ma'am. May I have your name please?" The female voice had a gentle and calming Hispanic accent.

"Melissa. Melissa Cody. I'm just passing through on my way to Window Rock."

"Yes ma'am. The Sheriff's office is on the way. Can you remain with your vehicle until the deputies arrive? Are you okay with that?"

"I guess so. I'm pretty rattled."

"Yes ma'am, I'll stay on the line with you until the deputies arrive. Can you take some deep breaths for me? That should help you calm down. I need you to stay calm for me."

Melissa took a long pull off her water bottle, then said, "I can hear a siren now. I think I'll be okay."

When the two McKinley County Sheriff vehicles arrived, one deputy asked Melissa to mask up and join him in his SUV, where she would dictate a statement, while the other three deputies set about marking the area surrounding the skull with yellow crime scene tape. Half an hour later, the deputy asked her to sign the statement and offered to have another of the deputies escort her the rest of the way into Window Rock.

"I think I'll be fine," she said. "But thanks for your kindness."

• • •

Immediately after the crossing into the Navajo Nation Reservation, a trailer- mounted flashing electric sign at the edge of the road read:

Curfew 8:00 pm – 5:00 am
Entire Navajo Nation

The sign had a sobering effect. The tribe was taking the Covid-19 crisis seriously, she noted, remembering that several weeks earlier, more people had died of the pandemic on the reservation of 180,000 than in the entire state of New Mexico. A religious rally at a northern outpost near the Arizona-Utah border had drawn members of the evangelical congregation from across the sprawling reservation, and as a result, the virus had spread like wildfire. And as she drove into the dusty town of Window Rock well ahead of the curfew, worrying signage outside her hotel reinforced the concern, warning of the rampant spread of Covid-19 on the reservation.

But the Quality Inn itself was more inspiring, clean and modern, and the lobby, though modest, was well appointed with comfortable furniture and woven wall hangings – symmetrical designs in turquoise blue, ochre and shades of orange. On one wall, she recognized one of R. C. Gorman's most famous prints – Zia Benita, a work she had been introduced to in university. From the far corner, a nicely trimmed and decorated Christmas tree cast its cheery light across much of the room.

"Your room is ready Miss Cody. Have you had a long drive today?" The clerk, crisply dressed, wore a facemask decorated with Navajo art. "If you've come from the east, did you see the excitement around Ya Ta Hey?"

A radio scanner on a shelf behind the clerk was spewing out police chatter that had to do with her experience of an hour earlier. Warily, she nodded. "I was there when the deputies arrived on scene."

"You were? Did you see the body parts?"

She blanched. "I saw a skull. I'm the one who reported it to 9-1-1."

"Well, since then, the police found part of a rib cage and two leg bones. The medical examiner is just arriving on the scene now."

"I'm glad I left before that." She looked around, searching for an escape from the disturbing update. "Can you tell me if my room is on the ground floor? I've got a fair amount of luggage."

"We have a ground floor room for you, yes. I see you're planning to stay for two months. You must be here on tribal government business."

"Not really. I'm here to do some volunteer work for the Indigenous Women Network of Arizona and New Mexico. I think they're commonly known as just IWN. They're not a government organization, but they work closely with, and support the Navajo government's Division of Social Services."

"I know all about the IWN. My mom works for Social Services." His eyes smiled above the mask. "If that's your grey Highlander under the portico, just drive it around the west side of the building. Your room is the fourth one in the next building, on the ground floor. You should be able to park right in front of the room. Do you need any help getting your luggage in?"

"I can manage, thanks. I've come from Santa Fe today, almost non-stop, so what I'm really looking forward to is a long hot bath. I hope there's a tub in the room."

"It's a tub-shower combination, so you'll like it. Breakfast is included in your room rate. It starts at 7:00 am and is served in the Diné Restaurant, to the right through those doors. Lunches and dinners are pretty good in there too. Otherwise the nearest place to eat is Taco Bell, about fifty yards to the west along the highway. But they're only doing take out through their drive-in window because of the pandemic."

"You've been really helpful. Thanks."

"You're welcome. My name's Paul. I'm here almost every day from 7:00 in the morning 'til 5:30 in the afternoon."

As soon as Melissa had settled in her room, she made a quick call to Bernice Begay, the Executive Director of IWN, to check in and arrange their first meeting for the next morning. Bernice, her voice warm and friendly, welcomed her to Window Rock and confirmed the meeting, but graciously didn't prolong the call. With that courtesy out of the way, Melissa was free to luxuriate in a hot, soapy tub.

Immersed to the neck, she felt her first doubt. What in God's name, she wondered, was she doing in this forlorn place anyway? A gritty little town on an Indian reservation, in the middle of a pandemic, in a remote corner of Arizona. True, she believed she was half Navajo, but this was only her second time on the reservation, which sprawled over vast portions of Arizona, New Mexico and Utah. She had no memory of the first time. She knew only that 26 years earlier she had been found, as an infant, in a sports bag at the base of an enormous outcrop, known to the Natives as *Tsé Bit'a'í*, or *the rock that has wings*, fifteen miles from the community of Shiprock.

Initially, she had been fostered to a couple living in Farmington, who had decided to call her *Tsiutah*, which meant "from the wilderness." But that hadn't worked out well. The couple were motivated mostly by government stipends for fostering children and spent much of their meagre income on Thunderbird, a white wine known for its cheap price tag and high alcohol content. Her first conscious memory, one she still harbored, was of cowering in the corner of her tiny alcove bedroom in the double-wide trailer, crying herself to sleep as her foster parents quarreled loudly and drunkenly in the kitchen. Fortunately, a social worker from the New Mexico Department of Children, Youth and Families was astute enough to see her trauma and removed her from the toxic environment. Nevertheless, her periodic struggle with depression was born there.

A couple from Santa Fe, Bob and Lois Cody, soon adopted her and had provided a loving home, seeing to it that she attended good schools in Santa Fe. She thrived with her new family, and by age 8 she had developed a sunshiny personality and did well in school, where she had eagerly participated in gymnastics and track and field.

At about age 10, when she asked Bob and Lois about her birth parents, they sat her down at the kitchen table. Lois took her hands in her own and told her tenderly what they knew; that she had been left at a spiritual place on the Navajo Reservation. There had never been a birth certificate registered for her.

"A reservation? Am I a Native?"

"We don't know exactly what your heritage is, but we're guessing that you're half Navajo by your dark hair and fair skin."

"But why would my parents just leave me in a bag in the desert?"

"We don't know that either, Sweetie." Bob brushed a strand of hair off her face. "Perhaps they thought that someone would find you who could give you a better life than they could."

When she was twelve, the Cody's enrolled her in Santa Fe Preparatory School, a renowned private school with a multicultural student population of 340 between grades 7 and 12. She remembered her six years there as happy, filled with music and dance and rich extracurricular activities. She did well navigating the rigorous academic program, designed to cultivate qualities of character, scholarship and citizenship, and she emerged confident and curious. Content with both her family life and her school life, there remained, however, moments when she brooded about who she was and who her biological parents were.

In her senior year, with Bob and Lois' encouragement and the help of her faculty advisor, she applied for and won a scholarship to the University of New Mexico, where, at the age of 22, she earned a BA in Native American Studies. At her commencement, Bob and Lois beamed with pride from their seats near the front of the hall.

She returned to Santa Fe and for the next four years she worked in the state legislature as a research assistant and communications specialist for Democratic Representative George Louie, a Native American from the Laguna Pueblo. She found the work there satisfying and her colleagues stimulating. She tested out a couple of lackluster relationships with male legislative employees, but neither felt right for her. Most importantly, during her tenure there, she became familiar with the North American-wide issue of missing and murdered indigenous women (usually abbreviated in literature as MMIW) and began wondering how she could advocate for indigenous women's rights.

She had spotted an ad seeking a volunteer at IWN in the online edition of the Navajo Times at about the same time that Representative Louie had become inappropriately friendly. She applied, had two telephone interviews, and here she was in Window Rock about to embark on an endeavor about which she knew very little, but to which she hoped to make a meaningful contribution. Who knew? Maybe she too was considered missing – stolen from her crib.

She rose early the next morning, turned on the TV and caught just enough of a local news item to learn that the skeletal remains she had happened across were those of a female about 19 years of age, and thought to be another victim of the plague of violence against Native women.

For her introductory meeting, she dressed in a modest but fashionable pant suit and mentally rehearsed what she might ask Bernice Begay. She had lots of questions, but her main role would be to listen, listen, listen.

Melissa stood at the bathroom mirror and finished brushing her long black hair. As she put the last touches on her makeup, she thought about her biological parents for the thousandth time. Who were they, and why had they abandoned her? She hoped this volunteer gig on the reservation where she had been found 26 years earlier might provide an opportunity for her to explore those questions.

Finally satisfied with her appearance and readiness, Melissa took one last look in the mirror and pushed her non-business thoughts aside. She hadn't yet turned away from the mirror when a thunderous explosion rattled her windows and knocked a lamp off the bedside table. Instinctively, she ducked beneath the bathroom counter, taking shelter there until she heard sirens stop in the parking lot outside her room.

CHAPTER TWO

Window Rock, AZ
November 16, 2020

Melissa parted the curtains a crack and peeked out her window. Two tribal police vehicles idled at the edge of the parking lot, their flashing red and blue lights refracting off the windows of other parked cars. A fire truck was parked nearby, its crew of helmeted firefighters in a huddle with three policemen. A fourth policeman was stringing yellow crime scene tape around the center of the parking lot and several parked vehicles, including Melissa's. A small crowd of guests and locals had begun to gather around the scene. She cautiously opened her door.

Melissa spotted Paul, the desk clerk, standing outside the police perimeter, calmly taking pictures with his cell phone. His calm demeanor reassured her that there was no immediate danger. She walked towards him. "What happened?"

"Probably a single stick of dynamite or small home-made explosive device. It's a form of protest by anti-colonialists."

She glanced back at the area being cordoned off by the yellow tape. The only apparent evidence of an explosion was a blackened scorch mark, about four feet in diameter, in the center of the parking lot. "Anti-colonialists?" A feeling of foreboding gripped her soul.

"Some people on the reservation can be quite radical. They resent white dominance over Native nations. They protest and demonstrate against the presence of the oil and gas companies on the rez and against what they see as colonial-capitalistic exploitation from companies like McDonalds, Taco Bell and the Quality Inn."

"Are they ever violent? Do people get hurt?" The feeling of apprehension still nested within her.

"Sometimes." Paul watched closely as one of the firefighters backed the fire truck out of the parking lot and the others walked over and climbed aboard, apparently satisfied there'd be no danger of another explosion or fire. "There are those who are mean and ugly. But for the most part, these activists just want to send their message. I don't think they want to hurt anyone. It's contrary to our central philosophy of *K'é*."

"*K'é*. You mean the concept of kinship?"

"Yes. When we say *K'é*, the first thing that comes to mind is our relationship with all the clans. But the philosophy goes much deeper than that. It also means that we have obligations to each other as humans. And that, ethically, humans also have obligations to the land, plants, animals and lakes. Everything is interconnected."

"So, to these people who made the explosion, what does blowing things up have to do with relations between humans and their environment?"

"I guess they see the incursion of colonialism and capitalism as an affront to the order of the universe. Many Diné people see the influence of white people as an erosion of our centuries-old connection with land and place."

"Tell me if I'm wrong, but my take on *k'é* is that it has mostly to do with importance of relationships between people but also with land. Land is a resource necessary for survival. Land is part of our identity. We have a relationship with land. 'Walk in harmony with the land' is the cliché I learned."

"You know something about *K'é* then?" asked Paul.

"A little. I have a bachelor's degree in Native American Studies from the University of New Mexico. I'm at least part native. It seems to me the *K'é* is the Navajo theory of everything."

"That's pretty much the story. We should have coffee and talk about that sometime. I'm studying the same thing at Diné College, here in Window Rock."

"I'd like to. But right now, I'd better get over to the IWN office. It wouldn't do to be late on my first day. Do you think those cops will let me move my car out from inside that yellow tape?"

'They probably won't be through taking photos and looking for evidence for at least an hour. But you can easily walk to the office. They're in a shared workspace called Indigehub. It's just down the highway about a quarter of a mile, right on the corner of Indian Route 12. You can't miss it. It's a long, low single-story building with lots of doors. Looks kinda like a motel."

"Maybe right after breakfast, then. I need something comforting to settle my rattled nerves. It's not every day I'm greeted by an explosion first thing in the morning."

• • •

Melissa took a seat in the sparsely patronized restaurant. She was still on edge after the explosion and glanced around to see how everyone else was doing. At the corner table, two men, swarthy and rough looking, probably in their early thirties, stared openly at her, whispering and clearly bantering between themselves. Equally clearly, their lascivious leers were meant for her.

With reassuring timing, a server, middle-aged and solid-looking, appeared at Melissa's table, offered a menu and said, "Good morning. The corn flour pancakes are excellent. They're served with fresh fruit and whipped cream."

But as the two men continued to gawk, Melissa changed her mind. "Uh ... actually, I don't have that much appetite." She smiled weakly at the waitress as she slid out of her seat. "I have an appointment in about twenty minutes anyway. I probably don't have time."

With her vehicle still penned in by the yellow crime scene tape, Melissa started down the highway and trudged along the shoulder toward the Indigiehub a couple of blocks away. About halfway there, the blare of a vehicle horn sounded behind her. As she glanced left, a pickup truck, with two men aboard, passed her and pulled to the shoulder just ahead of her.

The passenger poked his head out the window, looked back and eyeballed Melissa.

Her heart rose into her throat. He was one of the two men from the Diné Restaurant. The driver would be the other.

"Hey, like a lift?"

"No thanks." She made her voice as powerful as she could manage over the lump in her throat. She looked around for other people. Traffic along the highway was sparse and indifferent. There were no other pedestrians in sight.

The passenger door swung open and the man stepped onto the dusty shoulder. He wore a baseball cap with some sort of logo on the front and was dressed entirely in denim, a wrinkled shirt and faded jeans sagging low at the crotch. "C'mon we don't bite. We'll take you wherever you'd like to go." He cupped his groin and gave his private parts a hitch upward. "It can be dangerous out here on the highway for a young woman all alone."

Heart racing, Melissa looked around for refuge. Taco Bell was about fifty feet away, a brick and stucco island on a small sea of asphalt. A line of two or three cars waited along the side for access to the drive-thru window. She turned and dashed toward the front door, remembering as she ran that Paul had told her it was open for take-out through its drive-in window only.

"Hey. Wait. We're only trying to be nice to you." The emphasis he placed on 'nice' sounded menacing.

If the front door was locked, Melissa thought, she'd have to dash to the side and ask for help at the drive-thru. She reached the door, grasped the handle and pushed. It didn't budge. "Oh help," she screamed, her fear mounting. Now she rattled the door in attempt to attract attention from within. To her surprise, the door opened outward a crack. She gave it hard pull and it swung open. One-inch letters above the handle read: *Pull*.

"Can you help me?" she shouted as she went through the door.

She turned toward the highway and saw that neither of the men had pursued her. The passenger standing by the side of the vehicle looked her way and shrugged with his elbows bent and his palms upward, as if to say "What the fuck?"

A young female employee came out from behind the counter. "How can we help you, miss?"

"Those men." She pointed at the truck. "They were harassing me. I think they wanted to harm me ... or at least frighten me. They succeeded at that."

The clerk looked out at the truck. "I don't think either of those dudes are from around here. But we see lots of weirdos along the highway. Can we offer you a ride somewhere?"

Melissa's breathing slowed and she caught her breath. She shook her head. "I'm only going to an office up on the next corner, but thanks. I think I can walk. It looks like the men are leaving."

• • •

The Indigehub did indeed look like, and probably was at some point in its history, a motel. The door, one of twelve or so, was artistically signed in Diné stylized letters announcing that this was the IWN office. Just to the right of the door, a bulletin board had a variety of 8 by 10 posters pinned to it. The one that caught her eye first was a colored illustration of two people, a man and a woman, both in traditional apparel, standing opposite each other with two sheep, head to tail, between them. The caption read: **Covid 19 – Maintain your distance – stay two sheep apart.** The others were all pleas for information about missing women. Two official-looking Navajo Police Department bulletins depicted photos and information relative to age, race (both Native American Navajo), height and weight, hair and eyes. The other three, less formal but prayerful and poignant, and obviously placed by families, also showcased pictures of young women.

From behind her desk, Bernice Begay – Executive Director – welcomed her in. "Sorry, you've had two scares already today and it's barely 9:00 o'clock. It's not always this exciting on the rez."

In her fifties, with brown eyes so intense they looked black, she had pulled her graying black hair off her face and had it tied in a severe bun with turquoise and pink yarn. Her facemask was black and featured images of four bloody handprints. The printing above the images read, "Missing and Murdered" and beneath the handprints, "Indigenous Women." She stood, the crinkles around her eyes reflecting a beaming smile. "I'm Bernice, but please call me Bernie. I've been looking forward to meeting you."

She wore traditional clothing, a long greenish-black cotton skirt with a matching long sleeve blouse, accessorized by a wide red belt with turquoise stones set in silver. She removed her mask for a couple of seconds and through a bright smile said, "This is what I look like."

The office had a Spartan feel, reflecting elements of both function and culture in its furnishings. Four trestle tables and ten folding aluminum chairs made up the utilitarian component. Two tables were equipped with Apple desktop computers. A third contained stacks of papers, file folders and a copier, while the fourth comprised the break area, with a large coffee urn and an array of Navajo decorated cups.

Melissa threw admiring glances at the attractive woven rugs hung on two of the walls, and then turned her attention back to Bernie. "And I've been looking forward to meeting you as well. Although I'm obviously a little shaken right now, I'm eager to get started."

"Are you sure? Do you need a few minutes?"

"I've had a few minutes, so I'm good to go, but thanks, it definitely rattled me."

"Of course it did. We never forget an incident like that completely, even when it turns out well enough." Her smiling eyes turned sober as she gauged Melissa's emotional state. "But if you're sure, I've developed a little agenda for your orientation. There's a lot to cover, some of it pretty nasty."

Bernie handed a sheet of paper to Melissa. "We can start with a chat here in the office. Then I'll drive you around town and introduce you to some people. Over the next couple of days, I'd like you to get out into the *Dinétah*, our lands. I've arranged for you to go on a ride-along with one of our tribal police officers next week. But before we get started, let's have some coffee."

While Bernie poured the coffee, Melissa studied two large, framed posters side by side on one of the office walls.

Navajo Nation: By the Numbers
- **180,000** tribal members on the reservation
- **27,000** square miles of reservation land
- **43%** Navajos subsisting below the poverty line
- **49%** household income < $25,000
- **44%** Adults have not finished high school
- **7%** Adults have college degrees
- **22%** Adults hold full-time jobs.
- **33%** Households have no running water.

Violence Against Indigenous Women
- **MMIW** – The greatest social problem among Native people in North America
- **Over 5,270** missing Native women in North America (only 1,500 registered in Dept of Justice database)
- **Domestic Disputes** cause of much violence on the reservation

A yellow post-it note hung on the bottom of the right-hand poster. The handwriting, in blue ink, read:

Navajo Nation
22,776 Covid Cases
783 Deaths to date

Bernie set a steaming cup in front of Melissa. "So, you now see our raison d'être. The chart on the right encapsulates the problem, missing and murdered indigenous women, for which we seek to be part of the solution. The chart on the left gets at some of the root causes. And the yellow note on the bottom is the intervening situation that complicates our efforts to get on with the battle. Our main mission is to end violence against women by conducting education, training, technical assistance and culturally sensitive support services. We also do some one-on-one counseling with girls and women who have been victims. With Covid raging across the rez, we're stymied when it comes to conducting workshops and training sessions. Even doing one-on-one counseling is tricky."

"Those statistics are staggering. I don't get the notation that only 1,500 names are in a federal database when there are over 5,000 missing."

"Actually, that number, 1,500, has recently been up ticked from fewer than 200. Last year the Bureau of Indian Affairs established seven MMIW cold case offices across the US. That resulted in pulling together data from a variety of sources which increased the number to 1,500. The nearest cold case office to us is in Albuquerque. It remains to be seen if federal cold case task forces will produce any results, but it's a start in the right direction. Still, no one knows exactly how many Native Americans are missing because so many cases go unreported. Others aren't documented, and until recently, there was no specific government database tracking the cases. I can't even tell you how many of these missing are Diné."

Two hours later, Bernie took Melissa on a tour of Window Rock in her long-in-the-tooth Ford Explorer. They drove slowly through the campus of the seat of Navajo Government, on the northeast side of town. Bernie pointed out the many significant buildings, all decorated with red and blue Christmas lighting – the Office of the President and Vice President, the Division of Public Safety and the co-located Navajo Police Department, the Departments of Justice, Workforce Development and Information Technology. She pulled to a stop in front of an attractive red sandstone building, its two stories designed to harmonize with the surrounding rock and mountain formations. "These are the tribal council chambers. I'd like you to meet the woman who works as a receptionist."

"The building is hexagonal," observed Melissa. "Is that so it will resemble a dome, like a state capitol?"

"Actually, it's meant to evoke a hogan, the traditional house of the Diné. Look at the heavy wooden timbers serving as lintels and trim. And the main door faces to the East, traditional in all hogans. The inside is just one large, architecturally beautiful room where the delegates actually meet. I hope we can show you that room sometime when the council's in session. But now we need to enter an annex off on the north side. That's where the office space is."

A security guard, unsmiling but not impolite, signed them in and referred them to a desk where Faith Singer sat. Middle-aged, with a well-organized desk and efficient movements, she looked like someone who could be counted on, and for a moment, Melissa missed her mother. Lois Cody would be terrified if she knew about her morning scare.

Bernie introduced Faith to Melissa. "Faith and her daughter are one of our success stories."

"Yup. Bernie and her team found my daughter after she'd been missing for two years."

"How?" asked Melissa. "And where?"

"Well, actually she was in jail when she was located," said Faith with a slight grimace. "In Phoenix. She'd been kidnapped off the rez, taken to Phoenix and trafficked into prostitution. When she managed to escape, she was arrested for public drunkenness and was serving 90 days."

"I'm so sorry. How did you find her?"

"With persistence," Bernie said. "Two of our volunteers had been working phones for days when they finally located her. But for every success story like this, there are at least twenty other girls and women missing from the rez with no trace. The oldest of our known missing women would be about 85 by now, and the youngest, fifteen."

"You must have been very happy, Faith. Is your daughter still at home?"

"Yes. She's working on her two-year degree at Diné College."

• • •

As they left the government area and drove south, Bernie said, "To provide a contrast to the success story of Faith's daughter, I can tell you that not long ago a 50-year-old housekeeper, named Charlotte, worked at the Quality Inn where you're staying. Charlotte had two children who remember her as a loving mother and a hard worker. She never called in sick and whenever they were shorthanded at the hotel, she cheerfully went in on her days off to lend a hand.

"One day, about a year ago, as she was stripping the beds in a vacated suite, two men entered the room and forced her at knifepoint to go with them in her own car. Another housekeeper saw the three of them crossing the parking lot. Police found the car three days later in Boise, Idaho, with massive blood stains on the upholstery and puddles of dried blood on the floor mats. Charlotte's body has still not been found."

Melissa was shocked into silence. She was still digesting those tragic facts when Bernie slowed and drove past a storefront whose window sign read: *K'é Infoshop,* its Christmas décor conspicuously absent. "I just wanted you to see this place, Melissa. This organization was founded by a small group of people who position themselves as anti-colonial, anti-government, anti-racist, anti-homophobic ... umh ... basically they're anarchists. But at the moment they've departed from ideology and are heavily engaged in mutual aid." She stopped the vehicle to give Melissa a closer look. "They're the driving force behind a huge volunteer effort to obtain and distribute food, water and supplies to isolated seniors and immune-compromised people who can't obtain necessities because of Covid."

"D'you think I'd be welcome if I dropped in to learn more of what they're all about sometime? My experiences this morning tell me that, despite my degree, I really don't understand the concept of K'é in sufficient depth."

"Anti-discrimination is another of their tenets. So, you'd be welcome. I'd encourage you to do that when you have time. They're strict about the rules and guidelines around Covid-19, though."

"So they're obviously left-leaning. Do they get any flak from officialdom about that?"

"Not really. Right now, they're pretty much viewed as heroes. Yesterday, one of their volunteers drove four hours just to deliver 25 gallons of water to an elderly woman who lives in a hogan with no running water."

Their discussion was interrupted when a white police utility vehicle pulled up next to them and sounded two abbreviated, upwardly inflected, whoops of its siren. Its right-hand window came down and the lone officer leaned out and said, "Come on Bernie. You're blockin' the road. I don't want to have to write you a warning ticket."

Bernie only laughed. "Ha. You'd just be fishing for another chicken dinner at my place."

"Eh. You got it. I'm tired of mutton. But move along anyway." With a grin he accelerated away.

"That's pretty characteristic of this community," Bernie explained. "Even though we're the size of the State of West Virginia, there's pretty much a small-town personality on the rez. But, as you already know, we do have some bad apples." She stepped gently on the accelerator.

Minutes later, traveling back toward the office, they passed a side street and Bernie turned to Melissa as she pointed. "That's where my daughter and I live. A mile down Shonto Boulevard, a neighborhood of about 200 homes. A mix of ... you know ... single-story frame houses, manufactured homes and trailers."

"Was that a barrier across the road?"

"If I'd been going slower, you would have noticed a warning sign. It's a moveable barrier of wood and barbed wire. And there's a 24-hour guard on it too. Because of Covid, no one but residents are allowed in. That's another measure the tribal government has implemented reservation wide. In any community with definitive residential neighborhoods, no one enters except those who live there. And those on essential business. Plus, there's another advantage to having eyes and ears at the entrance 24 hours a day," Bernie said. "It may just add another layer of security against the ever-present spectre of missing and murdered indigenous women."

Melissa looked back over her shoulder to see if she could catch a glimpse of the barricade again, and as she did, a ripple of apprehension raised the hairs on her arms. A premonition of some unknown calamity seized her.

CHAPTER THREE

Highway 191, Northwest of Window Rock, AZ
December 3, 2020

Desolate. That would be an understatement, thought Melissa, as she drove north on US Highway 191 toward the little Indian town of Chinle. But the high desert is not without its own stark beauty. Ochre, red, brown, spotted with green vegetation, isolated buttes, mesas and pinnacles on all horizons, the occasional lonesome hogan or tiny cluster of rusty house trailers. Even the dead cars around the trailers added a touch of character.

Halfway through the hour-and-a-half drive from Widow Rock, the dramatic sight of a towering cumulonimbus cloud with a flat grayish-black bottom appeared through her bug-splattered windshield. From four years of observation and experience, as she made her monthly, hour-long commute from the university in Albuquerque to her home in Santa Fe, she had become accustomed to the rhythm of these desert squalls. Now she looked forward to coinciding with this one as a diversion from the monotony of the drive. Light rain dappled the windshield but soon morphed into a downpour, overpowering her wipers and reducing visibility to within a few feet in front of the vehicle. Two claps of thunder followed by lightning flashes commanded her attention and she pulled onto the shoulder to let the line of thundershowers pass.

Within minutes the storm had moved to the south, leaving in its wake only light rain and the fading rumble of thunder. Melissa swung back onto the highway. Thirty-five miles to Chinle. Bernie had already warned her: *Stay alert, but find something to occupy your mind or you'll get highway hypnosis.*

Her first three weeks at IWN had been good. She had met all four members of the Board of Directors, three Diné women and one Hopi. She'd also had the opportunity to meet four of the staff members who worked from home. With the exception of Mable Watchman, the chair of the board, who was able to drop by the office, the sessions had all been via Facetime or Zoom.

She had also had a chance to get her feet wet in the main work of the network. She'd worked with two staff members to design and set up an interactive training session on domestic violence and sexual assault to be delivered to a target audience of adolescents and young adults, via Zoom, sometime within the next month.

She'd also had the incredible opportunity of observing parts of two sacred, Diné rituals, The *Kinaaldá*, which marks the transition of a young girl into womanhood after her first menstrual period, and *The Blessing Way*, which honors a woman's pregnancy and her journey into motherhood. Even though she'd seen only a portion of each of the multi-day rites, she came away from both of them profoundly moved. The resonant singing and chanting, the marathon dancing, the sacred powders and paints, the hair combing of the honoree, her ceremonial dressing in traditional garb, the distribution of corn pollen, the sand paintings – it all made for a deeply emotional experience. She had been consumed with sorrow when told by one of the singing women that the increasing influence of popular American culture as well as a growing intent to modernize the Navajo Nation were pushing much of this rich culture aside.

She wondered again about her birth parents. Had her mother taken part in these rituals? About two weeks before leaving Santa Fe to come to the Navajo Nation, she had mailed a saliva swab, along with her application fee of $100.00 to Ancestry.com in hopes of obtaining information about her biogeographical ancestry that could eventually put her on a trail to her parents. Receipt of the application was acknowledged by e-mail with the pledge that her report would be available online within approximately six weeks. How long ago was that? It felt like she should hear something from them within the next week or two. In the meantime, now that she was on the reservation, she had a loose plan to get up to Shiprock and see if she could find whoever had rescued her from that sports bag all those years ago. In the short span of three weeks, Bernie had become a close friend, and Melissa had discussed the idea with her. "Absolutely," Bernie had said. "But let me make some phone calls first. I'll try the Farmington Daily Times to see what they may have in archival storage that might shed some light on it. Their online digital records don't go back that far, so let's see if they can find anything on microfiche."

As she thought about finding her birth parents, the same premonition of disaster she'd experienced a couple of weeks earlier took up residence in her mind. What if she learned that her mother had been raped and she was a product of that? Given what she was learning about male violence against women on the rez, that was a possibility. Or what if both her parents were unstable? What if they were druggies ... or criminals?

The southern fringes of Chinle as she approached were not impressive. A wide stretch of highway, pimpled on both sides by the non-descript, bland architecture of gas stations, fast food franchises and sundry shops, all separated by expanses of litter-strewn sand, had a distinctly gritty appearance. The town took on more definition, though, as she neared the center. Sidewalks, curbs and tall streetlights lent a slight air of poise to what some might think of as a whistle-stop. And signage indicated a hospital somewhere off the highway. The fairly modern-looking campus of Chinle High School was on her right as she turned onto Route 7 toward Canyon de Chelley National Monument, the popular tourist attraction, which she supposed provided the main reason for the burg's existence. A well-manicured athletic field splayed out just east of the school's buildings, with a large reader-board proclaiming it the home of the Chinle Wildcats. It shared the same wide mast-tower as the Canyon de Chelly Holiday Inn, next door.

Two miles down Route 7, a green and white sign informed her that, due to Covid-19, Canyon De Chelly was temporarily closed. This didn't matter to Melissa, not today anyway, as her destination lay just ahead on the right – a low modern brick building, again embracing a hogan theme, headquarters for the Chinle District of the Navajo Police Department.

Melissa was met in the foyer by Brenda Goldtooth, a short, slender officer clad in a dark tan uniform. "We've just finished our roll call for the afternoon shift so I'm ready to go," she said. "Do you need anything before we take off? Water? Coffee? Bathroom stop?" She had slightly almond-shaped eyes, characteristic of Navajo heritage, and she wore a navy-blue baseball cap with a large police emblem on the crown, along with small gold studs in her ears. Her facemask was standard hospital issue, blue and white with accordion folds. The cumbersome black tool belt, with its array of weapons and gear gave her a wide-in-the-hips appearance. A coiled black cord across her chest connected a UHF portable radio riding on her hip with the microphone attached to an epaulette.

"The bathroom," Melissa replied. "Then I'm eager to get started on the ride-along."

Moments later, they climbed aboard the patrol vehicle, a Chevrolet Blazer, and set out for Highway 191. Almost as soon as they were moving, Brenda began what would become an intermittent running commentary. "The NPD has only 199 officers to patrol an area the size of West Virginia. Each one-person patrol has well over 100 square miles to monitor. When I started this job four years ago, a typical day was issuing a traffic ticket or two, busting the occasional drunk and intervening in domestic disputes. Things have gotten a little dicier in recent years. Nowadays the domestic disputes frequently involve violence, drug abuse is a problem by both natives and white workers in the oil and gas fields, and sexual assaults are way up."

As though to reinforce her brief spiel, the radio crackled with a call for Brenda to respond to a report of a sexual assault in progress near the dam at Many Farms Lake. "Look for a black sedan thought to be stuck in the mud. That's where the assault is reported to be."

Brenda hit the switches for the blue lights and siren and squealed the vehicle around the corner onto 191 northbound. "That's about fourteen miles from here. Tighten your seat belt. We should be there in ten minutes." She stomped on the accelerator and the speedometer needle climbed to 100 MPH.

The roadside scenery raced by in a dizzying blur. Ahead, a slow-moving truck crept up a slight grade, just steep enough that any oncoming traffic could not be seen.

Brenda approached to within two car lengths of the truck before braking. "C'mon. Move it. Get outta the frickin' way." She added the blare of the vehicle horn to the wail of the siren. Melissa stiffened and braced her hands against the dashboard. The truck edged part way onto the shoulder and the police vehicle sped past.

"We were close enough to the district headquarters when we got that call that dispatch'll send another unit, so I'll have backup. Often if we have to respond from a remote location, there's no backup scenario. We call it the 'y'er on y'er own scenario.' If we find 'em, you stay in the car while I deal with whatever we have to deal with."

"No problem." Melissa's fingers turned white as she gripped the edge of her seat.

Nine minutes later Brenda took a sharp right and wheeled the police vehicle onto a dirt road. Half a mile up, at the site of the earthen dam forming the lake, she cut the siren and turned left onto a muddy, rutted road skirting the northwestern perimeter of the brackish lake. Slowing the vehicle to a crawl through the ooze, she commented, "I always respond to these calls with loose expectations. Often times, they're not what's indicated on the radio. This could be a false alarm. Probably is. But, on the other hand, there's always the chance of something really dangerous." She unsnapped the holster on her right hip.

They plowed through mud and gravelly ruts for nearly a mile, until they spotted an older model black Chevrolet Impala parked just off the track between the road and the lake. Brenda stopped her vehicle, turned off the blue flashing lights and grabbed the radio handset to report that the subject vehicle was just ahead. She'd wait for backup before making a move.

"Seems quiet," said Melissa.

"All the same we're playing it safe. My colleague, Joe Tom, is not far behind us."

When the other police vehicle pulled up behind them, Officer Tom gave a hand signal to Brenda and began walking slowly, handgun drawn, toward the left side of the Impala. Brenda stepped out of the vehicle. "Stay here. Keep down," she said to Melissa. She drew her .40 calibre Glock and cautiously started on a course toward the right-hand side of the Impala. Both officers stopped about thirty feet behind the car. The passenger door was wide open and sagging somewhat, as though it had been sprung from its hinges.

"Police," shouted Officer Tom. "Put your hands where we can see them and get out of the car."

Nothing happened. The only sounds were those of birds in the nearby piñon trees.

Brenda repeated the command. Still no action.

The two officers moved forward, each to his respective side of the vehicle, and peered cautiously into the back windows, then stepped to the front.

The vehicle was empty. Brenda placed her hand palm down on the hood and said, "Cold. Vehicle's been here a while." There were no license plates, front or rear, and a search of the interior revealed no vehicle registration or proof of insurance.

Brenda and officer Tom agreed to search along the lake for a couple of miles in both directions. Brenda set out clockwise in her vehicle and Tom went counter-clockwise.

After about thirty minutes of skirting the shoreline and turning this way and that, Brenda pulled the vehicle up onto a slight rise overlooking the muddy lake and scanned the short beaches with a pair of binoculars. "Nothing," she said. "We should've brought some fishing gear."

Melissa heard distant thunder and remembered that periodic showers were in the forecast for the entire day. "What now?" she asked.

"I'll call it in and we'll get on with patrolling. I think we'll head north toward Mexican Water. I haven't shown any police presence up there in a few days."

The 50-mile drive up to Mexican Water was winding, hilly and scenic. Brenda talked about crime on the reservation. "The biggest problem, and potentially the most hazardous kind of call we respond to, is domestic violence," she said. "But, as I mentioned earlier, there's no shortage of drug and alcohol incidents. The domestic violence incidents are usually fueled by booze or drugs."

Melissa made some notes in her phone to later remind herself of the trends in violence against women.

"Just to give you a flavor of the violence, over the past three days in the Chinle District, a man in Fruitland was accused of stabbing his mother several times, a woman went missing in Round Rock, there was a homicide near Piñon High School and a suicide in Lukachukai. For the past several months, we've also been busy enforcing the lockdown and curfew rules around Covid-19. When I applied for the Navajo Police Academy, I never imagined the job would be this demanding."

"It must be a strain."

"It is, but it's also satisfying. Unlike a municipal police officer, when I'm on patrol I'm practically my own boss and I enjoy getting to know the people in these scattered communities out here. Of course, the flip side is what I already said, the 'y'er on y'er own scenario' when I get called to a potentially violent incident. That can make your blood pressure go up."

They pulled into the unincorporated community of Mexican Water, a clutch of commercial buildings along the highway, two of them wearing garlands of Christmas lights. A trading post (really a convenience store with gas pumps), a clean-looking restaurant, and a laundromat. Beyond that, a small Baptist church and several double-wide trailers, obviously housing units, rounded out the built-up area of the hamlet.

They had burgers and coffee at the counter in the restaurant and made small talk with the server, a good-humored Native woman who seemed determined to make Brenda laugh. "Just seeing your car sent half my customers home," she said. "Two thirds of the rest are out back waiting to come out of hiding." Several weathered sheep farmers sat mutely on the other stools.

As they paid their bill, Brenda said, "One thing I want to show you while we're up at this end of the reservation. It's only a few miles from here. Hop in the vehicle."

Brenda drove East on Highway 160. The monotonous scenery along a straight stretch of two-lane highway was punctuated by a formation of low but rugged looking hills off to the north. A smattering of drilling rigs dotted the terrain to the right and pumpjacks pecked away like bobbing birds at petroleum wells on both sides of the roadway. On the right side, a green and white highway sign loomed up and announced that Shiprock, New Mexico was 50 miles ahead. "Oh my God," exclaimed Melissa. "I didn't realize Shiprock was that close."

"You know Shiprock then?"

"Not really. As an infant I was found at Shiprock Peak in a sports bag. It's a long story. I've never known who my parents are, but I suspect they were from the Shiprock area."

Brenda took her eyes off the road for a moment and looked at her with new interest. "Will you have time to get over there anytime during this IWN gig?"

"I'm loosely planning that. And the boss is encouraging it." That she could be entertaining second thoughts about finding her parents went unsaid.

"Okay, we're turning left just ahead. What I want to show you is two miles down a dirt road, nestled in a small basin at the base of those hills to the left."

Ten minutes in, the road turned into little more than a dusty track as it climbed slightly into the low hill mass. A cyclone fence bordered the left edge of the road. They had reached a spot with an open view down into the narrow basin thirty or so feet below them, and Brenda stopped the vehicle at a spot where they could see into a field of gravel and sand. Melissa saw a fenced compound of some sort, about two acres in area. A collection of about twelve forty-foot trailers, were scattered randomly about. They appeared to be living quarters and perhaps office space. Pickup trucks were parked here and there around the compound, and a passenger bus, its engine running, sat near a gate on the left side of the perimeter fencing. Like a file of soldiers, a row of chemical toilets behind one of the trailers afforded the only symmetry in the encampment – if that's what it was.

Melissa detected a faint odor of cooking. "What is this, an oil camp?" she asked.

"All those petroleum rigs and wellheads gave it away, did they? This is the camp where the drilling and pump maintenance crews live. There's probably close to sixty men who live here for four weeks at a time. They're mostly under thirty, make good money, and have little to do in their off-time except play cards, watch videos, drink and do drugs. And, of course, they're horny as hell. The nearest place to find hookers is in Farmington, 25 miles past Shiprock. Two hours from here. That's a problem."

Before Melissa could respond, a blue and gray pickup, with **Security** lettered on the doors, pulled up and halted, leaving its trail of dust to roll forward and dissipate. The driver dismounted and swaggered toward the two women. "So, Brenda. What brings ya?" He wore a gray uniform shirt with patches on both shoulders identifying him as a security guard. His bearing was aggressive and his tone of voice authoritative and condescending.

"Hi yerself, Bill. Just showing Melissa, here, around. She's new to the rez."

"Well howdy, Melissa. Did Ms. Supercop tell you she ain't got no police powers at this camp? And therefore, no frickin' business bein' here?"

"Your manners are as impeccable as usual, Bill. But I'm not here to exercise police powers."

"How do I know you're not conducting surveillance of some sort?"

"That's a good idea. You nervous about what we might see?" Brenda reached into the police vehicle, pulled her binoculars out and made a show of scanning the encampment.

"You stupid bitch. I'll call corporate in Houston and report this. I'm sure that'll get you some shit from the tribal police big shots."

"You do that, Bill. I haven't set foot within the camp and have every right to scan my beat with binoculars. Go back and make your phone call."

"Well, that was friendly," said Melissa as Bill drove away.

"Yeah." A rumble of thunder came from deeper in the hill mass. "You might say there's a little tension between these workers and many of the people of the Navajo Nation."

CHAPTER FOUR

Window Rock, AZ
December 5, 2020

Although the sun had been down for nearly an hour, the girls could still see and appreciate a corona of orange and red light on the western horizon, typical of December evenings in Window Rock. But at just over 6,000 feet above sea level, the air was cooling rapidly. It would hit freezing by midnight.

Julie Longwalker and Beth Chee, both seventeen, had left Thursday evening bible study at The Christian Reformed Church on Teecto Road and were walking home together. Their families lived in neighboring houses about a half-mile to the west, although Beth's parents were seldom there.

As they bundled up against the chill, they chatted animatedly about The Three Forms of Unity, the subject matter of their evening lesson. Julie asked Beth how much she understood about the 52 sections of The Catechism. "Not very much yet," Beth said. "I think we'll learn about each section over the next year, one per week. I'm afraid that by the time we get to 52, I won't remember anything about the first 51."

Julie's responsive giggles caused her long black hair to ripple over her shoulders in raven waves. Beth, who wore her hair in the more conservative *chongo*, a tight Navajo-style bun, was laughing at her own joke when an extended-cab pickup truck with four white male occupants pulled up alongside them.

Julie and Beth kept walking at a brisk pace along the shoulder of Shonto Boulevard. The driver downshifted the truck and crept along beside them. "Hey girls, hop in. Let's go for a ride."

Terrified, they moved further onto the shoulder and kept walking.

"Hey tall girl," one of the passengers shouted, addressing Julie, the taller of the two. "You look just like Sacagawea. Me and my buddy are Lewis and Clark. You wanna guide us up the river?"

Another said, "If you come with us, we'll give you fifty bucks each. That's a lot for Indian girls. More than you're worth."

Julie and Beth grabbed hands and ran.

The driver deftly kept apace of them, then swung the vehicle to the right just missing the girls, but blocking their way forward. When they attempted to skirt around behind the vehicle, the doors flew open. Three of the occupants leapt out and grabbed the girls, throwing them to the ground.

Julie and Beth kicked, fought, struggled and screamed. Doors opened at a couple of houses on the other side of the street and several yard lights came on. But the young men, fueled by testosterone and alcohol, were strong and managed to wrestle both girls into the back seat of the crew-cab. The tires screeched as the driver made a hasty U-turn, and sped back to the east. At the intersection with Indian Route 12, he made a hard left and accelerated north, toward Fort Defiance. In the backseat, the girls, still struggling with all their might, were easily pinned down by the three burly oil workers.

● ● ●

At 7:45 the next morning, a sheep farmer from Lukachukai, on his way in to Window Rock on a supply run, spotted Julie, disheveled and disoriented, staggering along the shoulder of Indian Route 12. Her clothing was torn, she had blood on her hands and legs and her luxuriant wavy hair had been cruelly, inexpertly, hacked off at the nape of her neck. The old farmer eased his ancient Ford F-150 pickup to a stop at the edge of the road and climbed out.

Incoherent, her eyes unfocused, Julie was only capable of muttering, "Where's Beth?" The farmer half persuaded and half hoisted her into the cab of his truck and enfolded her in a sheepskin wrap which he kept behind the seat. He drove her twenty miles to the Tsehootooi Medical Center in Fort Defiance and escorted her into the emergency department.

The hospital was quiet and the staff took Julie, without triage, directly into an examination cubicle and settled her on a gurney. A nurse started an IV, while a young physician and another nurse treated her for shock. They measured her vitals and examined her from head to toe, discovering numerous contusions, bruises, some swelling around her jaw and one ankle, and vaginal bleeding, but no apparent broken bones. The doctor, Juanita Joe, ordered a full body scan set of X-rays and then did a digital pelvic exam. The police would want evidence collected by means of a rape kit, but given Julie's emotional state, Dr. Joe judged her incapable of rationally consenting to the highly invasive procedure, so she chose to await the arrival of her mother, who had already been notified by telephone.

• • •

Melissa had enjoyed most of her breakfast in the Diné Restaurant. The slice of fry bread was delicious and crispy, albeit a little greasy and probably way too caloric. Eggs fried over medium, so that the whites are firm and the yolk still runny, are hard to screw up and these, fried in butter, were delicious. The two links of sausage made her hesitant, as both looked a little pinkish. She prodded one tenuously with her fork, then abandoned it as the ring tone on her cell phone sounded.

"Good morning, Melissa Cody speaking."

"Melissa. It's Bernie Begay." Her voice was tremulous. "My daughter, Julie, has been beaten and raped. She's at the hospital in Fort Defiance."

Melissa threw her hand over her mouth, then quickly removed it. "Oh my God, Bernie."

"I don't think I can drive. I'm too shook up. Can you take me up to the hospital?"

"Of course. Let me just go back to my room and brush my teeth. Then I'll pick you up. I won't be more than ten minutes."

Bernice was talkative, probably a defense mechanism, during the fifteen-minute drive to Fort Defiance. "We live in constant fear of this kind of thing. More than half the Native women in this country have been sexually assaulted at some time in their life, and the rate of rape for Native women is two and a half times higher than for white women. Julie and her friends know that we're not safe. It's not that I want any of these young women to live in fear, but to stay safe, they need to be constantly reminded of the threat that's present. Christ, it's so unfair."

Melissa searched for words and found none. Finally, she said only, "I'm so sorry, Bernie." And then asked, "Did this just happen this morning? Was she on her way to school?" She looked at her watch: 8:55 a.m.

"It happened sometime last night. I guess a sheep farmer found her on the road this morning about twenty miles north of Fort Defiance. When she didn't show up last night within an hour of finishing her bible study class, I panicked. I called the Tribal Police, but they said not to worry. If she still wasn't home by midnight to call them back."

"My God. You must have been sick with worry. Did you call the police back?"

"Yes, but by then neighbors from down the street had come to my house and told me two girls had been abducted by white men in a pickup truck. They couldn't tell for sure, but they thought that one was Julie because of her height and long hair. I knew then. I just knew. It's been my worst nightmare since she was a baby."

"What about the guard at the barricade. Wouldn't he have done something?"

"I don't know. They probably bribed him to let them through." Bernie's eyes were red with lack of sleep and tears.

By the time they reached the hospital and were shown to a cubicle in the emergency department, Dr. Joe and a nurse were still fussing over Julie. A Navajo Nation policeman in his grayish-tan service uniform stood by. Melissa recognized him as Frank, the cop who had told Bernie to stop blocking traffic a few weeks earlier. A plainclothes detective, also from the tribal police, gently asked questions of Julie, who was now somewhat coherent.

But the second she spotted her mother, Julie ignored the detective and tearfully blurted, "I'm sorry, Mom. I'm so sorry."

Bernie went to the gurney and embraced her daughter. "It's okay, you don't have anything to be sorry for. It's not your fault. You know that."

Through her veil of tears, Julie asked, "Is Beth here too?"

"I don't know. But we'll find out." Bernie's eyes moved to Dr. Joe who shook her head almost imperceptibly.

Without saying anything further to Julie, Bernie looked to the two policemen.

The detective said, "Ms. Begay, can we speak to you in the lobby for a couple of minutes. We won't keep you long. I know you need to be with Julie."

"Yes. Of course. May I have my friend with me? This is Melissa Cody, a volunteer with our program." She reached down and patted Julie's arm. "I'll be right back, Sweetie."

Although the hospital lobby had plenty of seating, the four of them stood, all masked, and all maintaining social distance. The detective spoke first. He gestured toward the uniformed policeman. "I think you know officer Frank Cly here. He was first to respond. And my name is Raymond Phillips. I'm with the Criminal Investigation Directory. We've met before Ms. Begay. I spoke at a couple of your public workshops."

"Yes. I remember. Forgive me, I'm a little preoccupied at the moment."

"Of course. We've been trying to reach the parents of Beth Chee, Julie's friend, but there's been no response to phone calls and no one answered when one of our officers went to their door. I believe they live next to you. Do you have any information about the parents' whereabouts?"

"Uhm. Beth's father landed a job as a long-haul truck driver about six months ago. He's almost never around. Her mom works as a housekeeper at the Hampton Inn in Gallup. Rather than commute daily, she usually stays there four or five days a week. Beth looks after herself, but spends a lot of time at our house. She eats most meals with us. What information do you have about Beth? They went to bible study together and I'm sure they were on the way home together when they ..." she choked back a sob, "...when it happened."

"None. I'm afraid we have no information about her at all. She's missing." He paused to let that sink in. "Ms. Begay, we'd like your consent for the hospital to collect trace evidence from your daughter by means of a rape kit. If and when a suspect is apprehended, the evidence could go a long way toward getting a conviction."

Bernie swiped at her face as her tears spilled over. "My poor girl. Yes, of course. I'll sign the consent. Those bastards. Does this mean you have suspects in mind?"

"Not really. The fact that apparently it was four young white males driving a late model extended cab pickup truck, suggests that they're probably oil or gas field workers at one of the man-camps on or near the reservation. Most likely the one near Mexican Water. There's around 65 or 70 single young men living there. Another much smaller one is at Slim Canyon, northwest of Chinle."

Melissa asked, "Does that mean you'll make some enquiries there? Look for the truck? Do some interviewing?"

"No ma'am. As I'm sure Ms. Begay could tell you, we have no jurisdiction over non-Natives working on the rez. We can't even so much as issue them a traffic ticket that would stick."

"But why? That doesn't make sense."

"It's very complicated. It goes way back to early treaties and arrangements with the Bureau of Indian Affairs, modified over the years by legislation. But the bottom line is we have no jurisdiction over the men in the camps. We can, and will, turn this file over to the FBI field office in Albuquerque, but whether or not they decide to send agents to investigate is another matter."

"But why? Why wouldn't they investigate a crime as heinous as this?"

"You'd have to ask them," he said with a trace of bitterness. What he didn't say nevertheless hung in the air: Because an element of systemic racism was involved? Because the media assign a lesser value to aboriginal women, so there's little public pressure on law enforcement to solve MMIW cases? *After all, They're only Indians.*

CHAPTER FIVE

West of Window Rock, Arizona
December 9, 2020

Twenty-five miles west of Window Rock, the *Healing Way* was held in the hogan of a *hataalii*, a singing woman. Tradition called for the rite to be held on the land, away from towns and villages. It was here that Ke'é was strongest and they could more effectively commune with Changing Woman and the spirits.

Julie Longwalker, dressed in a ceremonial robe, sat reverently watching the wizened old medicine man as he methodically created a sand painting on the hard-packed dirt floor of the hogan. As he carefully dipped his hands into small vessels containing colorful grains of sand, he chanted and spread the grains on the floor. Beautiful pictures and symbols emerged as he sifted the sand between his weathered fingertips. Three women also chanted as the man painstakingly finished the painting.

Following her release from the hospital several days earlier, Julie had gone to the Christian Reformed Church and had sat alone in the front pew to pray for peace of mind, and for forgiveness of the men who had so deliberately and brutally violated her. From the fragments she remembered, it had all been such a big joke to them. They hadn't seen her as a person when they grabbed and tore at her. She might as well have been a sack of stolen grain. Only after three of them had spent themselves into her, did they finally go silent. Then they were awkward with each other and one of them had pushed her bruised and beaten back into the truck, where he had put his feet on her to keep her down, as if none of them wanted any reminder of their terrible theft. Now, hopefully, the traditional medicine of the Diné would contribute to her healing.

Mesmerized, completely caught up in the ceremony, Melissa sat next to Bernice Begay, who watched piously as the ritual unfolded. The sand was meant to absorb negative energy while the songs, prayers and chants all called upon the spirits to heal Julie. The rite would last for several days, would move outside at times and would involve not only prayer and chants, but also drumming, songs, stories, and the use of a variety of sacred objects by numerous celebrants. Sadly, when the ritual was over, the beautiful sand paintings would be destroyed, symbolic of wiping out the traumatic event which led to the *Healing Way*. Melissa wished that she could stay for all of it, but given that Bernie would remain by her daughter's side throughout the solemn process, Melissa would have to leave this spiritual healing to take care of things at the office.

•   •   •

Melissa studied the Navajo image on her coffee mug while she waited for the copier to run off thirty copies of an agenda for the forthcoming workshop. The image was clearly a hand painted likeness of a sand painting. The serrated diamonds symbolically and symmetrically emphasized the four cardinal points, four seasons, four parts of the day and four sacred mountains which delineated the boundaries of the Navajo land. She remembered an illustrated lecture in her ethnology class at UNM in which the professor proposed that four, or one of its multiples, is employed frequently in the laying down of patterns because it is expected to meet the approval of the gods.

The copier emitted a series of beeps, indicating that the job was finished, just as a loud chime signified an incoming e-mail on her laptop across the room.

She strode quickly to her desk and opened her inbox. The top item in bold letters was from Ancestry.com, and the subject line read:

Your Biogeographical Report

Her heart skipped a bit as she opened it.

The first screen depicted a pie chart showing the makeup of her probable ethnicity:

Native American -52%

Italian - 21%

Irish -16 %

Scandinavian - 9%

Iberian Peninsula - 2%

Aha! Confirmed. She was at least half Native American. Navajo, she assumed. She hurriedly went through a number of other screens, mostly maps and graphs that depicted American and European locations associated with each ethnic group in the report and one chart showing migration patterns from Europe to North America. She stopped and took a deep breath while she read the table that showed possible DNA matches to living relatives in the same database.

Feeling like a kid at Christmas, Melissa scrutinized the head and shoulder pictures and the names of two persons identified as possible first or second cousins with a confidence factor of "Very High:"

Susan Meadows
Curt Barclay

She Googled Susan Meadows and came up with a list of seven websites containing women with that name. She found one whose head and shoulder picture matched that in the report. She appeared to be about 30. No e-mail address was indicated but there were two street addresses, one in El Paso, Texas and the other in the nearby suburb of Horizon City, Texas.

Melissa then Googled Curt Barclay. She found quite a list of web pages using the name Curt Barclay. But after investing 45 minutes to read through them, she concluded that none could be the one she sought. At least half the articles were obituaries or biographies of a deceased professional baseball player, and many of the others were men who either appeared to be too old or who were not a geographic fit.

She gave up on Curt Barclay for the moment and thought about typing a snail-mail letter to both of the addresses for Susan Meadows. But did she really want to pursue this possibly ugly can of worms?

Yes, she decided. To hell with the negative scenarios. She'd been curious about her real family for 16 years. She'd write the letter, even if it meant waiting a couple of weeks to learn about possible relatives, assuming her missives were even answered. She'd mail the letters from the Quality Inn this evening.

CHAPTER SIX

Near Navajo Route 5035
December 6, 2020

She awoke in total darkness. Thinking at first that she was blind, she groped around trying to get a sense of where she was. Nothing felt familiar to her touch. She lay flat on a mattress, or some kind of pad, so she sat up from the supine position, rolled over onto her knees and crawled slightly forward to continue feeling around. She had a quilt or something draped around her, but still she shivered in the cold. "Hello," she said. "Is anyone here? Can anyone help me?" Her fingers touched something cool and pliable. Plastic? A plastic bottle? She gripped it and gave it a shake. Liquid sloshed within the bottle. With her fingers she found the cap and twisted it off to smell it. No odor. She tested the liquid by allowing a drop to hit her tongue. Water. She took a longer gulp.

She continued to feel around the mattress until her fingers searched out another plastic container, about four inches wide and rectangular shaped like the Tupperware her mom used for food storage.

As her eyes adjusted to the darkness, she made out more of her space. The mattress rested on the floor occupying the center of a rectangular room. "Is anyone here?" she asked again. She didn't recognize her own voice. It seemed croaky, disembodied. And her teeth were chattering. "Help," she said. This time it sounded like a wail.

The plastic container had a lid. She toyed with it and it came off easily, and with it she detected the scent of moist fruit. Was it apples? Pears? Grapes?

With her index finger she prodded. The fruit was fleshy, in a liquid bath of some kind. Using both her index finger and thumb she explored further. Semi firm, circular. A slice of something with more slices beneath it. Pineapple rings? She recognized the sweet, syrupy smell now.

Now that her eyes were adjusting, she saw a little natural light filtering into the room from five holes in the ceiling, each about the diameter of a baseball. Scant daylight beamed through them, allowing her to realize that she was in a metal box of some kind, the walls corrugated, the ceiling and floor flat and smooth. Realization dawned on her – she was locked in some sort of container. A stab of fear pierced her gut. A moment later, panic, as her brain worked furiously to figure out how she had got there.

She tried to stand, and made it to her feet, her entire body stiff and sore, and chilled from head to toe. She was completely naked beneath the quilt. She dropped back down to the mattress. "Please," she sobbed, her voice husky and unfamiliar. With no one to hear her, she pleaded with God. "Oh, please God, help me." She could see the steam from her own breath as she spoke and curled into the fetal position for more warmth.

Gradually, more daylight diffused through the five holes, suggesting that it must be morning. But how long had she been here? And where was here? She could see the whole of her confinement space now. She looked around for her clothes and found none. She sat up, entwined in the quilt, and drank more of the water from the bottle. Did anyone know she was here? Could anyone help her? What about Julie? Where was she?

As more light crept into the space, and her head cleared somewhat, she ate two of the pineapple rings and put her mind to work, trying to remember what had happened. She'd been to bible study with Julie. And then she had woken up here. But how?

She needed to pee. She looked around for a toilet. In the increasing light, she spotted a plastic bucket in a corner of the ... container? A shipping container. She'd seen them around the receiving warehouse of the tribal government in Window Rock. This must be what the inside looked like. A roll of toilet paper sat next to the bucket.

As she squatted over the bucket, she realized that her pubic hair was matted and stiff. She wiped with tissue and looked at the reddish streaks. Dried blood. Now she remembered what had happened as she and Julie walked home from Bible studies. She sat on the mattress and cried. If she was here, where was Julie?

She and Julie had been friends since they were five, when Beth's family moved into the trailer home on Shonto Boulevard. Julie and her mom lived next door in a modest two-bedroom, frame house. Beth and Julie had hit it off right away. Their parents never quite became friends, separated as they were by different levels of education and the nature of their work. Julie's mom, Bernie, had been an elementary school teacher, but now she worked to fight the MMIW problem.

Neither of Beth's parents, on the other hand, had finished high school. Her father, William, floated from one minimum wage job to another, with long stretches of unemployment between, and although the rez was dry, he always seemed to have a large cache of beer in the fridge. Two years ago, a cousin from the Blind Canyon clan had helped him land a job for Schneider Trucking as a long-haul driver. He had seldom been at home since. Beth's mom, Flower, also had hopped from job to job. Typical of Native women she worked hard, reared children and attempted to preserve and transmit Navajo customs and traditions to her children. But by the time Beth's two older brothers had left home when she was 14, Flower was burned out. She spent little time on either teaching the culture of their people or on mothering. Her job at the Hampton Inn in Gallup kept her from home five or six days a week. Consequently, Beth spent more time with Julie and Bernie than she did in her own house.

Beth wrapped herself in the soiled quilt again. She spent the day alternately despairing, praying, and napping fitfully. But her brief sleeps provided no escape from the anguish. Nightmares and flashbacks of the rape from the night before consumed her. When she had eaten the last of the pineapple slices, the light coming through the five air holes in the ceiling had faded and the air was cooling. Then she heard a vehicle approach and stop outside the container. She called for help several times.

Moments later, she heard the jangle of keys outside the door. Then with a clang, the wide door swung open. Fading daylight and fresh air engulfed her. She wrapped herself tighter in the quilt.

A tall man filled much of the open space but he was backlit so she couldn't make out his features.

"Help me," she said feebly.

"Oh, I'll *help* you Sacagawea."

She recognized the menacing voice of the man in the truck who had called Julie Sacagawea the previous night. He didn't even differentiate between them, apparently. She cowered backward on the mattress and tried desperately to convince herself that he was there to help, but at another level, she knew better.

She saw his face more clearly as he moved into the container. A white man. Rugged looking with arrogant chiseled features. He wore Levis and a quilted vest. He was carrying another water bottle and a food container. On her knees, she moved off the mattress and back into the corner opposite the latrine bucket. "Don't hurt me again," she whimpered.

"I'm not here to hurt you, girl." He placed the containers on the floor near the mattress. "Take the pee bucket outside and dump it," he said. "It stinks like hell in here."

Beth scrunched herself further into the corner, drew her knees up to her chest and hugged her arms around them. "Please don't touch me."

"Take the bucket outside, I said." He grabbed her arm and yanked her to her feet, pushing her toward the bucket.

She struggled to keep her body covered with the quilt and staggered toward the opening holding the bucket by its bail. The man had a hold on her upper arm and guided her out into the fading desert light.

She spotted the pickup truck, and behind it, the bobbing hammerhead of a pumpjack. Thinking the vehicle must be the same one in which she and Julie were abducted last night, she said, "Where's Julie?"

"She's headed toward Wyoming with Lewis and Clark." After the pail had been emptied, he steered her toward the truck and pulled the back door open.

For a fleeting second, Beth allowed herself to think that he would take her home. Instead, he gave her a rough shove toward the interior, and as understanding dawned, she folded in on herself and wailed in unrestrained agony. Her Bible study group had talked about the importance of restraint, of waiting for marriage, for the sort of love and commitment that would deepen a physical relationship when the time was right. Instead, this man only wanted to humiliate and hurt her. She doubted if he even found her attractive. Julie's mom had warned them about abductions and rape, had occasionally told them about cases that worried her. His excitement came from forcing her, and if Bernie was correct, possibly even killing her before he was through.

"Stop that fucking howling and climb in. We'll do it here. You should be happy. It's cleaner than that mattress you'll be living on for the next little while."

He shoved her belly down on the back seat and pinned her in one spot by pushing with all his weight until her face disappeared into the upholstery, her screams muffled. His grunting movements were quick and brutal and had nothing to do with pleasure. When he finished, he reached into the front seat and handed her a bundle, folded grey sweat pants and a red Seattle Mariners sweat shirt and paper towel. "Here. You'll be warmer in these."

Beth had stopped wailing, could only barely breathe. Her throat burned and her nose felt as if it might be broken. Now mute, her face bloody and terrified, she took a wad of paper towel and swiped at the seat.

CHAPTER SEVEN

Near Mexican Water, AZ
December 16, 2020

Guy Primeau stepped outside the fenced enclosure and fired up a cigarette. Changing out the main crank bearing had been a tough, hot job. His face was streaked with grease and sweat. He drew deeply on the cigarette and watched with satisfaction as the horsehead bobbed up and down, lifting out four gallons of emulsified crude oil and water with each stroke. At moments like this, when he'd finished an exacting procedure, he was proud of his trade and of his work in the oil patch. And at $48.00 an hour he always had plenty of dead presidents in his wallet and very few places to spend them out here in the wilds of Northern Arizona. His bank account back home at the Royal Bank of Canada in Verdun, Quebec was growing at an insane rate and his Registered Retirement Plan at Raymond James Ltd. showed a balance of over $175,000 on his last statement. Not bad for a 29-year-old.

But Guy had been sleeping poorly, and since the incident 10 days earlier, he'd had little appetite. Although he hadn't participated in the rape of the two Native girls, he'd been there, and he hadn't stopped the others. Guilt and remorse over his involvement gnawed incessantly at his gut. His brain felt overwhelmed with 'if onlys' and 'what ifs.' Now as he flicked the cigarette butt off into the desert, he pictured again the scene in the gravel amid the creosote bushes and desert broom, north of Window Rock.

Mark had pulled the truck off the highway and had driven down a gravel road for a good mile before stopping. "C'mon guys. Let's do 'em," he'd said.

Guy had remained in the truck, despite the egging on of his companions, his eyes tightly closed and his hands balled into fists, tears leaking down both cheeks. It was wrong. Just wrong. Worst of all, he'd done nothing to help the girls. He didn't even know what had happened to them both in the end. Had they made it home?

He gave his head a shake to banish the vision, and then he packed his tools and stood outside the enclosure waiting for the crew bus to pick him up for the short run back to camp. If only he could expunge the memory. He wondered if this might be what they called PTSD.

Back in camp, he skipped dinner, as he had done most nights since the incident and sat at the counter in the club trailer staring into a beer. He was on his third when a clutch of boisterous men came bursting in from the mess trailer. "Hey Primeau," one said, "fuck's the matter with you, Dude? Haven't seen you at dinner in days."

Guy desultorily blew the foam off the top of the beer. "Haven't felt like it."

"Shit man. Whatever's bothering you, you probably ain't gonna find the answer in that beer. If it's a girl back home, why not start your Christmas leave a few days early and go back to Canada for a coupla weeks? Patch things up, Dude."

"It's not about a girl. Just leave me alone."

"Awright. Some of us are heading into Farmington to get laid tonight. Wanna come along? Might get yer mind off whatever's riding yer ass."

"Naw man. I'm staying here tonight. Catch a little TV. Schitts Creek is on Netflix."

But the television didn't hold his attention either. His preoccupation with the memory tormented him. How, he wondered, would he get peace of mind before this shit drove him crazy? Even though he hadn't been to church in a couple of years, his French Canadian, Catholic upbringing governed many of his values and much of his behavior. He always tried to do what was right. But camaraderie and male bonding in the rough and tumble world of the oil patch was also a powerful force. He couldn't rat on his buddies, could he? Or did he have an obligation to do so? Would it ease his burden? And if so, who was he trying to help—only himself, or the actual victims?

He left the recreation trailer, where two other guys were engrossed in Schitts Creek, and walked thirty feet to another trailer. One end of this one was reserved as a quiet place, meant for those workers so inclined to reflect, meditate or get in touch with their souls through prayer. Guy stared pensively at a blank wall, painted a pale blue, and weighed his alternatives for the umpteenth time. He could ask the first-aid guys to refer him to a shrink in Shiprock. There he could seek counseling. Probably not a good idea. What would he tell the first aid attendant about the problem? Word would get around that he had asked to see a head doctor. He'd be ridiculed out of the camp.

He could find a priest and unburden his soul by going to confession for the first time in ... what was it?... six years? But where was the nearest Catholic parish? Probably in Shiprock. He opened his phone, went to Google Maps and entered "Catholic Church near present location." Even further than Shiprock. Sacred Heart Catholic Church in Farmington, New Mexico, 80 miles away. It would take nearly two hours to drive there.

Final option, he could report what had happened to management or to the police. Let the chips fall where they may. That didn't seem like a good idea. For starters, he wasn't sure which police organization to call. And he'd probably get beaten within an inch of his life by the roughnecks in this camp if he told the site manager.

He had no perfect idea.

Guy stared at the wall for another hour before he finally decided to go to confession in Farmington. He had Saturday off. He'd call the parish and see if he could get an appointment for early Saturday afternoon. It wouldn't be a problem to take one of the smaller company pickup trucks. They were always available for personal errands.

• • •

Father Gerome Rowe met Guy at the side door of the single-story red-brick church on North Allen Avenue. He welcomed Guy and then said, "Let's use my office for this today. I think the confessionals are a little too formal, and to some parishioners, too intimidating. We can be casual in my office, it's private, and besides it's much more spacious and lends itself to social distancing."

The office was not huge, about 10 by 15 feet but it did afford plenty of personal space across Father Rowe's wide mahogany desk. The ubiquitous plaster crucifix hung on the wall behind the priest, while the other walls were decorated with religious art, including a nicely framed print of Leonardo DaVinci's The Last Supper.

"Why don't you go ahead and get started, Guy?" Father Rowe said gently.

"Okay ... Uh, Bless me Father, for I have sinned. It's been ...uhm... about six years since I last received the Sacrament of Reconciliation."

Father Rowe nodded sagely, but non-judgmentally.

Guy explained his involvement in the rape of ten days earlier in detail, starting with the innocent drive to Window Rock to "see the scenery," the progressive drunkenness of the foursome, the hunt for girls and the final, reprehensible act in the desert.

Father Rowe asked only, "Where did you get the booze? The entire reservation is dry."

"We took it with us in the vehicle. We have plenty of access to alcohol at the camp."

"I see. Okay, I'm going to give you a penance, say the Rosary prayer. You can do that later. But I'd like you to say the Act of Contrition, now, with me."

"I'm afraid I don't remember it, Father."

"It's on this printed card. Just read it aloud."

Once Guy had read the prayer, Father Rowe said, "Okay. I'm giving you absolution. You can leave here today knowing that you're absolved. And you can celebrate that." He chuckled. "But try not to engage in any other sins while celebrating."

Then he leaned on his elbows and steepled his fingers, growing serious. "Guy, you're absolved of your sin, but this is a very serious criminal matter in the eyes of the law. I want you to report this incident to the police. Rest assured that I cannot and will not violate the confessional seal of confidentiality, so I can't say a word about this to anyone, but you really need to report it."

CHAPTER EIGHT

Window Rock, AZ
December 20, 2020

Detective Raymond Phillips, of the Navajo Police Department, stood and greeted Special Agent Wendy Burkenshaw of the FBI's Albuquerque field office. *Well it's about time, he thought.* When she strode to his desk and sat down, he said, "You're it? Two weeks after the incident and the FBI sends a single agent?"

She wore gray slacks and a blue denim shirt. Her short-cropped hair gave her a somewhat masculine appearance. "We're really strapped. But I'm here to work with you. What do you have on the missing girl?" She glanced at an open file folder in her lap, "Beth Chee."

"We're batting zero on that. We've had patrol units check at every remote hogan and house between Window Rock and Tsaile and up the Chinle Wash to Mexican Water. No one has seen a sign of her. Other than neighbors along Shonto Boulevard, no one heard or saw anything suspicious on the night of the rape."

He sighed deeply and glanced out the window at the stately Tribal Council chambers. "We've photographed the tire marks at the scene of the abduction. And also borrowed an evidence tech from the Apache County Sheriff's office to scrape up samples of the rubber residue. Both the photos and the residue have been sent to the state laboratory for analysis."

"Yeah. We got those results today." She glanced down at the file folder again. "They indicate that the tires were 15-inch Goodyear Wrangler Duratracs. Unfortunately, that's a very popular tire for light trucks and SUV's. There're probably hundreds of them on this reservation."

"For sure," said Raymond. "And the perps could have come from off the rez. Still, we'll have our patrol units watch for and record vehicles sporting that kind of rubber at our Covid check stops. We'll also snoop around parked vehicles. So," he added, "You willing to go up to the camp near Mexican Water and ask some questions of the site management?"

"You mean now? That's over a hundred miles from here. I just drove in from Albuquerque."

"A hundred miles is a trip to the convenience store for bread and milk for many people on this rez."

Wendy nodded wearily. "Okay. Just let me get checked in at the Quality Inn. I'll meet you back here in thirty minutes."

•   •   •

Raymond and Wendy opened the camp office door and stepped in without knocking. The entire trailer was a one room office with three desks, several computers and three tall, well used file cabinets.

Derek Behrendt, the site manager at the camp, lifted his face from the laptop and grimaced as he peered over the top of the reading glasses perched on the tip of his hooked nose. The gate guard had already notified him that a pale blue sedan with US Government license plates had pulled into the compound, its driver with FBI identification. He hadn't been pleased. And he was even less pleased now as he glared at the two visitors. "What brings you here, Detective? You know you haven't got any jurisdiction on this camp." He pointedly didn't invite either of the visitors to be seated.

"Just a friendly visit, Derek. This is Special Agent Burkenshaw from the FBI. She has some questions for you."

"Sharon," Behrendt said to his secretary, who sat across the cramped office. "Get legal in Houston on the phone. Put your handset on speaker so they can listen and chime in if necessary."

"That's fine with me, Mr. Behrendt," said Wendy, her expression one of practiced indifference. "But probably not necessary. We're not accusing you of anything. Just seeking information."

"Be brief. I'm swamped with administrivia today."

"Firstly, do any of your vehicles in this camp run Good Year Wrangler Duratrac 15-inch tires?"

"Practically all of them. What's this about?"

"Just looking for some routine answers to routine questions, Mr. Behrendt. Would you know if any crew persons were in or near Window Rock on the 5th of this month?"

Behrendt snorted. "I don't keep track of my men when they're on their own time."

"Is it possible that any of your men could have been driving a company pickup truck in or around Window Rock on the 5th?"

"Sure. It's possible. But, again, I have no idea."

"Mr. Behrendt," Wendy said. "We're investigating a rape and a missing young woman. Serious matters. It's possible that some of your crew people may have information about the incident. Would you be willing to grant us access to the personnel records of the persons who work from this camp? We may want to look into the backgrounds of some of your men."

"I'll answer that," said a male voice from the telephone speaker. "This is John Bergan, Corporate Counsel in Houston. Our privacy policy precludes granting access to employee information."

"I had hoped you'd be willing to cooperate in helping us search for leads in this investigation. But if not, I can probably get a court order to search those files."

"I doubt you could justify that to a judge," said Bergan. "You're just on a fishing expedition."

Wendy suspected he was right. There wasn't any evidence at this point to support a court ordered search warrant. "All right, Mr. Bergan, if you can't or won't grant us access to full personnel records, can we have a roster containing just the names of the men who work from this camp?"

Berhendt shook his head and the voice from the speaker said, "'Fraid not, Agent. You'll have to find another tree to bark up."

"Then you won't mind if I conduct some random and informal interviews with men in camp now?"

"We absolutely do mind," said Bergan.

"Right," said Behrendt. "This discussion is over. I've got work to do."

As they climbed back into her vehicle, Wendy noticed a small folded square of paper under the driver's side windshield wiper. She left it there and glanced around. Although she saw no one nearby, that didn't mean no eyes were on them. She would wait until they were well outside the compound to retrieve the paper.

CHAPTER NINE

Window Rock Arizona
December 20, 2020

"Melissa, we're on a biology break from the *Healing Way*," said Bernie, who had connected to the IWN office from her cell phone. "I got a hit on my query to the Farmington Daily Times. They found an article from August 3rd, 1994 reporting on an apparent abandoned infant girl found at Shiprock Peak. A 10-year-old girl by the name of Rebecca White carried the infant in the basket on her bicycle to the Northern Navajo Medical Center in Shiprock."

"Well, I guess that would be me. So, I had my first bike-ride as an infant. No wonder I like the out-of-doors as much as I do. Listen, I really appreciate your pursuing this, but aren't you afraid you'll break some of the magic of the ritual by doing mundane business before it's finished?"

"I've been in a trance-like state for two days. It doesn't hurt to revisit the real world for a few minutes. We'll resume the rite shortly. Julie's doing really well. Her face is radiating pure joy today."

Melissa noted the relief in Bernie's voice as she related that.

"But listen there's a little more. My contact at the Times also checked the police blotter for the same date. The Shiprock District of the Navajo Police conducted an investigation. Child abandonment is a serious matter in our tribal laws. Unfortunately, they hit a dead end. Here's another thing, though. My contact also did a search for the name Rebecca White in the paper's archival materials. Seems that in 2010, a 27-year-old woman of that name was convicted of armed robbery in Farmington and sentenced to 15 to 20 years in the New Mexico Women's Correctional Facility, in the town of Grants. That's halfway between Albuquerque and Gallup. I have no internet access out here, so I'll leave that with you. Maybe you can go online and learn more. Meantime, I'd better get back to the ritual."

"That's more information than I thought I'd know in such short order. Thanks so much Bernie." Melissa took a few minutes to lean back in her chair and absorb this information. So, who could this Rebecca White be? What was she doing at *Tsé bit' ai*, a sacred spot? Were others there with her? Or was she alone? And most important, if she pursued this lead ... would it take her down a path she didn't want to tread?

She Googled the New Mexico Women's Correctional Facility and clicked on several sites, until she learned that the facility had closed several years earlier and had been converted to a men's prison, run under contract by the Corrections Corporation of America.

Privatized prisons?

Melissa went to Google to understand more. Private prisons, she learned, are contracted by government agencies who need more prison capacity but don't want to invest in capacity building. Those who favor privatization argue that corporate entities can run prison facilities more efficiently and economically than governments. The counter argument was that private facilities could not be held accountable to the public to the same extent that government agencies were.

Another fifteen minutes of web surfing revealed that most women offenders in New Mexico were now incarcerated at the Springer Corrections Center, just off Interstate 25, 130 miles Northeast of Santa Fe.

She planned to go home for Christmas for ten days or so and could easily make a side trip up to Springer. If she could visit Rebecca White, maybe there was more information to be had about her origins. Curiosity outweighed her fears of what she might learn of her parents.

But then she found this notice on the New Mexico Corrections Department website:

Visitation: Due to Covid -19, effective immediately, all in-person visitation is suspended until further notice. This includes the suspension of contact, non-contact, and attorney visits in all prison facilities. Inmates are not allowed to receive phone calls or electronic messages in any form.

Damn! She was left with little choice. She'd just have to write a letter to Rebecca White.

The instructions on how to address mail to inmates at Springer specified that the inmate's NMCD number and date of birth should be included in the address.

For several more minutes she searched the website for names of inmates, which she hoped might also include their NMCD inmate number, but she came up empty.

Finally, she drafted a short, two-paragraph letter addressed to:

Rebecca White
NMCD number - unknown
Date of Birth – Estimated sometime in 1983
Springer Corrections Center
PO Box 10
Springer, NM 87747

CHAPTER TEN

Man-Camp near Mexican Water
December 20, 2020

Three miles west of the camp, Wendy stopped her vehicle on the shoulder, stepped out and removed the folded paper from its pigeonhole beneath the windshield wiper.

She quickly scanned it, then handed it to Raymond, saying, "We'd better come back up here tomorrow."

The handwritten note read:

To FBI Lady
Please meet me in the café at the Mexican Water Trading Post, tomorrow afternoon at 4:30. I have some important information for you.
G.P.

"Do you know someone with the initials GP?" she asked Raymond.

"Not off hand. But it's obviously someone who works out of the camp."

"Right, so are you free to come back up with me tomorrow? I suspect you're known in that restaurant."

"I should be. Yeah, let's meet this G.P. person there tomorrow. We can come in an NPD vehicle."

•   •   •

The restaurant had only six tables, spread well apart for social distancing. Wendy studied the few other patrons, three locals sitting together engaged in jovial chatter; two white truckers sitting apart at the counter, their rigs gurgling at idle outside; and a teenaged girl sitting alone, munching a cheeseburger at a corner table. A yellow mongrel roamed from table to table, wheezing, his sad eyes pleading for scraps.

G.P, whoever he was, was fifteen minutes late. Wendy and Raymond, sitting across from each other at a table near the door, sipped coffee and made small talk.

The conversation on the two hour drive up from Window Rock had focused mostly on the case. What had happened to Beth Chee? They exchanged theories and hunches. Could she have been taken off the reservation alive? If so, she could be anywhere, even thousands of miles away. Unless, of course, the perps were in fact from the oil camp. Then she likely would not have been taken far. Was she being held somewhere as a captive? A sex-slave? Wendy knew that they were both thinking that she was very likely dead, but neither of them wanted to raise that possibility yet. What was the information that G.P, whoever he was, wanted to share? Identities of suspects? Could G.P. himself have been an accomplice? Had he overheard chatter in the camp?

Now, having exhausted the speculative suggestions, they sat in silence, each keeping their own counsel, until finally Wendy asked, "How did you get into policing?"

Raymond stared pensively out the restaurant window, down the lonely ribbon of highway for a few seconds, then he said, "You want the long version, or the short version?"

She looked at her watch. "Is there an intermediate length version?"

"I'll try to craft one." He took long swig from his coffee cup, and returned it to the table before wiping his mouth with the back of his hand. "I grew up in the town of Aztec, New Mexico. About fifteen miles northeast of Farmington, surrounded by reservations. This one to the west, the Apache and Ute reservations to the east. And just to the north of us was Aztec Ruins National Monument—"

"I've visited the monument. Never could figure out why they named it *Aztec* when it features *Pueblo* ruins."

"Yeah. Actually, it was the Anasazi who built the ancient masonry structures there. Because they lived in these pueblos, they are often referred to as Pueblo, as if that was their tribe. Anyway, because we were surrounded by several Native cultures, I became interested in Native American history and anthropology. Between graduating from high school and starting college, I took a year off and hitch-hiked around much of the country visiting various reservations. I got as far away as the Sioux tribes in North and South Dakota and the Salish in the Northwest.

Is this too much background for you?"

"Not at all. I'm interested. I grew up on Long Island in New York and didn't know diddly-squat about Native Americans until the FBI assigned me to the Southwest. Keep goin'."

"I was really interested in the different policing models that exist at the various reservations. Some are policed by the Bureau of Indian Affairs Police; some have mutual support agreements or contracts with local county or state police. Some have their own tribal police department. And there're variations to these ideas. Sort of crossovers. It all depends on a tribe's arrangement with the BIA." Raymond paused to gauge Wendy's interest in this rambling narrative.

She was fiddling with her phone, but caught his glance. She smiled and said, "Let's hear the rest."

"I decided the tribal police model was best. That way the police would be sensitive to the norms and values of the Diné, the people, and those should be reflected in the police work on a reservation. I knew the Navajo Nation used that model, and when I was 20, I saw a recruiting ad in the Navajo Times and jumped on the opportunity. The rest is history."

"It must be a constant challenge to balance your understanding of the ways of the people with some of the laws you have to enforce."

"It is. We have to enforce both tribal and state laws. And this reservation spans three states. But it's essential that people, bad guys as well as good guys, be treated with the respect and understanding that's demanded by our K'é philosophy. See what I mean about a long story? What's yours? Your story I mean. How did you happen to join the Feebee?"

"A much shorter story. I've always been pretty much a tomboy. So, I enlisted in the Army right out of high school. I was pretty gung-ho. I wanted to go to jump school and Ranger school. I got through Airborne training okay. Became a five-jump commando. But washed out of the Ranger course after three weeks. In those days, very few females could cut it physically. So, I got out after my three years, which included one deployment to Iraq, and enrolled in John Jay College of Criminal Justice in New York City. My G.I Bill benefits paid the freight. FBI recruiters visited the campus during my senior year. As you say, the rest is history."

Having talked themselves out, they sat in the restaurant in companionable silence until the server came to their table carrying a carafe and asked if they wanted their coffees topped up. Raymond took a last sip from his cup, then carefully placed it next to the two overlapping rings it had already left on the table. Three overlapping rings now. Symbolic of the overlapping jurisdictions on this reservation. "No thanks," he said. "Marge, do you happen to know anyone from the oil camp with the initials G.P?"

The server pushed a strand of hair off her face with her free hand. "Those roughnecks come in here from time to time. But I don't know any of their names. Why? You get stood up?"

"Startin' to look like it."

A whiff of frying bacon was almost enough to divert Wendy, but she said, "Maybe we should go out to the camp again. Amortize our travel time."

"That'll probably be no more productive than yesterday. But sure, maybe we'll get lucky and bump into G.P."

They were headed east. Halfway between Mexican Water and the turnoff to the camp, the police radio in the vehicle came alive with chatter about an apparent industrial accident. A fatality at a wellhead near Teec Nos Pos, 25 miles further east.

Raymond hit the blue lights and siren. "I'm obligated to go to that site," he said. He pushed the press-to-talk button on the mic and reported that he was on the way.

"Why's that?" Wendy asked. "Sounds like there are uniforms already there. From both the NPD and Apache County."

The corners of his mouth turned downward slightly. "Arizona statutes require a coroner or medical examiner's presence on the site of any sudden death of a person otherwise in good health and anytime there is a disease or accident believed to be related to the deceased's employment."

"And you're a coroner?"

He tightened his grip on the wheel and flicked on his high beam headlights as they plunged into the increasing darkness. "That's a contentious issue on the rez. The tribe has been asking for federal funds for several years to establish a Department of Medical Examiners. While we wait for action on that grant request, criminal investigators with the NPD are required to handle deaths in the capacity of a coroner."

"That must make it tough to recruit detectives."

Raymond swerved the vehicle abruptly to avoid an animal dashing across the roadway. "You got it. We spend about 35% of our time serving as coroners. Rank and file police officers are not eager to become criminal investigators. They're discouraged by the nature of the additional duty."

"Hmm. I can see where that might be a problem."

"Actually ... It sucks."

As they sped eastward, the brightest things in the night sky were the numerous white glows of floodlit rigs, much of the light refracting off the low clouds. For efficiency and economy, the drilling rigs operated twenty-four hours a day, crewed night and day, while the established wellheads required only periodic maintenance and were usually unmanned. "It's like driving through a galaxy," she said. "Sort of pretty in an eerie way."

"Yeah. It's a good thing this particular field is in a sparsely populated corner of the reservation. Further south and east, there are constant complaints about the noise and light pollution caused by the drilling. On the other hand, the tribal government likes the revenue produced by royalties."

Off the road to the left, several flashing blue and red lights accented the aura of white light. "That'd be the accident site," said Raymond. He slowed the vehicle, watching carefully for the dirt road that would lead off the highway and into the field.

They were greeted just outside the wellhead's fenced enclosure by Officer Brenda Goldtooth, who stood beside her white SUV police vehicle. Nearby, another police cruiser was parked, this one belonging to the Apache County Sheriff's Department, its red lights flashing. A company crew bus stood idling nearby, its windows filled with the peering faces of male oil field workers.

"Whadda we have?" Raymond asked.

"A white male around 30. He'd been working alone and was found by the driver of the crew bus when it arrived to pick him up. There are no signs of foul play that I can see. He could have fallen from one of the fixed ladders." She pointed to a nearby metal ladder mounted to the rig. "Or maybe it's a drug OD."

"This is FBI Special Agent Wendy Burkenshaw. Lead us to the body, please," Raymond said.

"This way, sir."

The young man lay on his back near the hammerhead, his unseeing eyes staring straight ahead, devoid of any light. His arms were akimbo, legs straight, head turned slightly to the right. A yellow hard hat lay inverted near the body. Trained to pay attention to detail, Wendy noted a small blue decal of a *fleur de lis* on the brim. Both Raymond and Wendy squatted down on their haunches and examined the face and torso more closely.

"Got an ID on him?" Raymond asked Brenda.

"Guy Primeau. A rig mechanic."

'G.P.' Raymond and Wendy looked each other in the eye, then stood.

"Well, I'd call this suspicious. Wouldn't you, Coroner?" asked Wendy.

"Yep. Means we need some crime scene techs here. We'll have to borrow them from the county. Also requires an external autopsy. We'll arrange to get him shipped to Flagstaff."

"Right," said Wendy. "If you suspect a homicide, which seems reasonable given his youth and fitness, then it falls under my purview. The FBI will foot the bill for the post-mortem."

"Well then. I guess you'll be getting an all-expense paid trip to Flagstaff in the next couple of days."

CHAPTER ELEVEN

Near Navajo Route 5035
December 21, 2020

Her assailant came almost every day. Beth had trouble keeping track of the days, although she tried to separate them into weeks. With no defining boundaries, they blurred together. But she thought she'd been held captive at least three weeks, based on her memory of each new assault. She no longer cried. Instead she felt dead inside. On the outside, her body ached with scrapes, bruises and cold. So cold. As she lay shivering, she curled into herself, and especially in the dark at night, she often wondered if she might actually die of cold, if her heart might just stop, or if she might lose the use of her feet altogether, so cold now that she couldn't warm them even when she crossed her legs to position one foot high on each thigh. They felt like two cold bricks, and no matter how tightly she rolled herself in the thin quilt, it wasn't enough to keep her warm, even with the clothes he had brought. Her nose, too, remained painful to touch, no doubt broken from being rammed so long and hard into the backseat of the truck. Lately, he hadn't bothered taking her to his vehicle, but only shoved her to her knees or slammed her up against the metal wall when he wanted what he wanted.

Whenever she heard the familiar growl of the approaching pickup truck, she sat far back on the mattress, her knees folded protectively up to her chest. First, he would extinguish the engine. Then the truck door would slam shut. Finally, the clanking of the container door would sound and then, one good thing—the welcome rush of fresh air. But for the first time, today, she heard two male voices, the one familiar to her, the other not. Had help finally arrived? Would she be freed? She almost dared to hope for that.

The door to the container swung open and two shadows stood backlighted in the open space. The familiar voice said, "Bring your bucket and step outside Sacagawea."

She rose off the mattress gingerly, stumbling as she put weight on her feet. Every muscle in her listless body hurt. Still, she retrieved the bucket and limped to the doorway. Outside in the light she saw the second man, slightly older and a little shorter and stockier than the familiar one. He stood with his hands in his vest pockets, which Beth eyed enviously, his expression curious but also slightly contemptuous or perhaps repulsed. If she had hoped for even a modicum of kindness or pity, she didn't see it.

"This is Captain Meriwether Lewis from the Lewis and Clark expedition," said the one who had repeatedly raped her. "He broke off from the rest of the group up in Wyoming and came down here just to meet you." He turned to the other man, "Can Sacagawea just call you Meriwether?"

Beth stood hunched and trembling, still wrapped in the quilt, praying that they wouldn't touch her.

The shorter man laughed. "Sure. I don't really give a shit. No sense standing on ceremony."

"We have a treat for you today," the familiar one said. He opened the back door of the truck and lifted out a large insulated cylinder, a two-liter thermos. "Hot water. And here's a towel and a cake of soap. Go behind to the other side of the truck and give yourself a bath."

Beth fumbled to grip the thermos, towel and soap and still keep the quilt wrapped tightly around her skinny body. She stepped around the truck and did as she was told while the two men smoked and joked.

The two liters of water didn't go far. She wished that there'd been enough to wash her hair, now matted and stringy, but the brief warmth on her skin had felt good, and for a fleeting moment she forgot what it meant that they had allowed her to bathe. She looked down the road, wondering if she could run on her useless feet, or if there might be some place to hide where they wouldn't find her.

"Sacagawea, that's long enough. Get back here. Now."

Overcome by hopelessness, she came cautiously back around the truck and stood awkwardly near the two men wondering who would be first and how she could bear the pain of it again. And why had he brought *Meriwether*? Was he selling her body to others now?

The first man stepped in front of her and with a single swipe of his hand pulled the quilt from her and threw it onto the ground. "Pretty nice stuff, eh Captain Lewis?" The two of them gaped at her bare, shivering body.

"A little skinny. But okay," said the shorter man, looking at her as if she were a stray dog, he wasn't sure he wanted.

"You think you can look after her while I'm off shift for the next five weeks?"

"Yeah, but what's your ultimate plan? You can't keep her here forever? Her health'll fail under these conditions. You're smart enough to know that. You gonna let her go at some point?"

"That wouldn't be very bright would it? She can identify me. You too, now."

"Seems to me you're painted into a corner. The FBI's already nosin' around the camp. Came yesterday."

CHAPTER TWELVE

Window Rock, AZ
December 23, 2020

Melissa was jarred from a sound sleep in her room at the Quality Inn by the harsh jangling of the room's telephone. Unused to this strident ring tone, she struggled for a few seconds to recognize both the room and the sound. Getting her bearings, she snatched the handset off of the night table. The digital clock showed 7:00 a.m.

"Good morning, ma'am. It's Paul at the front desk."

"Morning. But please don't call me ma'am. It makes me feel old. We're probably about the same age. My name is Melissa."

"Yes ma'am ... I mean Melissa. There's a man and a woman to see you here in the lobby. Can you come down?"

"Who on earth's calling on me at 7:00 in the morning?"

"It might be important. The man is Raymond Phillips, a detective from the tribal police. I know him. He's with a white woman with blond hair. He didn't introduce her."

"Okay. I met Mr. Phillips about two weeks ago at the hospital." She sighed. "Ask them to have a coffee or something. I'll be down in about 20 minutes."

Melissa opened the curtain a crack to get a measure of the weather outside. The window faced west, where stars still shone, but directly overhead the sky was beginning to lighten up, enough that the lights in the parking lot had gone off. Apparently, a cloudless morning, it nevertheless looked cold outside, as one would expect in late December at 6,000 feet. She pulled on a pair of jeans and a sweatshirt, dabbed at her face with a hot washcloth and finger combed her hair. She applied a light coat of lipstick and made her way down the breezeway toward the lobby.

She supposed they wanted to talk to her about Julie or Beth, who was still missing. But what did they want of her, and why so early? She found them seated in the Diné Restaurant with Bernie Begay. She crossed her fingers and hoped they had good news about Beth.

Raymond Phillips introduced the blond as Special Agent Burkenshaw, of the Albuquerque field office of the FBI. Her left hand, with which she held the paper cup of coffee, was devoid of jewelry, the fingernails unpolished and trimmed right to the nub.

"Call me Wendy," she said to Melissa.

The dining room was sparsely patronized, not surprising for 7:20 in the morning during a pandemic. A couple with open iPads sat several tables away, obviously doing business, and a man dressed like a rancher sat alone eating fry bread with jam.

"I'm sorry to roust you so early," Raymond said. "Agent Burkenshaw has to get on the road by 8:00 and she wanted to speak with both of you before she leaves. I'm afraid we don't have any compelling news, though."

"Yes. Just routine questions, I'm afraid," said Wendy. "Ms. Cody, do you know either Julie or Beth well?"

"Nope. I only met Julie in the hospital after she was ... while she was being examined there. And I visited with her and Bernie in their home once between her release from the hospital and her going to the *Healing Way* ceremony. I have never met Beth."

Wendy said, "I had a chance to meet with Julie briefly, yesterday. There was very little she could tell me about her horrible experience on the night of the 5th. Has she been able to share any information with you, Mrs. Begay?"

"Julie remembers very little about the incident that could be helpful, only what she's already told you."

"Not unusual when a victim has been extremely traumatized," said Wendy. "What can you tell me about your daughter's friends, her performance in school, her activities when not in school? Anything at all that might prove useful for us?"

"She was doing well in school, and she's committed to her church youth group ... participated in a bible study program with weekly meetings. Beth was her best friend. Neither of the two had ever dated."

"How about the other kids in the bible study group. Know anything about them?"

"No. Maybe you could enquire at the church."

"I will when I get back. I've got to go to Flagstaff for an au—" She stopped herself. "For a meeting today. I should be back tomorrow."

"I'm sorry that I'm not much help," Melissa said.

"You'd be surprised. Every little bit of information can be useful." She took a sip of her coffee, paused to reflect, and then lifted a blue file folder from her cheap briefcase. She opened it in her lap. Her forehead furrowed as she studied the contents for a few seconds. "This is what we have so far. I'm going to share some lab information with both of you. But keep it confidential. Can you do that?"

"Of course."

"Certainly."

"The rape kit has been analyzed at a laboratory in Denver. Mrs. Begay, is it okay with you for Melissa to hear this?"

"I think so. Melissa has been my rock. Given me lots of support."

"Okay. The results show the presence of others' DNA extracted from Julie's vagina. The evidence is that two different males violated her." She glanced at Bernie, who had blanched, and covered her mouth with her hand.

"We also have a DNA specimen from one of the same two males from under Julie's fingernails. Unfortunately, there are no matches in any DNA databases, which suggests that neither of the men has ever rendered any, for any purpose. This means that, as yet, we have no identities to go along with the DNA."

"Just out of curiosity," asked Melissa, "Have you had a chance to speak with Beth's parents? Have you obtained any useful information from them?"

Raymond Phillips said, "The father is still on the road somewhere. We've been unable to reach him. The McKinley County Sheriff's office in

New Mexico notified Beth's Mom at the Hampton Inn in Gallup, where she works, but she hasn't been interviewed in depth yet." He neglected to add that, according to the McKinley County Sheriff's Office, she seemed harried and preoccupied – unable to concentrate on the news that her daughter was missing.

"I'll go down to Gallup to interview her in a couple of days," Wendy said.

"Is there a reason why you haven't interviewed her before now?"

"It's complicated." Wendy said.

CHAPTER THIRTEEN

Flagstaff, Arizona
December 23, 2020

As she approached the new offices, Special Agent Wendy Burkenshaw recalled how drab and depressing the former County Medical Examiner's facility, across town, had been. This one, a repurposed warehouse on East Huntington Drive, had been tastefully refaced in gray sandstone. The large utility doors, which could be seen from the parking area, were gray metal and trimmed in an attractive turquoise blue. She admired the effect as she walked down the pathway, through a garden with wood, stone and water features, toward the public entrance, double glazed doors again trimmed in turquoise. Clearly this building had been designed for the comfort of the public, the professionals and the bereaved who had occasion to visit.

The spacious lobby, bathed in a warm orange paint, had its ambiance enhanced by skylights, and a decorated Christmas tree stood in one corner. The receptionist greeted Wendy by name and showed her into the office of Dr. Brian Cooley, the chief Medical Examiner of Coconino County.

"Ah, have a seat, Agent." He rose from behind a cluttered desk, his six-foot-two height easily accommodated by the high ceiling. "It's been a while since we've seen you. How do you like our new digs?"

"A bit more uplifting than your last facility."

"For sure. Our support staff weren't very enthusiastic about our dingy old building over on Fort Valley Road, but they enjoy coming to work here. Even the procedure room is pleasant, or as pleasant as can be, given its purpose. Coffee?"

"No thanks. My time is tightly budgeted today."

"Okay, come on. I'll show you the remains and what we found." He grabbed a clean white lab coat from a credenza drawer, slid it on and led the way past several other offices to the doorways opening onto the autopsy room.

The spacious room, bright with natural light beaming in through skylights and amplified by pristine white walls, contained two stainless steel autopsy tables, one occupied by a body covered in a white plastic sheet. The attitude of the feet showed that the body was face-down.

Dr. Cooley pointed to a stainless-steel cabinet and said, "You'll find gowns and booties over there. I'm pretty sure we'll have your size." With the jocularity necessary to cope in his job, he added, "If not, we can pin up the bottom. That'd be quite fashionable."

Wendy did her best to ignore the sickly, cloying odor of the chamber and gowned up, joining Dr. Cooley at the head end of the table.

He gestured broadly across the room to another set of doors. "Our cooler," he said. "We have 1,600 square feet of storage, more than twice the space of our old place, and enough now to serve contract clients beyond the county."

"You mean like us? The FBI?"

"Yes. The FBI, the BIA, the BLM and the Navajo and Hopi tribes. Nearly half our procedures are done on a contract basis for those agencies." Abruptly getting down to business, he said, "I'm going to spare you the extensive disfigurement of our complete dissection today and just show you the posterior head and neck. Those are most relevant to our findings."

Wendy took a deep breath and fought off a wave of nausea. As many autopsies as she had seen, she still couldn't shake the shock of a cold chill ripping from her stomach and sinking to her groin.

A swish of plastic, and then she was staring at the back of a lifeless head and shoulders. From this perspective, the corpse bore no resemblance to the young man she had seen two days earlier at the wellhead near Teec Nos Pos. Glad she didn't have to peer into those unseeing, lifeless eyes again, she was nevertheless repulsed by the two long incisions off each shoulder, descending at forty-five-degree angles until they met at the point of a single, longer incision running down the spine and disappearing under the plastic sheet above the lumbar level.

"The external examination revealed extensive edema around the posterior neck, so after doing the thoracic dissection, which rid the body of pooled blood, we concentrated here on the neck." With a pair of hemostatic forceps, he lifted the pointed flap of tissue formed by the intersection of the two shoulder-to-back incisions, and stretched it up over the lower posterior scalp. "Now if you'll lean in closely, Agent, you can see that the C-2 and C-3 vertebrae are acutely fractured. It's hard to tell without some additional dissection, but the spinal cord is probably severed."

Wendy could clearly see the two splintered vertebrae. Her stomach did another flip. "So, your conclusion, Doctor, is that the cause and manner of death was blunt trauma to the back of the neck? Are you suggesting this was a homicide?"

"Not conclusively. I wouldn't totally rule out another mechanism of injury, like perhaps a fall onto a metal object. But for the damage to be as profound as this, the fall would have to have been from some altitude greater than his six-foot height. My impression is that he was struck from behind by a narrow metal object, like a tire iron or a pipe. Perhaps a piece of rebar. And with great force, I would add. I may be more definitive once we have the tox screen and the tissue studies back, but for now I would call this one a *probable* homicide."

"That's enough for me to muster some investigative resources, Doctor. Thank you.

I'll need a copy of your tentative findings and any photos you've taken. Also, get his DNA to the FBI Forensic Laboratory in Quantico. And Merry Christmas to you."

Wendy stopped in the lobby and hit a speed dial button on her phone. Raymond Phillips answered on the first ring.

"Detective, are the evidence techs still on site at the wellhead?"

"No. They left yesterday. They didn't find anything. I'm still in Window Rock, but I've directed that the crime scene be preserved. The tape is still up and a uniform is guarding the wellhead 24 hours a day."

"Good. See if you can get the technicians back out there. It's a probable homicide. We're looking for a narrow pipe-like object, something like a tire iron or a piece of rebar."

He groaned. "Really? Do you have any idea how much piping might be on a wellhead site?"

"This would be loose. Not connected to any fixtures or other plumbing. I'd expand the perimeter of the crime scene and have a thorough look around the surrounding 300 or 400 yards as well."

"Okay. I'll ask them to check the shoulders of the highway between the wellhead and the camp as well. But with only two days until Christmas, the county boys aren't going to like going back out there."

"If they're professional, they'll agree that this is essential. I'm on my way to the Federal Magistrate Courthouse here in Flagstaff to see if I can get a judge to sign off on a search warrant for the camp. We'd now be looking for a murder weapon and an opportunity to interview crew members."

"Well, the company shuts down drilling operations for a week over Christmas and New Year. Gives the men an opportunity to be with their families, so starting tomorrow, the only men who'll be in the camp will be security and possibly Derek Berhendt. He lives just off the rez, in Bluff, Utah."

"That might be perfect. With the crew members off site, we could show up the day after Christmas with additional FBI resources and search the trailers and vehicles without too much interference. I'll ask that the court order include access to the personnel records. Hopefully we can get into those online from anywhere, then return to the camp after the New Year for interrogations, if necessary."

• • •

Wendy bounded up the steps to the second-floor offices of the US Magistrate Judge in Flagstaff's AWD Building. She showed her fed creds to the sleepy security guard, and was shown into the office of the Chief Deputy Clerk, who glanced at her watch – 2:00 pm on the day before Christmas Eve. "How can I be of service to the FBI today?"

"I need a place to sit for an hour, or so, and assistance with the forms for filing an affidavit for a court order in a criminal matter on the Navajo Reservation."

"I'm sorry, Agent. But we don't accept filings at this location. You'll have to submit the affidavit to the Sandra Day O'Connor US Courthouse in Phoenix. They close in three hours. And will only be open for half a day tomorrow."

"I didn't realize that. I'm actually from the Albuquerque Field Office. Is there any way I can do it by phone?"

"No. But you can e-file. If you want to take a seat over there, I'll get someone to help you. You can either use one of our computers or your own laptop. If you have all your ducks in a row, we can get it off before they close tonight. But you should follow up with a phone call tomorrow morning to be sure it's acted on before they break for Christmas."

Her helpful attitude caught Wendy by surprise. "Oh. Thanks so much. You're a credit to government employees."

CHAPTER FOURTEEN

Window Rock, AZ
December 24, 2020

Melissa Cody had just hefted her largest bag into the back of the Highlander when her cell rang with the familiar Marimba tone. "Glad I caught you," said Bernie. "Are you on the road yet?"

"Nope. Just loading up. Gonna' go into the restaurant and grab a large coffee to go before I take off on my three-hour run to Santa Fe."

"You want to stop by here and have that coffee? There's a letter for you here from Rebecca White at the Springer Corrections Center in New Mexico."

"Wow. That was fast. I guess there's little else to do in prison. I'll be right over."

The freshly brewed coffee Bernie offered was rich and foamy. The gray envelope, postmarked and stamped with a prison censor's approval, lay in the center of the table. Bernie asked, "Shall I leave while you read that?"

"Oh no. Please stay." Melissa tore open the envelope and withdrew a single sheet of low quality, buff colored paper, with wide blue lines – the kind on which a second grader might do his first alphabet exercises. The penmanship, a mixture of cursive and printing, reflected a person who hadn't practiced a great deal.

Missus or miss Cody

Yeah I remember finding a baby at shiprock It was up kinda behind a big rock in a adidas bag. I didn't no wher it came from still dont. but a lady left driving a p.u. truck. I was 10 and me and two boys had went there on bikes tho we shouldn't have done. There names are willie yazzee and ronald George. Willie is dead. He got killt in knife fight I dont no about Ronald he maybe is still in Shiprock. I took the baby to the hospital in Shiprock town. Thats all I can tell u.

Rebecca White

Melissa read the note slowly. A wave of sadness washed over her, for Rebecca, a disadvantaged, uneducated woman currently in prison who, at 10 years old, had the perspicacity to grab a wailing baby and rush the infant to a hospital. She gave the baby a life – Melissa's life. With moist eyes, she handed the note to Bernie. "You can read it. It's very sad." Then she put her elbow on the table and rested her chin in the vee between her thumb and forefinger.

Bernie scanned the missive quickly, then said, "Will you go to Shiprock to try and find this Ronald George?" Then, as an afterthought, "Since Shiprock is within the bounds of the reservation, I'll ask the tribal police to see if he has a rap sheet."

"Okay, thanks Bernie. Yeah, I guess after Christmas I can return by the northern route and stop in Shiprock. At the very least, even if I can't find this guy Ronald George, I can see where I was found. That would be almost like returning to my birthplace for the first time."

Melissa was no further than half a mile from Window Rock. She'd just crossed into New Mexico, when a chime from her cell phone indicated she had an incoming e-mail. She pulled onto the shoulder and checked the screen. The message was from "smeadows," Susan Meadows in El Paso, the possible first cousin in the Ancestry.com report.

The message read:

Hi Melissa. How exciting to learn that I may have a cousin I've never known. Ancestry.com seems to open a lot of interesting doors for lots of people. It would be fun to get together sometime. El Paso and Santa Fe aren't that far apart.

This may be very good news for you. I have an uncle, Willie Cole, who went to high school in Farmington, only 25 miles from Shiprock. His Dad was based there as a superintendent in the oil patch. He sometimes jokes about the local girls he dated when he lived there. If we're truly first cousins, that would likely make him your father. That is unless I have other uncles that I don't know of lurking about (ha ha). Uncle Willie lives in Elberton, Georgia now. He's a high school vice principal. Never been married. His e-mail address is williecolevp@elbertonnet.com.

I would encourage you to e-mail him. He's a very outgoing, friendly gentleman, and although it would be like a bolt out of the blue to him, I'm sure he'd be totally open to discussing possibilities with you. If you'd like, I can soften the surprise he might have by telling him about the possibility before you send your e-mail.

This is so exciting.

Best, Susan

Melissa hastily responded with a return e-mail asking Susan not to alert 'Uncle Willie.' She'd take the time to craft a carefully worded e-mail, once she got settled in for Christmas in Santa Fe.

She could think of little else for the entire duration of the three-hour drive to Santa Fe. Two hits in one day: a letter from Rebecca White and now the e-mail from Susan. Could it be possible that after twenty-six years she was on the verge of discovering the secret of her birth parents? Moreover, now that it seemed like a possibility, did she really want to? What if there were too many ghosts in the closet? Susan seemed like a skookum woman and she made it sound like Uncle Willie, possibly her father, was an okay guy. But what if her birth mother was not so nice??

She also worried about Bob and Lois Cody, her adoptive parents who had given her the gift of a loving home and wonderful childhood. How would they feel about her connecting with her birth parents? She chewed on that for a hundred miles, hardly noticing anything on the road ahead or to the sides. Time to talk to them.

• • •

Santa Fe looked different to Melissa as she drove through the outskirts. Had her perceptions altered that greatly in the few weeks she had been in the wide-open spaces of Arizona? But things felt more familiar as she neared Old Pecos Trail and her childhood neighborhood in the South Capitol area. Despite having lived on campus at university and in an apartment of her own in Santa Fe while she worked at the legislature, home was still her parents' house. Twenty-four years ago, they had bought from the plans of this gated community. Now, with its golf course and social clubs, they could little afford to buy. But they'd been lucky, and it was only dawning on Melissa how lucky she too had been to land here with these gentle people.

The front door swung open as Melissa pulled up into the driveway. Lois flew down the path and yanked open the door before Melissa had turned off the engine. "You get out of this car and give your Mom a hug. To hell with Covid-19!"

Mid-embrace the two women spied Bob, leaning on the door jamb of the house. His slow, easy grin spoke volumes about his love and respect for his wife and daughter as he ambled towards them.

"Need help with your luggage Melissa? I suspect your Christmas present for me weighs a ton."

"Hey Dad. Sorry no presents, there wasn't a golf pro shop on the rez." Her father's obsession with the game of golf had grown with the hours he had spent on the course since his retirement last June.

"Well then the hugs better come quick and often." They stood a long while in a firm hug.

Melissa's bedroom was still her room, the one where she had grown up and perhaps was now grown out of, but she did love it. She had slept here, studied here, giggled with girlfriends here and sometimes, in the dark, wondered who she really was here. As she flopped her luggage on the bed, the persistent conflicting thoughts of the past few hours almost made her dizzy. Wasn't she content to be Melissa Cody, privileged daughter of Lois and Bob?

As she threw her underwear, sweaters and jeans into empty drawers and hung her two blouses in the closet, Melissa's mind switched gears. How moved she had been at the *Healing Way* for Julie. How magnificent the dawn was over the mountains in the early morning. She felt connected to the land and people of the Navajo Nation. She couldn't deny that she was drawn there.

With a light tap on the door, Lois stuck her head around to say, "Dad is about to pour drinks. You coming?" Then, "It's nice to see you settling into your old room. We've missed you this last month."

"A drink will go down nicely. Glad that drive is over with. Anything I should be doing to help with dinner?"

"It's all ready, Sweetie. You know how easy our traditional Christmas Eve posole rojo is. What could be simpler than pork and hominy stew?"

They sat in the cozy living room, the corner kiva fireplace with a few logs alight, to take the evening chill off the room. Greenery and bunches of bright red chili pepper ristras were the only holiday decorations, but the broad windows showcased the sparkling dusting of snow in the lighted yard.

"So, my sweet daughter, tell us all about your month on the reservation." Bob stretched his lanky frame to an optimum position of comfort in his large leather chair.

"You know Dad, I did a lot of reading before I headed off for this volunteer position and I thought I was prepared. But I wasn't, and still am not, ready for the bombardment of information, experiences and realizations I've encountered over the last four weeks. My knowledge of the people, the culture, the social problems and the geography of the Navajo Nation is incredibly superficial, despite my degree in Native American studies." She shook her head as she considered her naivety. "Textbooks somehow don't reflect the here and now realities of being a Native today. I can't remember our discussing the issues at our dinner table either. Mom, you know a lot about Navajo art and crafts from your volunteer work with the annual Indian Market here. Did you ever learn from your fellow volunteers about the way of life on the reservation?"

Melissa was deliberately deflecting the conversation away from the issues that were really eating away at her, the raped and missing Beth, the lack of clean water on the reservation, the poverty, the harsh living conditions and the rat's-nest of conflicting police jurisdictions and politics. And her own efforts to locate her birthparents. Christmas Eve was not the time to have that heart-to-heart with her parents.

"Both the Santa Fe Indian Market and the International Folk Art Market took real blows this year when they had to cancel because of Covid-19," said Lois. "We were heartsick, not only for the event itself, but for the loss of income for the artists. The Natives who are accepted as vendors really rely on this event for a big chunk of their annual income. I've met so many of the artists over the years, and I really admire their work." Lois cast a look around the living room and dining room where her pottery acquisitions added warmth and visual pleasure. "There's not much time to chat during the market, but in stolen moments I've learned some amazing stories first-hand about how their culture is passed down orally from one generation to another. Also, weaving, pottery and jewelry-making skills. I'm intrigued by how spiritual their work is, and by the legends that inspire the work. Many of the artists work in what we would judge to be difficult circumstances, with no such thing as a studio. The studio is outside in good weather, and in bad weather in a small house with the kids crawling around. There's often no clean water or not enough food, and yet they arrive at the market with the most exquisite rugs or jewelry. The new co-ops are thriving, offering space for work and day care."

"And on top of all that, the Navajo have given us the most beautiful gift of our lives and that gem is you, Melissa," Bob said. "There's no finer jewelry around here."

Here it was, the opening that Melissa needed, wanted and craved, not exactly at this moment, but she dove in, unprepared and breathless.

"You're such an old Sweetie. You and Mom are my home place, my heart place and I love you." She raised her glass of Pinot Grigio and grinned at them over the rim. "But I do want you to know that I've been doing some investigating to find my birth parents. Being on the reservation has piqued my interest, and I confess I've always wanted to know my origins and genetic make-up, beyond the sketchy story of being found as an infant on the reservation. I hope that you're OK with that."

As silence fell around the table, Melissa tried to read her parents for clues as to their reactions. Lois's eyes were glassy. Bob looked mystified. He spoke first.

"Tell me more about the 'why?' Melissa. Your mom and I have always answered your questions as openly and thoroughly as we could. I honestly didn't know that the issue of your origins had troubled you all this time. I feel badly about that, not badly that you want to know, but badly that it has troubled you for some time."

"It hasn't been like that, some awful wondering. Just sometimes at night when I lie awake in bed thinking. You know, teenage angst stuff about not fitting in and wondering if I'm really some sort of alien. More recently, wondering about marriage and kids and my genetic pool. I want to become as fine a human being as you and Mom are."

The tears waiting in Lois's eyes spilled onto her cheeks. "Melissa, my darling, of course I've wanted to be the only mother you'd ever need or want. But the reality is that I'm a barren woman who relied on the spirits to bring me a child, and I share you with the woman who bore you. I knew the minute we saw your pinched, frightened little four-year-old face at the agency that I needed to love and nourish you. You had such quiet intelligence in those brown eyes of yours even then. We're very proud of you, and this business of wanting to know your heritage is because you have wisdom. It's infinitely sensible. I just hope that there's more joy than pain in this journey for you."

"Oh, Mom." Melissa almost knocked over her dining chair, quickly rising to give her mother a hug. "You've always been my biggest fan – other than Dad of course." Breaking her clutch on her mother she moved towards Bob sitting at the head of the table, stoic as usual, but with glistening eyes. She lay her arm across his shoulder and kissed his balding head. "What do you think, Dad?"

After a thoughtful pause, Bob said, hesitantly, "We knew of course that one day you'd probably want to know your genetic makeup for health reasons. And we thought you'd be curious about your birth parents and exactly why they gave you up, especially in the dramatic way they did. We intentionally waited for you to begin your own search if you chose to. And you have. We're not threatened by this in any way. Mom and I know that we've done our job, and we couldn't have asked for a better daughter. We'll support you in any way we can. I think that goes without saying."

"Can I ask a favor?" Melissa reclaimed her chair. "I leave it to you as to how and when you share this with the rest of our family and your friends, but can we not bring it up tomorrow on the Christmas Zoom call? I'd rather not be center stage. I expect there'll be the same numbers and chaos, with everyone being, shall I say *festive*, even on camera."

"Gotcha," said Bob. "Now, let's get the dishes done before Santa comes. Tomorrow we can talk about your job. I suspect it's a real eye opener.

CHAPTER FIFTEEN

Man Camp near Mexican Water, AZ
December 26, 2020

Derek Behrendt, arms crossed at chest level, stood on the stoop of his office-trailer glaring at the three Ford Explorers and one thirty-foot motorhome, all bearing Federal government license plates, as they rolled through the gate of the compound. In his fist he held the folded and wrinkled court order just presented to him by Wendy Burkenshaw.

Standing together a few feet from the office trailer, Detective Raymond Phillip and Wendy watched as the little convoy came to a halt. Ten men and women disembarked from the vehicles, six in white coveralls and blue rubberized booties. Four were in mufti, but wearing blue windbreakers with **FBI** emblazoned in gold letters across the backs. Raymond said sardonically, "I can't help but note that it took the FBI two weeks to respond to a brutal rape and missing girl by sending a single agent. Yet now that we have a probable murder of a *white* man, the cavalry comes charging in, in force."

"I take your point," Wendy said.

The small FBI task force consisted of six forensic evidence specialists and two IT specialists. The other two in windbreakers, both male, were special agents. Wendy briefed them as a group, then climbed into the back of the motorhome, which would be their command post. She set up her laptop and established a secure video connection with her superior in Albuquerque, Special Agent in Charge, Dave Akerman.

"The team is here" she advised him. "They're already in the process of interviewing the few oil people and security personnel around, and copying the hard drives of the office computers."

"Good."

"We'll obtain access to the corporate shared drive containing the personnel records and start going through those from here in our command post. Meanwhile, the forensic specialists in their cute little white suits will comb through the vehicles on the compound, rifle through the garbage dumpsters and search the sleeping quarters."

"Roger that." His visage on the colored screen revealed dark circles under heavily browed eyes, a furrowed forehead and a bald pate inadequately camouflaged with a ridiculous combover. "Make efficient use of your time. I had to prostrate myself and practically give away my first born to get those resources out of Denver and Phoenix. We need to return them as soon as possible."

"Okay, sir. Anything further?"

He looked away, obviously glancing at another computer screen. "Yes. Just for your information, the Surete du Québec – that's the provincial police – made the notification to Guy Primeau's next of kin in Verdun. They also determined that he had $100,000 in life insurance. Part of a group policy through his employer, the oil company. The sole beneficiary is a slightly older sister."

"I'm sure we'll be able to confirm that as soon as we get into the personnel files. That would automatically make his sister a person of interest."

"Yeah, but the Surete also looked into that and determined she has a solid alibi. Hasn't been out of Verdun since the pandemic started. They're now pursuing the question as to whether or not she could have contracted with someone in the States for a hit."

"Seems doubtful to me. The whole reason we have this search warrant is based on the probability that he was offed because he knew something about the rapes here that he was about to divulge to me."

"Me too, actually."

An hour later, one of the forensic techs entered the command post gripping a pair of tweezers from which a gold earring dangled. "Found this under the back seat of one of the pickups. You may have grounds to expand the search parameters. Under the magnifying glass it looks like there's a tiny piece skin tissue stuck to the hook. This was probably ripped from someone's ear either inadvertently or deliberately."

"Right you are." The earring was in the shape of a cross with a piercing hook. "We'll get this off to Quantico for analysis. Meantime, start looking for DNA in that vehicle."

"We're already combing it for loose hairs. We dusted it for prints as well, but it's been wiped clean. The license plate number is **2 OIL 773**."

"Okay, thanks. I'll see if we can find out who's been driving it over the past several weeks."

From personnel records, Wendy determined that vehicle usage and maintenance records were managed by Sharon Hathale, Derek Behrendt's secretary. Although she too was off for Christmas, she lived on the reservation in Kayenta. Wendy got her on the phone on the third ring.

"I can answer that question without coming in," she said. "**773** is assigned to Mark Snyder on the A crew and Roger Pringle on the B Crew."

"And which crew would have been on duty on the 5th of December?"

"The A crew was on the whole month of December. After New Year's, the B crew will be here until February 1st."

"All right, so this Mark Snyder would now be home on Christmas leave."

"Yes," Sharon said. "I can go online and find his home address if you'd like."

"Thank you. But, I did that as we spoke. Looks like he lives in Tacoma, Washington when he's not in camp."

"That sounds right, but good luck finding him. He said something about using his Christmas leave to take his girlfriend to a remote cabin somewhere in the mountains. He was pretty excited about it."

• • •

At 5:15 p.m., Derek Behrendt stepped into the command post and demanded. "What the hell are those snow bunnies doing? They're bagging cigarette butts out of the dumpster."

Wendy looked up from her computer screen and rubbed her eyes. "They're looking for anything that may contain DNA we can test for matches with the rape victim in Window Rock."

"This is bullshit, Agent. That's beyond the scope of your warrant which says you're looking for evidence related to the possible – and I emphasize *possible* – murder of Guy Primeau."

"That's right, Mr. Behrendt. But we've found material that may belong to one of the rape victims. That allows us to expand the search. It gives us probable cause for exception to the search warrant limitations. You can check that out with your legal beagle in Houston. If you don't like it, I can secure the site, await the DNA matching and then request a new warrant with expanded parameters. That could take a week or longer, given that we're between Christmas and New Year's. In the meantime, your operations would be frozen."

"Fuck! Just do what you gotta do and get those fuckheads out of my hair." He stormed across the compound to his office.

CHAPTER SIXTEEN

Santa Fe, New Mexico
December 27, 2020

Melissa met Pam at Frenchy's Field Park on the southwest side of Santa Fe. Over a span of four years, the two had become great friends and confidantes as colleagues at the New Mexico State Legislature, when Melissa had worked for Representative George Louie. This was the first time in six weeks they'd seen each other, and as badly as they wanted to hug, they had to settle for bumping elbows.

"Let's head upstream along the river," suggested Pam. "The nicest section of the Greenway is the part that goes straight through town."

River was an overstatement. The Santa Fe River, a tributary of the Rio Grande, was more a wide stream as it coursed through the city, but its banks, carpeted in green and well treed, hosted a charming 4.5-mile long pathway.

"So, what's new at The Roundhouse?" asked Melissa, referring to the state capitol, the only one in the United States built in a circular architectural pattern.

"You mean who got married, who got divorced and who's sleeping with whom?"

"Well, now that you frame it that way..."

"Jeez, girl. You've only been gone for six weeks!" Pam laughed, jiggling her cascades of red curls. "The legislature doesn't even convene again until January 19th. Why don't you tell me what they've got you doing out there on the reservation?"

"Mostly helping to plan workshops, and training sessions around preventing and combating MMIW. The vision is to end violence against indigenous women by strengthening the community response. Through education. It's satisfying work, but I'm just beginning to understand the scope of the problem – it's North America wide. And heartbreaking." A flash of pain passed over her face.

"I know. Have you heard of the Highway of Tears in British Columbia?"

"Maybe I read something about that online a few months ago? That long stretch of highway in the north, where dozens of young women and girls have disappeared?"

"It's a 450 mile stretch of highway between Prince George and Prince Rupert in B.C. A remote and isolated area. In the last fifty years, since 1970, hundreds, not dozens, of women and girls have disappeared along that roadway and only a few bodies have been found. There's a disproportionately high number of indigenous women on the list of victims."

As they neared the downtown district, they passed through an underpass, the stream still gurgling gently beside them. Several runners passed them in the opposite direction.

Pam added, "Needless to say, poverty, drug abuse and domestic violence are all contributing to the problem. And I suppose it's the same on and around many reservations, but low rates of car ownership don't help. It means the only way they can get to work or school is by hitchhiking. In a remote area like that, it makes them more vulnerable."

"I don't know the details about the Highway of Tears," said Melissa. "But it's agonizing in its familiarity."

"Yeah. One reason so few bodies are ever found is because it's such a wild and remote area. Remains dumped along the highway are often carried off and scattered by the animals. Bears, wolves, cougars, what have you."

"You've done your homework about that place. Have you traveled up there?"

"I haven't. But look, we're only a couple of blocks from the Plaza. Let's pop over there and get a coffee. I'll tell you the story over a table face to face."

"Aren't the restaurants around the Plaza closed because of Covid?"

"Some are. But we can still get outside seating. It'll be brisk, but we're dressed for it."

They found a table under the building overhang at the Thunderbird Grill and ordered lattes. Both were served in wide mouth cups, and artfully decorated with foam swirls on top.

Pam pushed the foam off to one side before she took a sip. "When my Aunt June was 20, between her junior and senior years in college, she took a summer job in Northern BC planting trees on a reforestation project. She met and married a First Nations man. They made their home in Prince George and within a year, she had a baby girl. They named her Dawn. One summer evening in 2008, when Dawn was 17, she left the house in Prince George to go for a bike ride with her cousin Alvin. He was the last person to see her. He left her near a bridge on Highway 16, two miles west of Prince George and pedaled home to get them each a jacket. When he pedaled back to meet her, he thought he heard the door of a pickup slam. But when he reached the bridge, there was no pickup truck, and his cousin was gone. Her bike was still there."

"And she was never found?"

"Not a trace. According to my aunt, the police did a cursory investigation, but they seemed pretty indifferent. For decades, the indigenous community in Canada has been fighting to have police agencies and government recognize that First Nations women and girls go missing or are murdered at a much higher rate than the national average. Aunt June has worked hard to persuade the police and the politicians to be more aggressive in investigating. She says, in many cases, the police take the view that these missing persons just wandered off. Like they're not really worthy of a deeper look."

Melissa felt sick to her stomach. She pushed her latte aside. "It's the same story in the States. It was only in 2019 that the Bureau of Indian Affairs established cold case offices and began coordinating more active investigations into MMIW."

"In Canada, there's been enough press interest and media ink about MMIW that the authorities have finally put together a number of special task forces to fight the problem and clean up old cases. But Aunt June is still agonizing over Dawn. The last time we spoke, her sorrow came through loud and clear over the phone. It left me with a pain in my chest so tight I could barely breathe. Holy shit, Melissa, how can you possibly bear to be so close to this depravity day after day?"

"It's true, when I took this gig I may have been idealistic in thinking I wanted to help combat the issue. But what I've learned is that the pain is unrelenting. There are nights when I just can't sleep. On the drive up here from Window Rock, I actually contemplated quitting. But I've met so many dedicated, sweet people who are, you know, decisively engaged in finding solutions. I can't, with a clear conscience, just walk away from it.

CHAPTER SEVENTEEN

Enroute to Gallup, New Mexico
December 31, 2020

The morning air was crisp, the light brilliant, with the mountains to the left of the highway well defined against the background of clear azure sky. Wendy Burkenshaw felt as if she could reach out and touch them, prick her fingers on their sharply pointed peaks. But she needed this driving time to prepare for the interview with Beth's mother, coming up in a few minutes. Given the McKinley County Sheriff Department report on their initial interview with her, Wendy's expectations for much useful information were low. She hoped that at least she could get Ms. Chee's DNA to check against that found on the earring.

The executive housekeeper was cooperative, but guarded. "Yes ma'am. You'll find Flower Chee in room 210. Take the elevator to the second floor and turn left, but please don't keep her more than thirty minutes or so. She has eight rooms to turn over today and this's only the second one."

The door to Room 210 was open. Wendy approached and entered without knocking. "Hello," she said loud enough for her voice to be heard over the whine of a vacuum cleaner.

The woman operating it wore baggy pants and a blue-bibbed apron over a short sleeve shirt. She turned. "Oh," she said, and switched off the vacuum. "You must be the FBI lady." She spoke through a plain white facemask, and after her first glance at Wendy, mostly kept her eyes lowered. "I can only talk for a few minutes. I can't be much help. What d'you want to ask?"

"I'm Wendy Burkenshaw, Ms. Chee. How about if we sit down. I'll be as brief as possible."

Ms. Chee pointed Wendy to the one upholstered armchair in the room and took a seat on the edge of the bed. She chewed on the inside of her lip.

"I'm sorry about your daughter's disappearance. It must be so difficult." She could see how difficult it was in the way Flower Chee wrapped her arms around her middle, as if to hold herself together. "But I need to ask some questions about Beth to help with our investigation. Let's start with Beth's friends, Ms. Chee. Can you help me understand who she hung out with? Was she interested in boys? Did she talk about friends? Boys in particular?"

"Far's I know, her only friend is the neighbor, Julie. The two of them go to some church thing together one night a week. But I don't know nuthin' about that. 'Fraid I don't have time to be no mother to her. I work my butt off here for $10.50 an hour just tryin' to keep some food on the table." Her eyes spoke of a chaotic and unstable life.

"I understand. It must be very difficult for you."

"You *don't* understand." Her anger fizzed to the surface. "You're a white woman with 'n education. You got no idea 'bout being an Indian woman with eighth grade, tryin' to pass on our ways to a daughter when I have time. But working in a white man's world six days a week."

"I'm sorry. You're right. I can't totally understand your life. Is it true that you stay here in Gallup four or five nights a week?"

"The hotel lets me stay in a room – more like a supply closet off the housekeeping office. Driving back and forth every day'd cost 25% of my take-home pay. And let me tell you, working here's not satisfying. People are always coming and going. Don't bother putting any effort in cuz management don't recognize it. They're too busy talking to each other to say 'thanks' to me. And if you can't handle the pressure, they'll just take you right off the schedule, not even giving you a chance to finish out the pay period." She paused long enough to dab at her eyes with the corner of her apron. "I'm sorry. I don't mean to unload on you. I just don't have time to be any mother to Beth. I hope you find her, but I think she might be dead."

"We hope not, Ms. Chee. What makes you think so?"

"A dream I had."

"Tell me about that dream."

"It was scary. So real. Beth and me were walking' along an empty road together. Hot air. Dry wind. Evening almost on. Out of nowhere a huge hawk with talons like ... I don't know ... big mechanical diggers or something, comes swooping down and grabs her."

"Was that the actual night that Beth disappeared that you had this dream?"

"Yes ma'am. It was. I woke feeling so empty. I knew Beth was really gone."

Wendy observed her carefully before speaking. Was this an example of the spiritual nature of Navajo culture?

"We hope she's not dead," she said. "We don't have any evidence to suggest that she is." She reached into her bag and pulled out an 8 x 10 glossy photograph of the cross-shaped earring found in the pickup truck at the man camp. "Ms. Chee, do you recognize this? Did this belong to Beth?"

"I don't know. I'm ashamed to say that. I'm a terrible mom." Silent tears rolled down her brown cheeks. Again, she brought the apron to her eyes.

"We found this earring in the back of a pickup truck driven by men from an oil company camp up on the north side of the reservation. The FBI lab is trying to get some DNA from it. Would you mind giving us a sample of your DNA? We only need to do a Q-tip swipe on your gums."

"What's DNA?"

"Uh. ... Well, it's the hereditary material we carry in the cells of our body. Every cell in our body has the same material, which can be examined and decoded under a microscope."

Ms. Chee narrowed her eyes, but nodded noncommittally.

"It's actually more reliable than fingerprints in identifying individuals. But close relatives have DNA molecules that very closely resemble each other. So, if we had a sample of your DNA we could probably tell if the DNA on the earring, if any, is a very close relative. In other words, if it's Beth's."

"Would that mean she's dead if it is?"

"No. No. It would just tell us that she was probably in that truck. We'd then have evidence to pursue the driver of the truck for questioning."

"Do I need a lawyer before I decide?"

"No, Ms. Chee. You're not under suspicion of anything."

"Well, I guess it's okay. Have you got one of them Q-tips with you now?"

CHAPTER EIGHTEEN

Shiprock, New Mexico
January 4, 2021

The parking lot and sidewalks were covered with three inches of fresh snow. Melissa parked as close to the door as possible without taking any of the stalls reserved for disabled persons. The MacDonald's restaurant, a clean and modern structure of red brick, sharply contrasted with much of the other architecture in Shiprock, an impoverished town far on the northeast corner of the reservation. She pushed the door open, dusted the snow off her jacket in the vestibule, then made her way to the service counter.

"Hi.WelcometoMacdonalds.MayIhelpyou?" The earnest counter clerk made it sound like a song with one multisyllabic word.

"Just a coffee with cream please," said Melissa. "I'd like to park in one of your booths to make a couple of phone calls."

The clerk, perhaps all of seventeen, didn't know how to respond to that. But a nearby supervisor, wearing a headset for drive-thru communications, stepped up and flashed a warm smile. "Of course, ma'am. We're not busy. Stay as long as you'd like. Where are you visiting from?"

Normally, Melissa might have said, *Well I was born here but now I live in Window Rock.* But wanting to avoid lengthy small talk, she said only, "I'm on my way from Santa Fe to Window Rock. I'm doing some work there for a few months."

"Cool. Are you staying overnight here in Shiprock?"

"Farmington. I'm staying there tonight." Her online search for accommodations had revealed less than glowing reports for the one motel in Shiprock. "But, do you by any chance know a man in his mid-thirties named Ronald George? I think he might live here."

"Ronald used to work here. It didn't work out for him and he left after six months. Said he was taking a higher paid job. That was a year ago. I think he lived just south of town, but I'm not sure if he's still there. How do you know him?"

Melissa couldn't believe her luck, an affirmative response to her very first query in Shiprock. But it was a very small town. "I don't really know him. He's a friend of a friend. I promised her I'd say hello for her if I ran into him."

"Well, as I said, I don't really know if he still lives here. Good luck with that."

The booth afforded a good view up the snowy main drag toward the row of single-story buildings that made up the tiny business district. Could she have been born in this place? Or had whoever deposited her at the rock formation south of town brought her from elsewhere?

If she had been born here, the community hospital where Rebecca White had taken her a day or two later might still have records of births for the first few days of August, 1994. She had no idea what her mother's name was, or if she'd been given a name at birth, but in a community this small, there couldn't be many births in any given week. Maybe a stop at the hospital would be worth the effort. On the other hand, since she didn't even have a birth certificate, maybe she'd been born in a home somewhere ... or in a car for that matter.

If Willie Cole of Elberton, Georgia was in fact her father, hopefully he'd be able to shed some light on all this. She had waited to e-mail him until yesterday, her last day in Santa Fe, and had checked her phone several times on the drive up. No new e-mails. He was a high school vice principal, apparently a responsible man. She had expected him to respond fast, maybe within 24 hours. But then again, if he was taken totally by surprise, maybe he'd need time to think, just as she had, in waiting a week to e-mail him.

Halfway through her coffee, she dialed Bernie Begay's number. "Hey Bernie," she said, "I'm in Shiprock. How's Julie doing?"

"Thanks for asking. She's pretty much recovered from her own trauma, but she's very blue about Beth. Keeps saying, 'Mom, I know she's out there somewhere. Can't we do something?' I keep reassuring her that the police, even the FBI, are looking for her.

"But hey listen, I tried to call you several hours ago and didn't get an answer, not even your voice mail. You must have been in dead space."

"Yeah. There's plenty of dead air between Española and Cuba along Highway 96. What's up?"

"The Navajo Police District in Shiprock got back to me this morning. I spoke to a Sergeant Descheene. He said there's no criminal record on Ronald George. But he knows Ronald. Said they play softball together in the spring and summer."

"Wow."

"Sergeant Descheene says Ronald George is a solid citizen, a pillar of the community. He works for the post office as a rural letter carrier. I then called the post office and they gave me his cell phone number. I'll send that to you by text."

"Fantastic. I hope I can reach him today, while I'm here. I'm staying overnight in Farmington."

"That's not all. When I told Sergeant Descheene why we're looking for Ronald, he said he'd pull up the file of your being found and reopen it as a cold case. He said they – the police – would be interested in finding the mother and pursuing prosecution. I'll send you Sergeant Descheene's number too, in case you want to talk to him."

"Jeez. I'm stirring up quite a caldron."

"Good luck finding Ronald. I'll send the text now."

Still in McDonald's, Melissa punched in the number for Ronald George. He answered right away. She identified herself and explained the purpose of her call.

"Holy cow. Are you kidding? I'm stunned, but I remember that day like it was yesterday. Are you sure you're twenty-six?"

"I'm twenty-six all right. Sorry to spring this on you."

"Not at all, I'm glad you called. Uhm, I'm afraid I can't really help you with finding your parents. But I could take you to the site and show you where we found you."

"I'd love that. But I'm only planning to be here today. I'm staying overnight in Farmington and heading to Window Rock tomorrow."

"I'll be finished with my route at about 3:00 o'clock. What time is it now? Ah 2:20. Why don't you meet me in about 45 minutes at the Subway on the south side of town? It's on Highway 491 at Tachoo Nii Blvd and easy to find. You can see their sign for about a mile. You can leave your car there and we'll go out to Shiprock Peak in my Jeep."

"Sounds good. I haven't eaten since breakfast in Santa Fe, so maybe I'll get there a little early and have a salad."

"Okay. See you a few minutes after 3:00. Just watch for a Blue Jeep Patriot in the parking lot."

•   •   •

As they drove south, Melissa found banter with Ronald easy. As they chatted about the legends and myths surrounding Shiprock Peak, she glanced sideways at his face. He was not only intelligent, but easy to look at, with coarse black hair, neatly trimmed, high cheekbones and a finely built nose, slightly wider than that of most Caucasian men. He had taken off his brown facemask when they met, outside, but he wore it again now that they were inside his Jeep. He was well put together.

They turned right onto a rough gravel road and passed a warning sign advising them that non-Natives were not permitted beyond this point. "Do I qualify?" asked Melissa. "I'm half Native American."

He laughed. "I'm sure you do. The tribal advocates that keep their eyes on this place know me and know my car, so it's not a problem. Their big concern is thoughtless tourists who might deface the sacred mountain with graffiti, or maybe just litter or leave tracks. Beyond that, they have superstitious reasons for not wanting tourists here. A man was killed while climbing the rock a number of years ago. The Navajos have a traditional fear of death and its aftermath. So, the peak is taboo."

"I thought it was off limits because it's sacred."

"It *is* sacred. *Changing Woman's* two sons, *Born for Water* and *Enemy Slayer*, killed the evil bird, *Tsé Nináhálééh*, who lived on top of the peak but fed on human flesh. Many other spirits inhabit the mountain. Including evil spirits, which are thought to have come to contaminate the mountain since the man was killed there."

As though a curtain had suddenly arisen from the desert floor, the iconic pinnacle filled the windshield with a spectral omnipresence. Melissa was inexplicably overcome with emotion at the sight of the haunting crag. Her eyes filled with tears. This mountain could have taken her life as an infant. But instead, its spirit *gave* her life by summoning the three children who rescued her.

Ronald turned toward her. "Are you okay?"

"I don't know.... I just feel so ... weird. It's like I've been here before and I'm supposed to come back."

"You have been here before. Maybe the spirits are talking to you. Saying, 'Welcome back.'"

"I know. I know ... but I don't remember. Couldn't possibly remember. It's like déjà vu or something. Like I'm supposed to be here ... like I've come home. It's so weird. But it makes me cry."

Ronald took a hand from the wheel and patted her shoulder. "It's okay to feel that way. This mountain touches people's souls all the time."

His touch on her shoulder produced another wave of warmth. She grasped his hand briefly, then, embarrassed, released it.

When they reached the base of the mountain, they were greeted by more signage warning them that climbing on the rocks at the base or scaling the mountain itself was taboo. One sign indicated that climbing the sacred peak could stir up the ghosts and create bad medicine. Ronald parked at the edge of the talus slope. They stepped out of the Jeep and stared upward at the majestic mountain.

Still feeling nostalgic, Melissa lifted her misty eyes to the summit of the peak, 1500 feet above where they stood. The sky was clear. The sun's rays slanting from the west cast the mountain in a golden glow. "Tell me some of the other legends about this place," she said.

"Well, one of the most famous fables is that the Diné people were transported from another place to live on the top of the mountain, coming down only to plant fields and get water. One day the peak was struck by lightning, obliterating the trail and leaving only a sheer cliff. The women and the children were stranded on the top to starve."

"So, what happened to them? Were they rescued somehow? I mean the people survived to become a great nation. How'd they get down from the mountain?"

"The legend doesn't answer that. I guess it ends in what you'd call a cliff-hanger. Literally." He glanced at her. "Sorry. Bad joke."

Melissa laughed anyway. For a few moments, they silently contemplated the great monolith basking in the late afternoon light.

Melissa broke the spell. "So, where did you guys find me?"

Ronald pointed to a large outcrop in the talus slope. "See that huge boulder over there?"

"Yes. Is that it?"

"You were in a gym bag behind that rock. It was a really spooky day with lightning and thunder and very black clouds. We heard you crying and thought it was ghosts. Willie and I both wanted to get outta here. But Rebecca had more balls than either of us. She climbed up there and brought the bag back down here."

"I guess I know the rest of the story."

"Right. Rebecca opened the bag and there you were, all pink and wrinkly, wrapped in an old army blanket. Your upper lip was trembling. I guess because you'd been crying so much."

"Thanks for bringing me here, Ronald. I think this'll really help me understand more about who I am." She stepped close to him and hugged him, Covid be damned.

When she had retrieved her car, Melissa made a stop at the Northern Navajo Medical Center on the north side of Shiprock. The woman at the admissions desk advised her that the records office had closed at 4:30 but would open again at 07:00 in the morning. Well, stopping here in Shiprock again tomorrow morning while headed to Window Rock would be okay. Maybe she could work out a way to see Ronald again if it didn't interfere with his duties as a mail carrier.

•   •   •

The outside temperature registered 29 degrees on the dashboard display as Melissa drove east to claim her hotel room in Farmington. The late afternoon light slanting from behind her, just before sunset, was brilliant, with an ethereal quality. A flash of movement to her left front caught her eye. She turned her head and watched a hawk drop from the sky like a missile. Some critter was about to die.

The sun sets fast in the southwest, and twenty minutes later just a hint of twilight remained in her rear-view mirror as the fading light was eclipsed by a set of headlights, obviously on high beam, rapidly approaching from the rear and filling her mirrors with blinding glares.

Melissa reached up and flicked the switch to change the inside mirror to night mode. That helped. But as the vehicle behind her continued to approach at high speed, her side mirrors both reflected intensely. She adjusted both of them to different angles. This reduced the dazzling light, but now the vehicle coming up behind her was switching its headlights between low and high beam repeatedly. It had a high center of gravity, a large pickup truck or a big SUV. The vehicle approached within a few feet of her rear bumper and began honking its horn. For the second time in only a few weeks, fear clutched her heart like a vice.

She slowed her speed slightly and pulled to the right, partly on the shoulder, to allow it to pass. But instead of passing, the other vehicle pulled abreast of her and swerved to the right in an obvious and flagrant attempt to stop her. Melissa tapped on the brakes to slow even further. But the other vehicle, which she could now identify as a dark-colored pickup truck, followed suit and stayed alongside.

She pressed hard on the accelerator and surged ahead of the pickup, swinging back into the right lane from the shoulder. She continued to accelerate until her speedometer registered a dangerous 75 miles per hour.

The pickup soon caught up and came up behind Melissa's Toyota Highlander. She felt a slight bump. The other vehicle had struck her rear bumper – a signal to pull over.

Near panic, she attempted to steer the car on a steady course with one hand, while also punching 9-1-1 into her hands-free cellular display.

Within five seconds a young male voice came over her speaker, "Nine-one-one. What's your emergency?"

"I'm being harassed by another vehicle – crowding me from behind – swerving toward me. Honking. They're trying to force me off the road ... or get me to stop. They—"

"What's your location ma'am? And can you tell me your name?"

"I'm on ... Oh God. They just bumped me again ... I'm on ...uh ... Highway 64 ... maybe five or six miles west of Farmington. My name is Melissa."

"Okay ma'am. Which way are you headed?"

"Jesus. They're behind me and still bumping my bumper. I'm doing 75 and they're right with me ... Can you help me?"

"Yes ma'am. I've already alerted the police. Which direction are you headed in?"

"East. About five miles from Farmington, I think. Oh God. This is crazy. They're sticking right with me and blowing their horn. Like they want me to stop. But I'm scared to."

"Okay, Melissa. I want you to try to maintain your speed and do your best to ignore them. The police have been notified of your situation. Please try to drive into Farmington and pull into the parking lot of the Walmart on the West side of town. It's just off the highway, again, on the west side of town."

"I'm still doing over 75 miles per hour. They're right on my rear end and honking like crazy."

"You're doing fine, Melissa. Just keep driving. Keep talking to me. The police will meet you at the Walmart."

The pickup alternately tapped her rear bumper and pulled alongside to swerve in her direction several more times. Melissa could see two occupants gesturing for her to pull over. She screamed and tapped her brakes again, in a panic, not really knowing what that would achieve other than to illuminate her brake lights.

Dumb move. The other driver became even more aggressive and banged into her rear bumper, then again pulled alongside and swerved into her, this time actually making metal to metal contact. The side-mounted mirror on Melissa's Highlander snapped off and thudded against the door a couple of times before falling away.

"Oh mercy," she said through clenched teeth.

"It'll be okay, Melissa," said the 9-1-1 operator. "Try to maintain your speed and keep your eyes to the front. One police unit is heading west to meet you and two are now in the Walmart parking lot."

Melissa sped past the first 'reduce speed' sign on the outskirts of Farmington. She could see flashing blue lights approaching from the opposite direction. "I see the police," she said breathlessly.

"Okay Melissa. Blink your high beams at them so they'll know it's you they're approaching."

She furiously pumped the lever controlling the high beams for several seconds. But the police car was abreast of her all too suddenly. She first became aware of its wailing siren as it roared past her moving westward. The truck came along side and slammed into her door panel again. "My

God, they passed me," she wailed, just as she entered the built-up area on the western side of Farmington. "They didn't do anything to help." She reduced her speed to 50 and tried to maintain both her course and regain her composure.

Now with opposing traffic flowing through the suburbs, the driver of the pickup was unable to come abreast of her vehicle, but he stuck to a tailgating posture.

Melissa slowed further. She could see the large Walmart sign several blocks ahead on the left. In the darkness, it cast a blue aura.

Without using her signal light, she swung hard to the left and pulled into the parking lot. The truck followed her through the turn, its high beam headlights burning brightly.

She spotted two police cruisers near the main entrance and aimed for them, her speed excessive for a busy parking lot. She bounced over two speed humps and ignored the pedestrians preparing to use the crosswalk at the front entrance.

She pulled up to the two police vehicles and hit her brakes.

The occupants of the pickup on her tail spotted the police and attempted a u-turn, foiled as a third police car came up behind them and turned sideways across the driveway.

The police from all three vehicles jumped out with guns drawn. Multiple voices shouted, "Keep your hands where we can see them. Get out of the vehicle. Now."

Melissa slumped down in her seat and took a deep breath, trying to slow her heart rate. Realizing the line was still open to the 9-1-1 operator, she said, "I think I'm okay. The cops are taking two men out of the vehicle."

"Okay, Melissa. Please stay in your vehicle. They'll want a statement from you. Good luck to you."

"Okay." Despite her attempt to compose herself, she sobbed. "Thanks so much for your help."

"You're welcome, Melissa. Bye."

As the supercharged rush of adrenaline ebbed, Melissa found her quaking, hands shaking as violently as if she were mixing martinis. She crossed her arms across her chest, partly because she felt suddenly chilled, partly to quell the trembling. She touched the phone button on her steering column and said, "Call Bernie."

She heard a series of clicks, one ring tone then the answer, "Indigenous Women's Network, Bernie speaking."

"Oh Ber-nie." Melissa tried to regain her composure and calm her warbling voice. "I'm in Farmington. I've been chased by two men in a pickup truck for the past ten miles." She broke down.

"Are you okay? Do you think you should call 9-1-1?"

"No.... I've been on ... the police are here now. They have the two guys. I was talking to the 9-1-1 guy the whole time. He got the police."

"Will you be okay? Should I call anyone for you?"

"No. I'll be okay. I just needed to talk with someone ... a friend, while I decompressed. Here comes a policewoman to speak with me now."

A female police officer, wearing a black facemask, approached the Highlander. "Do you feel like talking with me now?" she asked. "Or can I call the paramedics for you?"

"I can talk." Melissa reached for the door handle.

"You can stay in your car ma'am. I'll slide in the front seat with you. You were lucky," she added. "It's generally not advisable for female motorists to be out on that highway alone after dark." She walked around to the passenger side and slid in.

Melissa felt foolish. She should have known better, given her intimate familiarity with the MMIW problem in this region. Then she felt a surge of anger. Why shouldn't she be able to drive without fear? "Who were ... are those guys? What happens now?"

"They're local oil field workers out lookin' for a good time. Read: they wanna get laid, even if it means terrorizing you. We're booking them into jail pending charges. If you're ready, I'd like to take a statement from you now. Or, we can do it tomorrow if you'd prefer. They aren't going anywhere but to jail. After we have your statement, we'll be talking to the district prosecutor about charges against these yoyos."

"I'm ready to talk now."

• • •

Melissa slept fitfully that night, her breathing periodically labored as she fought off nightmares about the events on the highway. A good breakfast with fresh fruit juice and camomile tea calmed her somewhat the next morning.

Fortunately, the Toyota dealership in Farmington had the side mirror in stock in their parts department, so she was able to have it replaced and be on the road by 10:00 a.m. The left door panel was distressing – a large dent and several scratches – but it would lend some character to the vehicle, she decided, and it would fit right in on the reservation, where the majority did not drive flashy vehicles. She phoned Ronald as she drove into Shiprock, and he enthusiastically agreed to meet for lunch. He could take about forty-five minutes from his mail route.

At the Northern Navajo Medical Center, a staff member asked Melissa a litany of Covid-19 screening questions at the door, her responses all negative. In the medical records office, a clerk named Barbara told her that records so old were stored in the archives in another part of the hospital. She added, "I'll get someone else to watch the shop for a few minutes and we'll go to the archive room together. I could use a break from the phone in here anyway. It's been ringing constantly."

The storage room smelled musty, like old library books. Floor to ceiling racks stood in ranks like a platoon of guarding soldiers, each rack with multiple shelves of stacked cardboard record boxes. "I love it in here," Barbara said, as they walked between the stacks. "It reminds me of a wine cave I visited in Provence while my husband and I were on honeymoon. In the village of Lourmarin. Smelled just like this."

Melissa shot her a curious look.

"Are you wondering how a Native, living on the rez, could afford a honeymoon in Europe?" She laughed. "My husband's a doctor. We were in our late thirties when we got married. His practice was well established already. But here we are, 1994. The top two shelves on this rack." She counted the boxes from left to right, pointing at each with her index finger. "August would be in these two. Let's take them to the work table over in the corner."

Barbara lifted the dusty lid from one of the boxes and sorted through the file folders inside, each containing a patient's last name followed by a first name and a terminal digital file number. "Aha, Doe, Baby Jane. Admitted 3 Aug 94. This would be you."

Melissa gripped the edge of the table with both hands. "Oh my gosh. I'm real."

Barbara laughed. "It certainly looks like it." She glanced down at the two pages of clinical notes.

"It appears that everything tracks. You were admitted at 4:42 pm on August 3rd. A young girl, aged ten, by the name of Rebecca White brought you in. It says here she found you at Shiprock Peak. You were first examined by the E.R. doctor on duty, and then by a pediatrician; his name was James Water. Both found you in good health. Dr. Water estimated you had been born between 16 and 20 hours earlier." Barbara looked up from the folder and into Melissa's eyes. "How're you doing?"

"Well, my heart's racing like crazy, but I'm just fine."

"You must have been really cute. Some of the notes suggest you were much fussed over by the nurses."

They both laughed.

"Because you had apparently been abandoned, the chief nurse for the E.R. called in the tribal police. It looks like they arrived, took a statement from the nurse, questioned Rebecca White, then left. You were placed in the nursery adjacent to the maternity ward and given neonatal care until August 16th. At that time, you were discharged and taken from the hospital by Social Services who would put you in foster care. That's it."

Melissa left the hospital in a daze of information. Lots of details she'd never known.

The drive to the Nataani Nez restaurant took only five minutes. She spotted the blue Jeep Patriot in the parking lot, and as she fumbled to open the door, she found herself tingling with anticipation. As a result of excitement at seeing the man she had only met yesterday, or because of what she had just learned at the hospital? Maybe both.

When Melissa approached his table, he uncoiled his long frame from the chair and stood to hold a chair out for her – proving himself gallant, as well as good looking.

"Good to see you again," he said. "It looks like you're bursting with news." A waitress hovered at the table. "I told Bridgette here I only have forty-five minutes, so she's ready to take our orders. The fry bread is great wrapped around a burger. Let's order then you can tell me all about it."

Melissa ordered the fry bread burger, against her better judgement, and between delicious, juicy bites, she rattled off all the details she had learned at the hospital. Ronald's eyes never strayed from her face.

"You're staring," she said.

"Sorry. This is very weird. Don't get me wrong; it's great that you're getting closer to finding your birth parents, but for me it's strange because I'm remembering vividly that day we found you. It was one of, if not *the* most impactful, days of my childhood. Simply being on the forbidden ground was scary. The thought that there were ghosts was scary. But finding a wailing little baby was even more scary. Right now, though, I'm completely discombobulated. I can't connect the image of that baby with the beautiful woman sitting across from me."

She felt herself reddening. "Thanks, Ronald. Believe me, there are many 'disconnects' for me too." Then, to prevent him from taking the flattery further, she launched into her terrifying experience on the highway and explained how it had affected her for the rest of the evening in Farmington.

"Jeez, I'm surprised you can be so calm about it today. You must still be traumatized."

"I tossed and turned and fought off demons all night, but I'm better now. Still, I'll avoid the roads around these parts at night in the future, much as it irks me to think that I have to."

Their parting came too soon. And just as Ronald drove off, Melissa's cell rang.

"I'm glad I reached you. It's Barbara, the records clerk at the hospital. I found your number on Google. Listen, half an hour after you left the medical center, a janitor brought me a yellowed and faded note that evidently fell out of the file we were looking at. This could be important. Can you talk now? Or are you driving?"

"I'm in a parking lot. Go ahead."

"It seems like one of the nurses noticed a teenage girl, Native, in the corridor outside the nursery staring at you through the glass. She came three days in a row. She stayed for about fifteen minutes each time. Just staring at your bassinet. Nobody knows who she was ... and I guess nobody challenged her."

"Good Heavens. My birth Mom?"

"Well, no one knows, do they? But this is interesting. One of the nurses noticed that she had a wide tattoo with a Navajo design – lizard symbols – encircling her left wrist like a bracelet."

CHAPTER NINETEEN

Shiprock, New Mexico
January 5, 2020

In light of the news about the teenager with the tattoo, Melissa went in search of Sergeant Descheene, the Shiprock District member of the NPD who had told Bernie he was resurrecting the 26-year-old child abandonment file as a cold case. The digital time and temperature display on her dashboard, read 1:30. Hopefully she could meet with the policeman and get back on the road in time to get to Window Rock before darkness fell at about 5:30. It would be tight.

Situated just a few blocks from the Nataani Nez Restaurant, she found the police station easily. She parked in a visitor spot and made her way toward the public entrance. Four flags on tall aluminum poles snapped in the breeze as she strode along the sidewalk. She glanced up, and at the sight of the banners of the USA, the Navajo Nation, and the states of Arizona and New Mexico streaming straight out somehow felt reassured, as though all was well. Weirdly, the simple red brick design of the single-story building, emblematic of most government buildings on the reservation, also gave her a sense of security.

Inside, a surly gray-haired receptionist curtly told Melissa that Sergeant Descheene was out on a case and probably wouldn't be back in the office for the rest of the day. Undeterred, Melissa smiled warmly and complimented her on her fashionable sweater, a white cardigan with a band of Navajo-patterned red, gold and blue around the middle. As she turned to go, the woman scribbled a number on a sticky note and tore it off. "His cell," she said. "You might catch him on that."

Back in her car, she connected with Sergeant Descheene and identified herself.

"I'm glad to hear from you," he said. "Can you come by the office tomorrow morning for a chat about your case?"

"I've really got to get back to Window Rock tonight. But I have some information that could be helpful. Can I tell you on the phone?"

"Sure. Go 'head." She heard him rustling papers.

"The records clerk found a note in my clinical file about a teenaged girl, identity unknown, who came to the maternity ward three days in a row and stared at me in my crib through the nursery glass. She had a tattoo encircling her wrist like a bracelet. The note described it as being wide and having a Navajo lizard pattern."

"You're right. That could be useful. I'll have someone get a copy of that note into the case file."

"Good. If you should locate my birth mom, or if she should come forward, I would want her to know that I can forgive her. And I wish we'd gotten to know each other. Maybe we still can."

"That's a nice sentiment, Miss. And as a Native American, I can relate to it. But from a judicial standpoint, forgiveness is not on the plate. Child abandonment is taken seriously by both the state of New Mexico and the Feds. If it had gone differently ... if those three kids hadn't found you, we'd probably be talking homicide. I suspect if we locate her, a prosecutor at the federal level would want to go for child endangerment, at the minimum, or attempted murder. Either carry a penalty of up to twenty years in prison."

"I understand. But I would probably still forgive her."

An hour later, as she passed the turnoff to the man camp near Mexican Water, she vividly recalled the horror of being bumped and rammed at 75 miles per hour. She hoped the two men would not walk away with merely a slap on the wrist and a reckless driving charge. A feeling of foreboding took up residence in her gut as her thoughts turned to Beth Chee. Was she out here somewhere, alive or dead, in this rolling Arizona desert? Either way, it had been a month to the day since the abduction of the two girls. Would she ever be found?

• • •

Three days after Melissa returned to Window Rock, she and Bernie worked together to plan an upcoming webinar on domestic violence. A nationally renowned attorney and subject matter expert on domestic and sexual violence had donated her time and would be the principal speaker during the webinar. As always, it would be a challenge to make the event available to a wide audience of vulnerable women and children. Many on the reservation had neither access to a computer nor the skills to tune in to a webinar, so most of the 110 chapter houses in the Navajo Nation planned to reach out to vulnerable populations within their chapters, asking them to attend meetings hosted in their facilities. The challenge would be managing the local gatherings in such a way that social distancing could be observed in the typically cramped quarters of the chapter houses.

Bernie was on the phone with a chapter official in Shonto and Melissa was working on the agenda on her computer, when Special Agent Wendy Burkenshaw came into the office.

She and Melissa exchanged greetings, and then Wendy waited politely until Bernie had finished her call.

"Good afternoon ladies. I won't take much of your time. I have a quick question for you." She pulled a file from her briefcase and withdrew an 8 by10 glossy colored photo. "Do you by any chance recognize this, Ms. Begay?" The image was of a gold cross-shaped earring, which lay on a table with a pencil beside it to provide a sense of scale. Melissa looked at the picture as well.

"Yes." Her voice broke. "Beth Chee has a pair of earrings like that. They're her favorite. She wears them frequently."

"That's what we thought. We retrieved this from the back of a pickup truck, but our lab in Quantico wasn't able to profile the DNA. Do you know if Beth was wearing these on the 5th of December? The night she and Julie went to the Bible study?"

"She was here with Julie that afternoon, but I couldn't say for sure she was wearing them that day. Like I said, she does ... did wear them often."

"I wonder if Julie can confirm that Beth was wearing them that day?" asked Wendy.

"She's home now," Bernie said. "You can go by the house and ask her. I'll call to let her know that you'll be there in a few minutes."

"Okay. This helps. Thank you."

●　　●　　●

On January 11th, seven days after her harrowing experience on the road between Shiprock and Farmington, Melissa was working alone in the IWN office while Bernie attended a board meeting from home via Zoom. The familiar marimba tone of her cell phone jarred Melissa out of her deep thoughts about the forthcoming webinar.

"Is that Ms. Cody?"

"This is Melissa Cody, yes."

"My name is Michele McNair. I'm a prosecutor with the 11th Judicial District of New Mexico. Our Jurisdiction includes San Juan and McKinley counties. Have you got a minute?"

Melissa felt her heart skip a beat. This had to be about that terrifying incident. "Yes. Is this about January 4th?"

"It is ma'am."

"Okay. You've got my undivided attention." She inhaled deeply. "But please call me Melissa."

"Okay, Melissa. I thought you'd want to know that the two men who threatened you are aged 24 and 28. They're both oil field workers from the Chaco Basin area."

"Chaco? Is that along Highway 160 near Mexican Water?"

"No. Chaco Canyon is more south of Farmington. It's an active exploration area with a lot of fracking. Quite contentious, really – both from an environmental perspective and the occasional rowdy nature of the crews. The nearest town – it's more like a village – is Nageezi."

"I remember driving through that little hamlet on my up to Farmington from Santa Fe."

"I'm surprised to hear that. It'd be easy to miss if you blink. Anyway, the reason for the call is to let you know the charges we're considering for the two who harassed you so viciously."

"Okay?" Melissa said, the inflection in her voice rising with all the questions that suddenly sprang to mind.

"We're looking at felony attempted murder, felony assault with a deadly weapon, and felony aggravated assault."

"Oh wow. That sounds pretty heavy duty. You obviously mean business."

"We do. We could throw some lesser offenses in the mix too. But that would weaken the complaint and maybe allow a judge to lower the bail. It would also allow the defense attorney to wheedle his or her way into misdemeanor plea-bargain conversations."

"I see. I don't know if I should feel happy or sad."

"Well, while you're sorting that out, the other thing I'd like you to consider is that your testimony would obviously be essential at trial. Do you think you can do that? Given Covid-19, the trial is likely to be virtual, once its set."

"Yes. I'll commit to that. And if the trial happens to be live in a courtroom, I could come up to Farmington."

• • •

Minutes after the conversation with the New Mexico prosecutor, Melissa took another call; this one from Ronald George. "Melissa," he said, "I hope you don't mind my calling. I've been thinking about you. Our lunch meeting in Shiprock a week ago ended too abruptly."

"I've been thinking about you too. I'm glad you called. I hope we can get together again sometime. Do you ever get to Window Rock?"

"Not often. My job as a letter carrier doesn't give me a lot of time for getaways. You know our oath, 'Neither rain, nor sleet, nor dark of night' ... etc., etc."

"Well then, I'll have to get back up there. Maybe you can show me some of the other highlights of Shiprock apart from the Subway and Nataani Nez restaurants."

"Sure. Next time I can show you the Burger King, or KFC. Oh ... but wait. The real highlight for entertainment in the town of Shiprock is on Monday and Thursday afternoons when trucks are unloading at City Market."

"I can hardly wait. Listen, I want to tell you something. Right after we had lunch last week and just before I drove off, I had a phone call from the records lady at the Northern Navajo Medical Center. She told me that there was a note in my file that described a young Native woman coming into the hospital." She told him about the young woman staring at her for three consecutive days through the window of the nursery.

"And they think that may have been your Mom?"

"Nobody knows. But here's the interesting thing. She had a conspicuous tattoo encircling her wrist like a bracelet. It had a Navajo design depicting lizards. Just before I left Shiprock, I phoned Sergeant Descheene at the local cop shop to tell him. He said that could be very useful information."

"I know Descheene. We play softball together. I'll follow up with him."

"Good. In the meantime, I'll try to arrange another time I can come up to Shiprock. Try to think of something we can do other than watch the grocery truck unload."

CHAPTER TWENTY

Interstate 5, north of Everett, Washington
January 17, 2021

Trooper Sarah Hudspeth of the Washington State Patrol sat in her cruiser, in the truck parking area at the southbound rest area just north of Marysville, clocking the freeway traffic with a handheld radar gun. So far it had been a quiet afternoon. Five hours into her shift, she'd issued four speeding citations and had responded to a fender bender at the Stillaguamish River bridge. An hour earlier she had assisted an elderly couple who'd run out of fuel and were parked on the shoulder of the interstate with their four-way flashers on. She pulled up behind them, and after ensuring that both vehicles were sufficiently out of the traffic lane, she used an accessory tube off the fuel pump of her own vehicle to deliver a gallon of gas into their fuel tank. She then gave them directions to the nearest exit with fuel stations. They thanked her profusely, their beaming smiles reflecting their gratitude. That moment had made her day. She derived a great deal of satisfaction from helping the public, and she much preferred that aspect of her demanding career to busting drunks and speeders, or worse yet, attending motor vehicle accidents with injuries or fatalities.

A sporty, metallic red vehicle flashed passed her in the outside lane. The brilliant paint job alone would have caught her attention, but for a rainy, sloppy day in January, in the Northwest, the vehicle was remarkably clean and sparkly. She faintly remembered a description of a red Audi, appearing on a BOLO that morning, its driver sought by the FBI. Her radar readout indicated that the car was just under the speed limit, but something told her to check the vehicle out more closely. As she accelerated into the merge lane from the rest area, she brought the BOLO up on her computer screen and noted the details; 2020 Audi R8. Tango red metallic in color. Washington plate number **069 MARK**. Registered to one Mark Q. Snyder.

She caught up with the Audi just south of Marysville and a mile before reaching the bridge over the main channel of the Snohomish River. The driver responded to her blue light and short siren burst by pulling onto the shoulder. Trooper Hudspeth radioed her location and the fact that she had just 10-26ed the Audi in the BOLO. She requested backup. She then switched her mic to the grill-mounted loudspeaker and said, "Sir, you and your passenger remain in your vehicle for a few minutes please. Please put your hands on the dashboard. I'll be there to chat with you in a couple of minutes."

Three minutes later, a Snohomish County Sheriff's vehicle arrived and pulled onto the shoulder in front of the Audi, effectively blocking it in. Two deputies dismounted and stood behind their open doors facing the red vehicle. Each had unsnapped his holster, but left the pistols holstered.

Trooper Hudspeth placed a black facemask over her mouth and nose, lifted her large blue 'Smoky The Bear' hat off the passenger seat and placed it on her head as she slid from the vehicle. She unsnapped her holster and walked briskly to the driver-side window of the red Audi. "Sir, may I see your driver's license and vehicle registration, please?"

"What's this about? I wasn't doing anything wrong. I was under the limit."

"Yes sir, you were. Please produce your driver's license with one hand then get your vehicle registration out from wherever it is. Ma'am," she said, looking at the young female passenger, "Please keep your hands on the dashboard."

"I don't get it," the driver said, reaching for his wallet. "I wasn't doing anything wrong." He handed the documents to Trooper Hudspeth.

She glanced at the driver's license. "Mr. Snyder, do you have anything in the vehicle I should be concerned about? Firearms? Edged weapons? Drugs?"

Now clearly annoyed, Mark said, "Hell no. When are you going to tell me what this shit is all about?"

"Then you won't mind if I have a look. Pop your trunk please. Then get slowly out of the vehicle – both of you. Keeping your hands where we can see them, walk to the front of your vehicle, remain on your respective sides of the car and face the deputies in the other police vehicle. Do you understand what I'm asking you to do?"

"This is fuckin' ridiculous," he said, climbing out. "Go ahead and search all you want. You won't find anything. And when you're finished and come up empty handed, I'm calling my lawyer. We'll lodge a complaint against you with the State Patrol, or the governor's office if necessary."

"You're certainly within your rights to do that, Mr. Snyder."

After taking ten minutes to thoroughly search the trunk, under the seats, the glove compartment and under the dashboard, Sarah went back to her cruiser and radioed her dispatcher with the status of the stop. No weapons or contraband were found in the vehicle.

She stepped forward, strode past where Mark and the woman were standing and spoke to the two deputies for a moment. Then she came back to within six feet of Mark. "Mr. Snyder, the FBI has some questions for you. Their agents will meet us in an interview room at the Sheriff's office on Rockefeller Avenue in Everett—"

Snyder rudely interrupted her. "This is bullshit," he shouted, now turning florid and clenching his fists. "Fuckin' bullshit. You ain't got anything to hold me on."

"I'm not holding you, Mr. Snyder, I'm delivering you to an interview with federal agents. Now sir, we can do this one of two ways. You can get back in your car, start it up and follow the two deputies downtown. I'll be right behind you in my cruiser. Or, I can place you in handcuffs, put you in the back of my vehicle and drive you downtown. Your choice."

"Shit. You're going to be real sorry once I've talked to my lawyer. What about my girlfriend. Does the FBI want to talk with her too?" he asked with venom in his voice.

"No sir. If you choose to drive your own vehicle, she can ride with you. Once we get to the County Campus Plaza, she can do whatever, or go wherever, she'd like. If you decide to ride with me in cuffs, she can take your car and go ... wherever. Or, if you'd prefer, we can have your car towed. Again, it's your choice."

"Nobody but me touches my car. I'll drive it to the fuckin' Sheriff's office."

•　•　•

With his navy-blue suit and red tie, and an American flag lapel pin, Special Agent Fred Wong looked more like a young politician than a law enforcement officer. His partner, Special Agent Sally McKnight, wore a red turtleneck sweater with a string of faux pearls. Thrown over the sweater, a blue FBI windbreaker emblazoned with gold letters looked incongruent with the rest of her ensemble, and somehow caused her to look less capable beside her well-dressed partner.

The two sat in folding chairs on the same side of a square, wooden table in a windowless room. Mark Snyder, wearing a malicious scowl above his leather jacket, sat opposite them.

A sheriff's deputy set a pitcher of water and three glasses on the table, then left the room.

Sally started the session by looking up at the video camera mounted near the ceiling in a corner and announced, "This is January 12, 2021 at 1530 hours in the Snohomish County Sheriff's Office interview room 1. Special Agents Sally McKnight and Fred Wong interviewing subject Mark Q. Snyder." She glanced over at Fred Wong and nodded.

"We'll start with some easy questions," Fred said. "Can you give us your full name, date of birth and current address?"

"Do I need a lawyer here?"

"It's your right to have one if you wish. But you're not accused of anything. You're not in custody. It shouldn't be necessary. As we proceed, if we suspect you of anything, we'll advise you of your Miranda rights, at which time you should definitely lawyer up."

"Are you saying I can't have one present unless you Mirandize me?"

"Not at all. You can have one any time you wish. I'm only saying it shouldn't be necessary at this time. Now, you want to answer that first question?"

"Yeah. Mark Q. Snyder. August 18th, 1989. I live at 12701 Narrows Way in Tacoma Washington."

"What's the Q stand for?"

Snyder reached for a glass and poured himself some water. Taking a slurp, he said, "Quentin. It stands for Quentin."

"How long have you lived at your current address, Mr. Snyder?"

"I guess about four years."

"Where did you live before that?"

"In Seattle. In an apartment near Golden Gardens."

"Did you grow up in Seattle?"

"Yeah. Went to Ballard High School."

"Any siblings while growing up?"

"Yup. Two brothers. Both older. You want to know my mother's maiden name too?"

"No. Just your oldest brother's shoe size." All three chuckled. Fred Wong handed off back to Sally McKnight.

"Mr. Snyder, are you employed by a Houston-based oil drilling company and currently working the oil fields in the San Juan River basin of New Mexico and Arizona?

"Yeah."

"Then you actually have another address, besides the one on ..." she glanced down at her note pad ... "Narrows Way in Tacoma. Don't you live at a camp near Mexican Water, Arizona about four weeks out of every eight?"

"I suppose you could say that."

"And what are your duties?" asked Sally.

"I'm a lead hand on the rigs. I supervise several roughnecks."

"And during your crew's time on site, are you the usual operator of a pickup with truck Arizona license plate number **2 OIL 773**?"

"I want my lawyer here. Now!"

"Very well. Feel free to call him, or her. Agent Wong and I will leave the room while you make the call."

Outside the interview room, the agents begged two cups of coffee from the guys in the squad room down the hall. "It's pretty bitter stuff," said one deputy as he filled two Styrofoam cups. "But if you have cast iron stomachs, you can probably manage it. Hey, we got donuts, though. They were fresh just yesterday."

Five minutes later, when they re-entered the interview room, Snyder was pacing back and forth on one side of the table. "My lawyer's not available until tomorrow. I'm outta here. Now."

"Okay Mr. Snyder. You're free to leave, but then we'd like to see you again tomorrow – with your lawyer – at the FBI satellite office in Tacoma at 2:00 p.m. We highly advise you to show up. Don't make us go looking for you. The optics of that would not bode well for you."

After Snyder had left the room, the two agents grinned at each other. With a handkerchief, Agent Fred Wong gingerly picked up the glass from which the suspect had drunk and dropped it into a Ziplock bag.

On the way out of the office, he said to the deputies sitting in the squad room, "We owe you for a drinking glass. Just send an invoice to the Seattle Field Office."

CHAPTER TWENTY-ONE

Near Navajo Route 5035
January 17, 2021

Beth had stopped her near-constant banging on the walls of the container. Her hands and feet had made only a dull thudding noise, not the sharp cracks she had hoped for, and she had bruised herself and caused even more pain. And however long and often she screamed or kicked on the walls, no one had ever come except her first captor and now the one called Meriwether, always announced by the tires of their trucks. Now she mostly lay quietly, praying, trying to stay warm, willing God or her own mind to find a solution. She knew the way of her people was to be in harmony with nature ... and to endure suffering, so she felt guilty for having any feelings at all. Hope. Self-pity. The feeling of family love she remembered from long ago.

She wondered if Christmas had come and gone, and she pined for the surrogate family life she enjoyed with Julie and her mom. Last Christmas, she had woken to the warmth of their house and had stayed there, while Flower, her own mother, worked for time-and-a-half holiday pay at the Hampton Inn in Gallup. The trio – Julie, her mom and Beth – had opened Christmas stockings stuffed with oranges, warm socks and gloves, and then they had breakfasted on a festive meal of homemade biscuits stuffed with scrambled eggs and chilies, lamb sausages, hot sweet tea and apple juice. The food had been in contrast to her own mother's idea of a fancy breakfast – Spam and potatoes fried together in leftover bacon grease. And even though she had grown accustomed to the sparse food the men fed her in captivity, which had caused her appetite to diminish, the thought of the Christmas morning meal last year triggered growling hunger.

The new man, Meriwether, had come about every three days, with the same meager food offerings she had become accustomed to. The fare varied little from day to day; pineapple slices, crackers, bologna slices, cheese, some days dry cereal. He refreshed the water and allowed Beth outside of the container long enough to empty her bucket into the sand, move her limbs and stretch.

She reckoned it was mid-day, and that Meriwether might come in several hours. That routine produced mixed feelings. Her heart pounded ferociously at the thought that he might yet force physical contact, although so far, he had not. No one had forced her since the taller man stopped coming. On the other hand, Meriwether's visits provided human contact. A small promise that the world still existed beyond the dark, cramped confines of the container. She looked forward to the few minutes he allowed her outside, so she could empty her latrine bucket. The fresh air and dim sunlight of winter, the opportunity to unfold and extend her limbs, reassured her. But her mind constantly competed for her two worst fears – one that he might not return, the other that he would. She had been imbued with the belief that man is inherently good. And she wanted to believe that this one, this Meriwether, was. But could he be a friend of the taller man who had hurt her and still be good?

For the past several days, she had suffered from a fierce headache. She itched all over and could smell her own body odor. How could Meriwether let her stay so dirty and stinking? Did he have no compassion? She had no means of washing, or brushing her teeth, or cutting her fingernails and toenails, which had both grown uncomfortably long. Just the weight of the quilt on her toenails caused her pain, and the nail on her small toe was cutting into the skin of the next toe on her left foot. She had tried to separate them by rolling a couple of small squares of toilet paper into a tube and inserting it between the digits.

Later in the day, as she had expected, the truck stopped and the door slammed. The container door swung open with a clank.

"I brought you hot water again," Meriwether said, not unkindly. "You can bathe again today. And this time I brought enough that you can wash your hair. There's shampoo too. You can go behind the truck again. I'll let you have privacy."

CHAPTER TWENTY-TWO

Tacoma, Washington
January 18, 2021

Special Agent Fred Wong turned on the *record* function of his cell phone and laid it flat on the table. He cleared his throat and said, "Okay, let's get started. This is 13 January 2021 at 1405 hours. Special Agents Fred Wong and Sally McKnight interviewing Mr. Mark Snyder, for the second time. We're in the conference room of the FBI satellite office in Tacoma, Washington. Mr. Snyder is accompanied by his attorney ..." he glanced down at the business card lying in front of him ... "Mr. Jake Gabriel."

Snyder, sitting across the table with the attorney, merely stared straight into the eyes of Agent Wong. Gabriel grunted, "Correct. Ask your questions, Agent."

"Right. Mr. Snyder, I believe you're aware that anything you say can be used in evidence against you in any judicial proceedings that should arise as a result of this case. You have a right to remain silent. You also have a right to an attorney. And you have your own attorney with you at this time."

"Yeah," said Snyder.

Fred nodded at Sally.

"All right, Mr. Snyder," she started. "Let's go back to yesterday's question. When your crew is on duty at the oil camp near Mexican Water, are you the usual operator of a pickup truck bearing Arizona license plates **2 OIL 773**?"

"Don't answer, Mark," Mr. Gabriel said. "My client will invoke his right to remain silent on that question."

"Mr. Snyder, just so you know what we're dealing with here, on the 5th of December of last year, two Native girls, both aged seventeen, were abducted by four men in a pickup truck in Window Rock, Arizona. That's a hundred miles south of the camp out of which you work, and on the Reservation." Sally paused to gauge any reaction.

Snyder shrugged. His lawyer scribbled a note on a yellow legal pad.

"One of the girls was found disoriented and wandering aimlessly along a highway almost twenty miles from where she was abducted. A medical examination revealed she had been raped. To this day she's suffering from PTSD. The other girl has not been found. She's been missing for over five weeks. So, as it stands now, we're looking at rape and assault charges against the perpetrators. If the missing girl should turn up dead, we're then dealing with a homicide." She paused again and settled her gaze on Mark Snyder.

He stared at a clock on the wall, while the attorney continued to furiously scribble notes on his legal pad.

"We were able to profile male DNA from a rape kit administered on the girl who was found. Now listen carefully, Mr. Snyder. Our agents also found DNA in the pickup truck bearing license number **2 OIL 773.** And this is an amazing coincidence, it matched the male DNA found on the girl. Now, records in the camp office indicate that when the A Crew, of which you are a member, is on duty, you are the principal operator of that vehicle. You want to help us out with any insights you may have into this amazing coincidence?"

Jake Gabriel intervened, "Stay quiet, Mark."

"Let's up the ante a little," said Sally. "Yesterday when we met in Everett, you drank water from a glass in the interview room. After you left, we removed that glass and sent it to the Washington State Patrol's crime lab in Seattle. We expect the report on that tomorrow. If it should develop that that glass contains a match to the DNA found in the victim and in **2 OIL 773,** we'll have sufficient evidence to obtain an arrest warrant on you. Now, if you choose to help us, a court just may be more lenient than otherwise. What do you say to that?"

Jake Gabriel immediately announced hoarsely, "I want a short conference with my client."

Sally and Fred both nodded.

Placing his hand beside his mouth, Gabriel turned and whispered something to Snyder. The two exchanged whispers for thirty-five seconds.

Finally, Gabriel said, "My client wishes to continue to invoke his right to remain silent."

Fred put both hands palm-down on the table and leaned forward. "Okay. Let's take it up another notch. On December 20th of last year, a rig mechanic by the name of Guy Primeau from the A Crew was found dead at a drilling site. A post-mortem revealed that the cause of death was probably a homicide. We believe he was about to reveal some information about the rapes on December 5th to the FBI and that he was killed to prevent that. If we were to get some help in solving that, we might be willing to ask for a charge of manslaughter instead of murder."

"Now you're just on a fishing expedition," shouted Gabriel. "My client will remain silent. In fact, we're out of here."

"Okay. I think you'd best advise your client not to leave town, though, Mr. Gabriel."

CHAPTER TWENTY-THREE

Window Rock, Arizona
January 18, 2021

When Melissa first noticed an e-mail from Elbert County Blue Devils in her in-box, she assumed it was spam, a fundraiser for an athletic team somewhere ... Elbert County, wherever that was. She was about to hit 'delete' when it twigged for her. Elbert County ... that must be Elberton, Georgia. Susan Meadows' Uncle Willie —possibly Melissa's own father – was a vice principal at a high school in Elberton. Her heart fluttered. "Oh, I wonder," she said involuntarily.

"News of some kind?" asked Bernie from the other end of the long table.

"Could be." Melissa opened the e-mail. "We'll know in a minute.

She held her breath as she hastily scanned the contents. "Oh my god."

"Good news?"

"Oh my god. I think so. Let me read it again. Slowly."

Hello Melissa.

I apologize for my tardy response to your e-mail of January 3d. I read it on the same day but needed time to digest it, I'm afraid. Never in my wildest imagination did I ever think one day I might receive a message like that. But I have to confess, after taking some time to absorb the full impact of your news, I am excited at the possibility that I may have a grown daughter.

I was only seventeen when I dated a Native American girl from Shiprock. She was about the same age. We only saw each other about four times because my family moved to Houston. My dad was transferred to the corporate head office of the oil company he worked for. I was heartbroken to leave her and for a while we stayed in touch by mail. But after a few months, her letters stopped coming. I had kept a little stash of her letters and a colored photo of her - one of the kind you used to be able to get out of coin operated machine in a booth. When she stopped writing, I tried to forget about her. I burned the letters and photograph. I can still picture her in my mind's eye, though. Beautiful, with shoulder length dark brown hair, almond-shaped eyes, high cheekbones and skin like silk. I am, though, embarrassed to say that I don't remember her name. I never met her family. We first met in the McDonalds in Shiprock. She was working as a counter person. We always met there to go out on our dates. So, I never saw where she lived. I think her Dad was a seasonal part-time worker in agriculture. Apparently, her mom raised the kids.

Anyway, I'd like to explore this possibility further, and I hope you would too. I've attached a recent photo of myself. It's from the Faculty pages of this year's Elbert County High School yearbook. So, it's current. If you choose to write back, I'd love to see a picture of you too.

Best Regards,

Willie

Melissa shoved her laptop down the table and said, "Here. Have a look, Bernie. I'm suddenly very close to tears." She fled into the bathroom and sat on the toilet lid to cry.

When she emerged ten minutes later, tears gone and makeup freshened, Bernie said, "C'mon, let's go out and find a nice background for me to take your picture. There's still plenty of light, and it's from the west so it will be perfect. I think the Navajo Tribal Park next to the government buildings would be an ideal setting.

Minutes later, Melissa stood before the graceful red sandstone arch for which the town of Window Rock was named. The sunlight slanting from the west highlighted the perfectly blue sky, which could be seen through the arch, and painted the rock face with a glimmering patina. Her position next to a statue of a World War II Native Code Talker created depth of field in the resulting photos snapped with Melissa's phone.

Back in the office, the two of them agreed on the best photo. "Just look at how the golden afternoon highlights your hair, Melissa. This Willie gentleman will be bowled over at the possibility he could have so radiant a daughter."

Melissa typed:

Mr. Cole, (Willie) (Possibly Pop)

Thanks for responding to my very forward e-mail. I can imagine what a shock it must have been. I am excited too and would like to pursue this possibility. I am enclosing a picture. It was taken just an hour ago at the Tribal Park in Window Rock on the Reservation, where I am working as a volunteer with an NGO that seeks to fight violence against indigenous women.

I'm really not sure what the next steps should be. But for now, can you tell me a little more about yourself? Where did you go college? (I went to the University of New Mexico and have a degree in Native American Studies) What is life like in Elberton, Georgia? What led you there? I've never been to Georgia.

Maybe we could have a video call on Zoom or Skype one of these days.

Sincerely,

Melissa

Within minutes, Melissa's laptop chimed to signify she had another e-mail. She opened it.

Hi again, Melissa,

Here's my take on what the next step will be. I will sign up for a DNA analysis from Ancestry.com. Let's find out for certain if I'm your biological father. I'll pay the extra fee to have expedited service. I have only one reservation. If it develops that we're related, I wouldn't want that to impact or affect your relationship with your adoptive parents in any way. You said in your first e-mail that you have discussed this exploration with them and that they're okay with it. But I just want to reassure you that I recognize that they're the only parents you've ever known, and I respect that.

I got my Bachelors of Education and teacher's certification from Texas A&M and then spent four years in the Army as an officer, including one deployment to Iraq in 2003 (which was not fun). I mustered out at Fort Benning, Georgia. The Army's transition office at Benning, which helped soon-to-be discharged soldiers find employment, sent me up to Elberton for an interview. The rest, to use a cliché, is history. Elberton is a pretty provincial place, with not much to offer single professional people. But Atlanta is only two hours away and that's where I go to have a life apart from the high school.

More later. I want to get this registration off to Ancestry.com tonight.

Warmly,

Willie (Maybe Pop)

CHAPTER TWENTY-FOUR

Northeast of Round Rock, Arizona
January 18, 2021

Melissa had finally found time to drop into the K'é Infoshop, the storefront Bernie had paused to show her during their orientation ride around Window Rock, six weeks earlier.

Johona Nez, the founding director, enthusiastically greeted her. She explained that the reason the four walls of the shop were painted different colors was that they represented the four sacred Diné colors – black, white, turquoise and yellow. Near the entrance, a painting hung conspicuously, depicting the hands of a woman wrapped around jail bars, her fingers clad in turquoise rings.

"She represents one of our members who was unjustly arrested in a police raid of a flea market while she shared her lunch with a homeless group," Johona explained.

Shelves laden with books and magazines occupied much of the available space in back of the former coffee shop. Melissa studied some of the titles: *"Corn is our Blood," "Indigenous Men and Masculinities," "Red Power Rising," "Diné: A History of the Navajo Nation."* Intrigued by the title *"Decolonizing Wealth,"* she pulled the black and red paperback from the shelf to examine it more closely. She found the blurb on the back cover evocative;

Decolonizing Wealth is a provocative analysis of the oppressive dynamics at play in philanthropy and finance. Philanthropy has evolved to mirror colonial structures, ultimately doing more harm than good. It has imposed harmful and oppressive policies that dispossessed and inflicted harm upon Native people and their culture. Award-winning philanthropist Edgar Villanueva draws from Native traditions to prescribe the medicine to heal our divides.

She skipped ahead to the last sentence in the blurb.

With great compassion – because the Native way is to bring the oppressor into the circle of healing – this book offers the Seven Steps to Healing to open the floodgates for a rising tide that lifts all boats.

She took the book to the counter and had bought it, eager to learn more about the author's stance that philanthropy is tantamount to colonialism and oppression.

• • •

Now, a week later, Melissa and Johona bounced and juddered along an unmaintained gravel road, in places merely two ruts, in others a bed of cobbles and small boulders, to make a delivery of water, food, firewood and essential supplies to an elderly woman. Creeping along at ten to fifteen miles an hour, in Johona's rusty 1996 Toyota Tacoma pickup, they had not seen another vehicle or any sign of humanity for over an hour.

"One of the real tragedies of this Covid crisis on the rez," Johona said, "is that with so many elders dying, it erodes the transmission of our language and culture."

"I can imagine, but how exactly?" asked Melissa, eager to learn as much as she could about the philosophy and doctrine underpinning the K'é Infoshop.

"Simple. The Diné have a very strong tradition of oral history. Our legends, our rituals, our clan histories, our language are all passed from generation to generation by parents and grandparents. It's through the oral traditions that our children really learn who they are. Losing even one elder before his or her time is like losing the archival section of a library.

"Keeping our culture alive has been a constant struggle ever since the residential schools' era, which only ended forty years ago. The assimilationists and missionaries deliberately sought to destroy and vilify Native culture, language, family, and spirituality. It's a legacy that lingers."

"So, the residential schools and missionaries spelled the beginning of the imposition of non-Native ways for the Diné people?" asked Melissa.

"Oh, hell no. It goes way back before the missionaries came parachuting in. I would argue that K'é started to break down when the tribe first negotiated with the U.S. government. Why do you think the Bureau of Indian Affairs was created, Melissa?"

"To promote native self-determination; To help native tribes to help themselves to enhance their quality of life; To promote economic opportunity for native groups; I'm spouting the party line, Johona. That pretty much summarizes the mission statement of the BIA; But I suspect you're going to tell me that originally its purpose was very different."

"Damn right," she said venomously. "When the BIA was founded in 1824 all of its policies were directed at subjugating and assimilating Native Americans. Even now, they are tacitly doing just that. How do you think those words you just quoted from their mission – promote self-determination, promote economic opportunity – are operationalized?" She glanced to the right to look Melissa in the eye. "They 'improve' our lives by allowing oil and gas companies to exploit our natural resources and give our tribal government royalties. And by assisting us in creating glitzy casinos on our land to improve our income and our way of life. These things still erode our healthy lifestyle in the pursuit of profit. They have the effect of assimilation into the white man's system. They fly in the face of our traditional ways."

Melissa glanced over at her. Johona was trying to calm herself with deep breathing. "I know what you mean," she said. "The capitalist idea of 'progress' often has the effect of undermining culture."

With her voice now under control, Johona said, "By the way, this woman we're going to see, Clara, is a product of the residential school system. She'll likely have some things to say about that, just so you know. But tell me – how do you feel about discovering that you're half Navajo? You must have thought a lot about that as you grew older and went to college. Did you ever wonder what it means to be part Native in a white culture?"

"I did ask those questions when I was at UNM. I majored in Native American Studies and sought answers in my anthropology and sociology classes. But I never even saw a book with a biracial protagonist until I was in my twenties, and what I took away from that book is that identity is something way beyond skin color and eye shape. I guess the bottom line is I am who I am. Period. Full stop."

Johona slowed the vehicle to five mph in order to creep through a boulder-strewn stretch of dry creek bed. "Now that's a message I hope you can hang onto." She pointed. "And there's Clara's hogan on the horizon."

Pale blue smoke emerged from a hole in the center of the dome-shaped shelter constructed of logs and adobe. Two cars without wheels sat corroding nearby. About thirty-five feet from the Hogan, an ancient, rusty Airstream trailer was perched on blocks, tethered to the house by a series of household extension cords, some patched with black tape.

As Johona brought the truck to a stop, several mongrel dogs, aroused from naps, snapped and snarled at the vehicle. They encircled it and pranced around yowling and barking like the embodiment of angry gods. A woman, hunched over, probably in her mid-eighties, emerged from the hogan and issued several sharp commands. The dogs quieted and skulked away.

"Never mind them beasts," the woman said, as Johona and Melissa opened their doors and stepped from the truck. "They don't see no one but me, 'cept when my son is here from Farmington. That's his trailer, but he mostly stays in Farmington with his girl-friend."

"Melissa, meet Clara," Johona said, dropping the tailgate of the truck. When Melissa and Clara had acknowledged each other, she asked, "Where do you want the firewood, Clara? We'll take the food and water into your hogan ... or do you want some of it in the trailer?"

"Just take it into the hogan. I'll go over to the trailer and start up the generator. Then we'll be able to turn on the light in the hooch and I can make you a nice cup of tea."

Once the goods were stored against a wall on one side of the hogan, Clara invited Melissa and Johona to have a seat on a colorful woven rug spread over the dirt floor. She served tea in three mismatched cups.

After the three had sipped silently for a few seconds, Johona broke the silence. "Clara, I told Melissa that you might share some of your memories from the boarding school."

Clara put her cup down on the rug. "Now why you go pokin' around that subjeck out of nowhere? I don't even like to think of it. I shake my head and close my eyes every time thoughts about that Sister School come creepin' in. I try to shut off my mind to it."

"I'm sorry I brought it up. I just wanted Melissa to hear about the boarding school first hand from someone who was there."

"Well, now that you did bring it up, I'll just say this. Them nuns were the meanest bitches in the world. Always calling us 'dirty Indians' and making us scrub floors, do laundry, march around like soldiers and never speak our language. If one of us uttered a word of Diné, we'd be beaten with a switch. And Sister Giovanna, the Mother Superior, was the meanest of all. She wanted to whip the Indian out of us. She said so. It wasn't no education. It was brainwashing and torture."

Melissa had read about the legacy of Residential Schools. She also clearly recalled a shocking exhibit on American Indian Boarding Schools she had seen on a research trip to the Heard Museum in Phoenix, with frighteningly realistic dioramas, pictures, artifacts, short films, and most impactful of all, a montage of little, rapidly changing head and shoulder shots of children, both male and female, all with identical bowl haircuts and uniforms, their individuality and ethnicity camouflaged by uniformity.

"I'm sorry," said Melissa. "It's obviously still very hurtful for you."

"Sister Giovanna said she wanted to clean us of our culture, called us savages. Well, I discovered you're lost without a culture. You're lost without love."

• • •

Within the hour, the three stood to say goodbye. Melissa and Johona were about to leave when a small gold cross earring, lying amid an assortment of dishes on a shelf, caught Melissa's eye. "Clara, forgive me for asking, but I just noticed this." She pointed to the earring on the shelf. "Do you wear this?"

"No. I found that yesterday when I was walking in the desert, 'bout a mile from here."

"Clara, I think this may have belonged to a girl who went missing on the 5th of December. It could be an important clue for the police. If I call the FBI agent who's working on the case – a woman – do you think you could show her the spot where you found it?"

CHAPTER TWENTY-FIVE

Federal Courthouse, Seattle Washington
January 20, 2021

When the three of them had each taken tenuous sips of stale coffee, left over from Friday and reheated, Sally McKnight said, "Sorry to get you in here on a Sunday, Douglas. But we think this guy Snyder is a flight risk. We need to get to him fast and we need your support in getting an audience with Judge Benson and persuading him to give us a warrant."

Douglas was G. Douglas Winchester, Chief of the Criminal Division of the U.S. Attorney's Office for the District of Western Washington, a fast-tracker, thought by many in the courthouse crowd to be a shoo-in for the next vacancy among the ten senior federal judges at 700 Stewart Street.

"Why Benson? Asking him to come in on a Sunday's like trying to get the sun to rise at midnight. He's a devoutly religious man, heavily involved in church activities and family time on Sundays."

"That's just why we want him," said Special Agent Fred Wong. "He has strong Christian leanings *and* he has daughters. Snyder's a rape suspect, suspected of raping two young women. Out of the ten justices in this district, Judge Benson is probably our best shot at a warrant."

"And we're willing to go to him at home," said Sally. "He needn't come in to the courthouse."

Winchester stroked his neatly trimmed mustache and nodded sagely. "Let's go over what you've got."

"During our first interview, he drank from a water glass, which we sent to the State Patrol Crime Lab here in Seattle. They didn't get any DNA from it – too much condensation on the glass when he drank from it. You should have seen the file with the other, circumstantial, DNA evidence. We sent it over on Friday."

"Yeah, I saw it. Lots of circumstantial evidence that points to Snyder, but nothing really definitive. What kind of order are you hoping to get from Benson?"

"At the minimum, we'd like a search warrant to obtain a DNA specimen from Snyder," said Fred. "Better yet would be a warrant to arrest him for suspicion of rape. Two rapes, and one could be up ticked to murder if the Chee girl turns up dead. We also have a strong feeling that he's behind the murder of another rig worker, by the name of Primeau, who was about to reveal information to the FBI agent on the scene. But we haven't one shred of evidence to support that. It's admittedly supposition, but if we can nail him for the rapes, he may cooperate and help us solve the murder of Primeau."

"Let's roll the tape back a minute. What if the Chee girl doesn't turn up at all for, say ... ninety days? Then it might be possible to harness the power of the circumstantial evidence to convince a jury that a murder occurred. But again, an explicit link to Snyder would probably be hard to prove, just as it would in the rapes alone. Even so – and I'm just thinking aloud here – I think you have definite grounds to consider Snyder an actual suspect, more than merely a person of interest. The fact that he's the principal driver of the vehicle in which the DNA was found, and he was in the general area, on the western half of the reservation, at the time of the rapes – both are compelling pieces of circumstantial evidence. But —"

"Okay," interrupted Sally. "Let's forget about an arrest warrant for now. Don't we have enough to go for a court order to obtain Snyder's DNA through a cheek swab? I mean the results should be black or white. They should either clear him of suspicion, for now, or be the clincher for arresting him."

"Yeah, I think so," said Winchester. "There are precedents in federal case law that support the issuance of DNA search warrants, even for witnesses. Of course, if he's lawyered up, his counsel will grumble about his 4th Amendment protection against unreasonable search and seizure, but a judge's order trumps that. Let's see if Benson will see us this afternoon."

"You're going with us?"

"You bet. I've always wanted to see his house on Magnolia Bluff."

"Good heavens. We pay federal judges too much," said Sally when the black government SUV stopped in front of the mansion on West Magnolia Boulevard. "That pad must have at least eight bedrooms and baths. It occupies the equivalent of about three city lots."

"It's old family money," said Winchester. "He gets about $220,000 a year from the government. He couldn't pay the taxes on this place with that. I'm told he has an Olympic sized swimming pool in the back."

As the three stepped from the vehicle, which looked incongruous among the Mercedes and BMWs parked in driveways along the leafy street, Sally paused to admire the view to the south and west; a commanding vista of Elliot Bay and Puget Sound. "Holy cow. That's all I can say."

Up the long, flagstone sidewalk, lined with hedges, the judge's oldest daughter met them at the open door. A bookish-looking girl of about sixteen, she showed them through the foyer and down a wide, carpeted hallway and into the judge's study, a richly paneled and book-lined room boasting a view of the back garden and turquoise swimming pool, from which wisps of steam rose in the wintery air. Judge Benson, wearing grey slacks and a navy-blue cardigan over a pale shirt, stood in front of a crackling fire smiling broadly. "Welcome, welcome good people. Please have a seat. Would any of you like a beverage?"

All three politely declined the offer of a drink, and then took seats in rich leather armchairs arranged in a semi-circle around a low coffee table.

Avoiding the powerful trappings of his large mahogany desk, Judge Benson dragged another armchair to the other side of the coffee table and eased his slender frame into it. "Now, I've studied the affidavit and supporting materials that you faxed over. What can I do for you?"

"Your Honor," said Douglas Winchester, "a lot of circumstantial evidence points at Mark Snyder as a suspect in the deplorable rapes of two young Native girls on the Navajo Reservation on December 5th. But not enough to give us probable cause for an arrest. You can see for yourself in the documentation we've provided, there's the pickup truck usually operated by the suspect, DNA matching that of one of the victims found in the pickup truck as well as that of a male whose DNA matched some found in semen in the same victim's body. We're asking for a court order to obtain a specimen of Snyder's DNA to rule him in or out."

"So," said the judge, "It looks like you two," he nodded at the two agents, "sought to obtain his DNA opportunistically, but that didn't work out."

"Right, afraid not," said Sally.

"I'm inclined to agree that a warrant for the DNA is justifiable. But, if he knows you want his DNA, I'm sure he suspects you're obtaining a warrant. How do you know he hasn't bolted in the last day and a half? Do you have him under surveillance?"

"Yes, Your Honor. His house has been under surveillance, front and back, since we spoke to him the day before yesterday. He went straight home from our interview and hasn't left since."

"All right. When you call on him, let's just make sure it's done right. Obtain the DNA with a swab and minimize the chain of custody as it makes its way to the lab. If he or his lawyer cries foul and refuses to cooperate, let them know, in no uncertain terms, that it would look dirtier for him."

"We'll have two extra law enforcement officers with us in order to restrain the suspect and forcibly obtain the specimen if he refuses to cooperate."

"Okay, you've got your warrant. I'd advise you to execute it tonight, before he has a chance to flee from Tacoma." The judge moved to his leather-backed chair behind the desk and picked up his Mont Blanc pen.

• • •

The wind tugged at their jackets and trousers as they approached the front porch. The typical January-in-Seattle drizzle settled on them but without serious intent. Sally glanced over her shoulder at the Tacoma Public Utilities van parked along the opposite curb. Five minutes earlier the occupant, an undercover cop, had advised Fred Wong and her, by radio, that he'd seen no activity around the house on Narrows Way all day. The other agent, stationed in the back alley had rendered the same report. Two additional agents had just pulled up to the curb in their government sedan. They would be the backup in case Snyder was non-compliant or worse, had a weapon. As always when approaching a potentially violent situation, Sally's pulse hammered her eardrums.

Fred Wong pressed the doorbell. They could hear the three tones sound somewhere within the front rooms of the bungalow. As they waited for a response, Fred pressed the button again. Still nothing after twenty seconds. Now he shouted, "Snyder, FBI with a warrant. Open up now or we'll use force to enter."

Another thirty seconds elapsed, and then Sally gestured at the two agents sitting curbside, and by radio, alerted the man in the alley to watch for an escape attempt out the back door.

The two additional agents arrived at the porch, one of them carrying a DoorStorm, a twelve-inch, rectangular metal device used by police forces to breach doors mechanically. As one agent inserted the shoe of the device into the crack between the jamb and the door itself, the automatic garage door activated with a grinding, thumping sound.

Before any of them could react, a motorcycle with a single rider burst out of the garage, slid through a left turn on the wet pavement at the end of the driveway and roared down Narrows Way toward State Route 16.

"He's bolted. He's bolted," Fred Wong shouted into his hand-held radio as he and Sally sprinted back down the sidewalk toward their vehicle. "Southbound on Narrows Way. A black motorcycle. One rider, believed to be Mark Snyder. Get a broadcast out on the Tacoma PD frequency."

He had already slid into the driver's seat and started the engine by the time he heard the "10-4. Copy." Sally dove into the passenger's seat just as he put the Chevrolet Suburban into gear and hit the switches for the lights and siren.

Sally buckled her seatbelt and as adrenaline shot through her shouted, "Go."

Fred floored the big SUV and it leapt forward, accelerating rapidly, siren wailing. Sally switched the vehicle radio to the South Sound Regional Radio Network to monitor Tacoma PD chatter related to the motorcycle, now with at least four police vehicles in pursuit.

They sped through the slight curve, where Narrows Way becomes North Jefferson Avenue, approaching 60 miles per hour. Sally had the radio mic in one hand and with the other tightly gripped what one old boyfriend had aptly called the "Oh Shit" grab handle above the door. White knuckled, she focused on the transmission from a police vehicle racing down a parallel arterial street. "Subject turned onto Hwy 16 westbound. High rate of speed. Weaving from lane to lane. Looks like he's heading for the Narrows Bridge."

Then from another vehicle, "Definitely headed for the bridge. Alert Pierce County Sheriffs. Guy's doing 90. Must have a death wish."

Fred made a screeching left turn. Easing off the speed only slightly, he plowed up the on-ramp, a hairpin turn of 180-degrees, to the highway. On the high-speed approach to the Tacoma Narrows bridge, they spotted a constellation of fast moving red and blue lights ahead of them, traversing the bridge itself. Reluctant to exceed 75 miles per hour in the conditions of light rain and increasing darkness, Fred said, "I won't attempt to get ahead of the pack and overtake him. We'll just hang back and monitor the situation as it develops."

"Roger that," said Sally, trying to control the slight tremor in her voice. "Better to just bird dog him."

Soon another radio transmission announced: "Subject just tore down the off ramp at Pioneer Way. Continuing to pursue but losing distance. Could be heading to Gig Harbor."

Sally flipped on the GPS map plotter and zoomed in on the village of Gig Harbor. "A maze of streets in there. If those lead vehicles lose sight of him, we could be toast."

"Yeah. Damn motorcycle. His fancy little red car would have been easier to keep track of." Fred deftly wheeled the vehicle onto the Pioneer Way off-ramp and steered toward Gig Harbor. Ahead several red and blue lights moved at a much lower rate of speed.

Then, through slight static, "This is Tacoma PD four-two-two. Lost him. I'm at the T intersection with Harborview Drive. I don't see him in either direction. No telling where he turned off."

CHAPTER TWENTY-SIX

Albuquerque, New Mexico
January 22, 2021

"It's hard to justify," said Special Agent in Charge Dave Akerman. "There are those in Congress who think that police use of drones constitutes a 4th Amendment violation. The American Civil Liberties Union, among other lobbies, presses Congress members hard to prevent the use of drones by police agencies."

"Sir," said Wendy Burkenshaw. "This would not be a surveillance op against any individual or group. It would be a search for a missing seventeen-year-old girl. There are bureau precedents for this. In 2013 an FBI drone located, and was instrumental in the rescue of, a five-year-old kidnapping victim. That was deemed justifiable by the congressional committee looking into use of surveillance drones."

"Yes, I know." Akerman got up from the conference table, stepped to a service alcove and poured himself a fresh cup of coffee. "Coffee, Wendy?" He continued with his thought before she could answer. "And again, in 2017, a drone was used to locate an Alabama boy held hostage in a bunker. But the fact remains, anything that smacks of the use of a drone for surveillance in either criminal or security matters attracts a great deal of scrutiny. How wide a search net have you already cast on the ground?"

"Within several hours of being shown where the earring was found, we had ten Navajo Police Department cops and twenty-five Apache County deputies doing a grid pattern search by foot and ATV for three days. They were augmented by two Arizona National Guard helicopters and around twenty local ranchers and sheep farmers on horseback. They covered all of this." Wendy opened a 1:25,000 topographical map on her laptop screen and traced an area about six-by-six miles overlaid on the marker where the earring had been found. "So, in three days we were able to go out three miles in each direction by ground; farther than that with helicopter sweeps. All with negative results. I think our only options are to shut down the search – and that would not be looked on favorably by the Navajo Nation – or get a drone or two up there to expand the search."

"That's a lot of resources you were able to muster. Tell me again how the earring was found."

"An old woman living alone in a hogan at this location ..." Wendy pointed to a spot on the computer screen ... "found it in a pile of ashes while on a walk in the desert. She led me and an evidence technician from the Apache County Sheriff's Department to that place the next the morning after I learned of her finding it."

"Did you find any other viable evidence at that spot? Any trace evidence?"

"We sifted through the ashes. No human remains, but it looked like a pile of apparel had been burned. The evidence tech found one plastic button and a small metal clip – heavily charred, but we thought it might be the strap adjuster from a bra. Those pieces as well as some of the ash residue were sent to the state crime laboratory in Phoenix. They were able to confirm that the metal object was a bra adjuster and that the button was a button and the residue was from jean fabric, but nothing beyond that."

"So are there still searchers on the ground?"

"Yes, but most of the deputies and about half of the NPD resources have left. The remaining members cannot cover a lot of ground. That's why I want the drone. I think it's our duty to exert every possible effort to find that young woman – dead or alive."

Akerman finger-smoothed his combover and turned to his Assistant Special Agent in Charge. "What do you think, Bill?"

"Well, we'd have to run it up the flagpole to Washington. Bureau policy is that, without a warrant, drones can only be used with senior bureau management approval. On the other hand, if we get the director's or assistant director's approval, we could probably get a bird over the area within an hour. Much faster than fucking around trying to find a judge to give us a warrant."

"Yeah. I'm just concerned that elements in the media and even the House Judiciary Committee could see this as warrantless surveillance of suspected criminal activity, given that the principal suspects in the girl's disappearance are occupants of the oil camp very nearby. But I think your argument about our obligation is compelling, Wendy. And this would send a good message to the Navajo Nation. Let's go for it. Bill, see if you can get the director or assistant on the phone."

"Thank you, sir," said Wendy. "I'm off for the site now. It's a three-hour-plus drive."

"I want you back there sooner than that." Akerman stabbed a button on the conference table telephone. "Judith, please arrange a chopper from Kirtland AFB to Round Rock, Arizona for Special Agent Burkenshaw." He paused to listen to the response. "ASAP. Within the hour if possible."

CHAPTER TWENTY-SEVEN

Northeast of Round Rock, Arizona
January 23, 2021

"I'm going to step outside for a break," Special Agent Burkenshaw said. For the better part of two days, she and Detective Phillips of the NPD, had been watching the video feed from an Inspire 2 surveillance drone as it made passes over the desert. Their post was inside the 30-foot government-owned motorhome that had been used a month earlier as a command post at the man camp near Mexican Water.

"Okay. I've got it," said Raymond Phillips. "Take your time. Give your eyes a chance to recover from the strain."

Outside the vehicle, parked at the spot where the earring had been found, two porta-potties had been set up, along with a medium general-purpose tent for eating and sleeping. Two other FBI agents and two NPD police officers sat at folding trestle tables in the tent, near a military type water trailer. A few feet from the tent, a five-kilowatt generator murmured constantly.

While Wendy sipped a cup of coffee, a Navajo Police Department Chevrolet Blazer rolled up and stopped, producing a cloud of dusty fallout next to the tent. Officer Brenda Goldtooth leaped from the vehicle and announced, "Chow's here. It was hot when I left the KFC in Round Rock an hour ago."

"Well, that's one thing about the Colonel," Wendy said. "The chicken's good hot or cold."

"If I'd known you guys would be here for more than a day, I would've suggested we ask the Arizona National Guard to set up a field kitchen here," Brenda said.

Wendy shook her head. "I'm glad we didn't. I wouldn't have wanted to have a picnic atmosphere. That might distract from the seriousness of what we're doing here."

"Good point."

The other door of the Blazer opened and a passenger stepped out.

"Melissa," Wendy said, expressing surprise. "What're you doing here?"

"I wheedled a ride-along with Brenda. I've become very interested in the search for Beth Chee. Thought I may be able to help in some way. Besides, I've never seen a drone before. I want to know how it works.

"You're welcome to hang out with us. You won't see the drone though. Right now, it's at an altitude of about 2,000 feet and working around eight miles north of us."

"Who's piloting it? Is it being controlled from inside the motorhome?"

"No. It's piloted alternately by members of a team located in Albuquerque. We have an open line with them, so we can talk to them. Most of the time it searches on autopilot on a pre-programmed pattern. But there's always a pilot standing by to take over manually."

"Have you found anything yet?"

"Unfortunately, no. But we're not giving up. Come on in the RV and watch if you'd like."

They took seats flanking Raymond Phillips and donned their facemasks.

On one of the monitors, the desert floor slowly rolled past from an overhead, 'God's eye view.' Another monitor captured the moving imagery of the desert through a 45% high angle cam looking to the front of the moving drone. "Where are we, Raymond?" asked Wendy.

"Just about due North, around nine miles."

Another voice came through a speaker, "This is Albuquerque. The bird is on a transverse leg right now and will make a 90 degree turn to the East to resume the pattern in another minute or so."

Melissa observed, "Looks like a few pumpjacks are coming into view on that high angle perspective."

"Affirmative," said the voice from Albuquerque. "We're just coming into the San Juan Basin oil field."

Ahead of the drone's trajectory, the three people in the motorhome saw low mountains, with a huge build-up of ominous looking dark clouds to the north. "Is that just a localized weather cell?" asked Wendy.

"Negative," said Albuquerque. "It's a line of thundershowers slowly making their way south. They could interfere with our visibility if their track intersects the drone's flight path. But we can always slow it down to a geosynchronous orbit until the squalls pass."

"Could you explain that in either English or Navajo?" asked Raymond Phillips.

"It just means if we lose visibility, we'll have the vehicle make small circles over one area until the storm has passed. That way we shouldn't miss anything."

Through the forward-looking high-angle camera, the terrain itself seemed to rotate sharply to the left as the drone executed its 90-degree turn to the right. The field of view of the forward-looking camera was much wider than the overhead perspective. Low mountains and hill masses could be seen on both sides of the drone's trajectory. The cluster of pumpjacks became more densely spaced and numerous vehicle trackways had worn away much of the desert vegetation in long intersecting patterns. The occasional derrick of an active drilling rig could be seen.

"What are the rectangular structures?" asked Melissa.

"Those are shipping containers," answered Raymond. "The oil company places them here and there in the field for storage of parts and equipment. They're damn ugly, aren't they? Sorry to say, it's just one more way this exploitive industry has desecrated our sacred land."

Both Wendy and Melissa nodded somberly.

"Hey Albuquerque," said Wendy. "Can you zoom in for a closer look at two or three of those containers?"

"Affirmative. What is it you're looking for?"

"I don't know. Just anomalies, I guess."

"Okay. Let me get directly overhead one of them and I'll use the God's eye view."

A container appeared to move directly into the middle of the overhead view monitor; then telescoped into a much larger image, almost filling the screen as the operator zoomed the lens in close.

"Nothing remarkable. Just a lot of tire tracks," said Phillips.

"Yeah. Can we have a look at another one or two?" asked Wendy.

"Okay. They appear to be randomly scattered about two or three miles apart. So give me a minute to fly over to another one."

When the bird reached its viewpoint and zoomed in on the third of the containers, Wendy spotted her anomaly. "What would those little holes on the top of the container be for?"

"Beats me," Phillips said. "They're obviously not lift points. And not inspection apertures either. Those would be on the sides or ends."

"Could they be for ventilation?" asked Melissa.

"Maybe. But being on top of the container, they'd allow rainwater in. That doesn't seem to make sense. Albuquerque, can you move out a bit to get a closer look at the ground around the container?"

"Sure. Here you go. We're just outside the doors now."

"Looks to me like there's been more vehicular traffic around this container than the others. More recent too. Albuquerque, what do you make of that?"

"I honestly can't say."

"Okay, I'd like you to hold the position over that container. I'm going to ask Special Agent Bill Hartley to come in and have a look. He's out in the tent eating Kentucky Fried Chicken. Give me a minute to fetch him."

Melissa gave up her chair so that Agent Hartley could have a seat. She stood behind the other three, leaning against the opposite wall, but with her attention rivetted on the screens.

Hartley had a seat, asked a few questions about what else they had seen in the area of the containers, then said "I suspect they're air holes. Something, or someone, may be alive, or may have been alive, inside that container."

"But why would the air holes be on the top where they could allow water in, rather than on the sides?"

"So they can't be reached by someone from inside. As in a prisoner."

"Jesus. Interesting theory. But I don't think it's enough to justify hauling in a hostage rescue team from Albuquerque or Denver just yet. Anyone have any ideas?"

"I think we should ask to have the HRT on standby with a Black Hawk at Albuquerque Airport. Ready to go if we develop more information," Hartley said. "Meanwhile, maybe we can request a smellicopter to check out that container for a carbon dioxide plume."

"Okay. I'll bite," said Wendy. "Where did you ever hear of such a thing as a smellicopter?"

"It's been developed by the School of Engineering at the University of Washington. It's a drone that uses a live moth antenna to seek out smells. Trials have been very successful."

"Holy shit. I know you couldn't have made that up. How do they get the moth to cooperate?" asked Wendy.

"They remove the antenna and attach it to the drone's sensors with two small wires. The antenna will stay alive for about eight hours after it's been amputated." Hartley paused. "Realistically, though, it would probably take too long to get the approvals and have it flown from Seattle to either Denver or Albuquerque to deploy to that container site. I suspect we'd be looking at tomorrow afternoon at the soonest."

"Right. Detective Phillips, how long would It take us to drive to the site of that container?"

"Thirty to forty-five minutes. It would be rough going, though. The roads are little more than tracks through the sand and gravel. Lots of boulders in the dry streambeds. We have about three hours of daylight left."

"Okay. Bill, you stay here and monitor the situation with the drone. I'll take the other agent along in the Suburban. What's his name?"

"Smitty."

"All right; Smitty and I'll go investigate that container. Raymond, can you and two of your NPD guys come along in a Blazer for backup?"

"Of course, but we do have jurisdictional problems. Rape and kidnapping are your bailiwick. And if the perp is a Caucasian oil field worker, there's not much we can do officially."

"I fully realize that. It's more than likely my case. But I'd like as many badges along as we can muster. Just in case. Let's jot down the coordinates from the bottom of the video screen. We'll plug them into the GPS on both vehicles."

"You got it. I'll get them cranked up."

Both Raymond Phillips and Wendy scraped their chairs back and rose. Melissa said, "I don't suppose I could ride along as an observer?"

"No chance," said Wendy. "Why don't you just hang out here and monitor the drone imagery along with Bill. Stay overnight if you want. We have cots out in that tent."

"Will it be KFC for dinner tonight?"

"No. We have a cooler full of tuna fish sandwiches in the tent. They were fresh just yesterday morning."

• • •

"Talk to me. Is anything happening at that container?" Wendy had maintained an open cellular connection with Bill Hartley in the command post. Her vehicle and the Blazer following were about halfway to the container site and grinding slowly over and around the medium-sized boulders in an arroyo.

"Negative. The pilot sent the drone off to check out a few other containers. See if any others had similar perforations in the roofs. They didn't. The vehicle has just come back to an orbit over the questionable container."

"Can that imagery be patched through to my cell phone?"

"The pilot says 'No.' Apparently the cellular signal is too weak at your location. I'm only reading you about six by six."

"Okay, I think our ETA is about fifteen minutes. The signal will probably improve as we get near—"

"Wait," interrupted Agent Hartley. "There's a pickup truck pulling up to the trailer. It's stirred up a lot of dust and is a little obscured right now, but it appears that ... Hold on. We've got a visual on a guy getting out of the truck. He's uh ... He walked up to the container and it looks like he's pulled a set of keys out of his pocket."

CHAPTER TWENTY-EIGHT

Near Navajo Route 5035

January 23, 2021

It had been days since Meriwether was last at the container. Most of the food he had left was gone. Beth had eaten the last of the slices of cold pizza just this morning but still had about a half-liter of water. She sat alone in the dim light that passed for daytime and considered her situation. How long had it been since she had last seen him? Longer than usual, she knew that much. Five or six days she figured. Could something have happened to him? Or had he decided to let her die in the container? The half-liter of water might last a day. After that, it wouldn't take long in the dry desert environment to become dehydrated. Death, she knew, came quickly when the body was dehydrated.

The muscles in her jaw tightened as anger welled up to replace the anxiety. How could anyone do this to her? She hated all of the men involved. And why had God allowed it? Was it some sort of trial, like Moses in the desert?

Then she got angry with herself for being angry. This was not how she was supposed to react, either as a Christian or as a Diné. She took several deep breaths to calm herself.

She forbade herself to think that he might not return, and as she wondered when he would come, her mind became a whirlpool of hope. He had demonstrated that he had some humanity, and he had talked to the tall man about releasing her. He had brought her the means to look after her personal hygiene. He had spoken to her with courtesy, if not with kindness. Surely he would come. If not today, then tomorrow.

As she stewed, she fiddled with the little fingernail file that swiveled out from the clippers. She was grateful that after she had bathed and washed her hair those days earlier, Meriwether had left the pair of fingernail clippers with her. She had been able to trim her toenails and clip her fingernails. Now she contemplated the tiny file and felt its coarse edge with her fingertip as she peered up at the five air holes in the ceiling of the container. Would it be possible to somehow use the file to enlarge those holes into one opening, big enough to squirm out and escape into the desert? She didn't know where she was. But she had seen pumpjacks nearby, so she had to be in the oil fields on the north side of the reservation. She could be found and aided by one of the oil field workers. But she still couldn't figure out how to reach the top of the container. She stood and yet again stretched one arm over her head. The ceiling of the container was at least two feet higher than her fingertips. Even if she overturned the slop bucket and stood on it, she wouldn't reach the ceiling. And she doubted that the little file was up to the job of enlarging the holes anyway.

She moved to the doors at the end of the container and, in the dim light, felt around the edges, looking for inside hinges. Perhaps a hinge pin could be worked loose with the little file. Another no go. The edges were smooth and tightly joined to the frame, the hinges obviously on the outside.

Back on the mattress, her mind returned to the vortex of swirling emotions; fear, promise, depression, confusion. Everything in this jumble of feelings and thoughts had affinity. Everything in the universe is interconnected, with no difference between the emotional, the spiritual, and the real world. Her tumbling emotions were not separate and random but connected to reality ... to spirituality ... and to Christianity. Her people, whether traditional, Christian, or a blend of the two, believed that spirit exists in everything and that all things and people are connected in some way. All people and things are part of the same whole. She would either live or die in this container. Because everything exists in relation to everything else, her death or her survival would have spiritual and present-world ramifications.

Her thoughts were interrupted by the familiar sound of an approaching truck. He had come back. Her breath caught in her chest and she felt a surge of adrenaline, fueled by hope as much as fear. She had been granted one more opportunity to escape. But what about next time? If she didn't succeed today, would she get another chance? She moved to the front of her mattress, then stood and with her foot nudged the slop bucket nearer the mattress. She picked it up. Should she throw the contents at him and run? Or was it better to act normally and watch for an opening, any opening? She stood by the door, ready. Waiting.

Minutes later, Meriwether stood in the open doorway. "Be quick," he said gruffly, as he replenished her food and water supply and allowed her out in the late afternoon twilight. "I can't stay here for more than a few minutes. Got other things to do." He briefly clutched his groin with one hand, and then walked to the side of the container unzipping his fly as he moved. "Gotta take a leak. But hurry up. Empty and clean that bucket. Then I've got to put you back in."

Beth, near the driver's side door of the pickup, gleaned through her confusion that the engine was idling. That hadn't happened before. Impulsively, she grabbed the handle and pulled open the door. Without thinking it through, she slid into the driver's seat. She found the shift lever and pulled it into Drive. She had never driven a motor vehicle before, but she had no choice. She acted as an automaton, irrational and unemotional, robotically following her instinctive programming – get away. Get away from here.

The vehicle rolled forward slightly, inching its way toward the container.

"Hey. *Hey!*" shouted Meriwether. He moved toward the truck. "*Hey*, Goddamnit. Whadda ya think you're doing?" As the vehicle nudged up against the container, Meriwether barreled toward the truck.

Out of the corner of her eye Beth saw him and panicked. She jerked the shift lever back and forth. It hit Reverse and the truck started moving backward at a snail's pace. At the same moment, Meriwether stumbled toward, and grabbed hold of, the still-ajar driver's door. Now frantic, Beth searched the floorboards in search of the pedals. She jammed her bare foot down on the accelerator pedal.

The vehicle lurched backwards, its rear wheels spinning in reverse, spewing loose gravel, pinging and pecking, across the length of the undercarriage. Meriwether fell away to the side, and Beth screamed. The truck was out of control in reverse, but she had the wheel, if only she could hang on. Without letting up on the gas pedal, she flung the shift lever back into drive and cranked hard to the right, oversteering. She spun the wheel hard in the other direction and accelerated rapidly. The rear end fishtailed in the loose gravel while the front end bounced up a small grade and plowed into the rough, uneven terrain, smashing through a mixed field of Creosote and Bursage shrubbery. Just as the rear end settled down, the right front bumper smacked the thick trunk of a Piñon Tree. Beth could hear the bumper scraping against the tire with a sickening screech.

CHAPTER TWENTY-NINE

Northeast of Round Rock, Arizona
January 23, 2021

Raptly, Melissa watched the video feed from the drone until her mind shifted gears. Would the tattoo on a woman's wrist lead to her discovering who her mother was? And would the man in Georgia, Willie Cole, with whom she had exchanged e-mails, turn out to be her father? Learning about her real parents was more than mere curiosity. Knowing something about them might provide insight into her genetic programming, those aspects of her character and health that could be attributed to heredity rather than environmental conditioning. Knowing more could help her become more secure in her identity – or not. And importantly, she'd have a better idea about what genes she'd eventually pass on to her children.

But there was risk involved in finding the truth. Her love for and life with the Codys was rich. Her childhood had been happy, and so far, her young adulthood satisfying. She had become well educated and enjoyed her work, both in the New Mexico legislature and now with the Indigenous Women's Network of Arizona and New Mexico. And although it was too soon to predict where her interest in Ronald might take her, she couldn't deny that she was attracted to him, and not only because he had helped to save her infant life.

If this enchantment should blossom, what would she owe him, or any other love interest, as explanation? It's hard enough for a young person to choose a mate, even when the parents are available to observe. But when they're missing or unknown – would a potential partner have the same concerns about her origins as she had?

She felt fulfilled and happy for the most part, and yet the answers to the questions that nagged her were fraught with peril. What if her biological parents were alcoholics or drug addicts? What if her father was not Willie Cole, but someone else, a sex abuser? A misogynist?

And what about Willie Cole? When would she hear from him again? It had taken her six weeks to get her own report from Ancestry.com but Willie had paid for expedited processing. What would it be like to discover that he was in fact her biological father? She hoped they'd try to get to know each other via Zoom, or maybe even during an in-person meeting, if this third wave of Covid-19 would simmer down. And then what? Would they have an ongoing relationship? Would they become close? How would her life change?

Her thoughts swung like a pendulum, in huge arcs from one side to the other until Bill Hartley, sitting next to her, bumped her elbow with his and pointed to the video monitor.

He shouted into his headset,"Wait. There's a pickup truck pulling up to the trailer. It's stirred up a lot dust and is a little obscured right now, but it appears that ... Hold on. We've got a visual on a guy getting out of the truck. He's uh ... He walked up to the container and it looks like he's pulled a set of keys out of his pocket."

Melissa's attention refocused fully on the situation as Wendy's voice come back through the open phone link. "Roger that. We're only about three minutes from the container. I can see the dust cloud from the truck."

"Roger. The guy has opened the door. A young female in a red sweatshirt has just emerged from the container. Looks like she's carrying a bucket." He paused for a few seconds. "The guy is relieving himself at the side of the container .... Jeez, I don't believe it. The girl's climbed into the truck and put it in gear. It's about to bump the container ... Now the guy's reacting. He's running toward the truck. He's ..."

"Break. Break," shouted Wendy. "We're just about there. Bill, get on the phone and get that HRT in the air. Get 'em up to this location."

"Roger that. I doubt if they're even assembled at the Albuquerque airport yet. But I'll see if I can build a fire under them."

Melissa watched, glued to the action, while Bill Hartley got on another phone line to ask that the hostage rescue team be immediately deployed to the container site. He read off the coordinates from the bottom of his screen.

"Look," Melissa shouted. Hartley was still on the phone with Albuquerque. She jabbed him in the arm. "Look, look." On the screen, the truck moved erratically, accelerating as it spewed loose gravel from the rear wheels.

"Wendy," Hartley shouted into the open cell line. "The girl's driving the truck. It's just plowed up an embankment into the rough desert scrub. She's heading south cross-country. She just had a collision with a tree and the vehicle is damaged, but she's accelerating in very rough, uneven terrain."

Wendy's voice came back. "Roger. We're just arriving at the container. Make sure that drone sticks with the truck. I'm stopping here to arrest that character who opened the container."

CHAPTER THIRTY

Tacoma, Washington
January 23, 2021

Mark Snyder knew he was seriously out on a limb. By fleeing as he had, he'd clearly telegraphed to the FBI his concern about what a specimen of his DNA would reveal. When they had approached his front door, as he had feared they would, he had no other option but to get away from them, bad choice though it was. Now what? He had evaded the police and FBI, for the moment, by hiding in his girl-friend's cottage in Gig Harbor, his motorcycle locked in her garage. Mary Anne was working the night shift at the Tides Tavern, so he sat alone at her kitchen table, an open can of Budweiser in front of him, trying to think of his next move.

He couldn't very well go home. And he couldn't go back to Arizona. Showing up for work at the man camp in seven days would certainly result in his apprehension and the forceable collection of his DNA. Then he'd not only go down for kidnapping and rape, but obstruction of justice for bolting, as well. What was left? He could think of only two options: turn himself in to the FBI, or flee the country.

Turning himself in would probably land him in prison for at least ten years. No way he could live with that. But where would he go and what would he do for a living if he fled the country? Maybe Mexico? With his experience and qualifications in the oil patch, he could get employment with the state-owned petroleum company PEMEX, at one of their offshore drilling sites in the Bay of Campeche. He wouldn't earn anywhere near the $115,000 a year he was pulling down now, but the cost of living in Mexico was less than half that of the US. And the señoritas in the Yucatan were reputed to be plentiful and loose.

His ringing cell phone jolted him back to the present. He glanced at the caller I.D. then quickly answered. "Jake. Thank God. I've been trying to reach you all afternoon. I'm in a bit of a pickle."

"So I understand." Jake Gabriel didn't even attempt to match Mark's light tone. He'd been practicing law long enough to know the likely outcome of a client who fled. "I heard from the FBI. Congratulations. You've graduated from person-of-interest to suspect. I gotta tell you. Running from them was stupid, Mark."

"Yeah, I know. It's a shit show. What I need now is advice."

"The best thing you can do at this point is turn yourself in and we'll try to cast doubt on the charges in court."

"I've thought of that, but I'm leaning toward Mexico. I'm sure I can get a job with PEMEX in their drilling operation."

"There are two problems with that scenario, Mark. First, if PEMEX wants to check references, that news would get to the FBI within hours and they'd be onto you. The US has an extradition treaty with Mexico, and the Mexican government is all too cooperative when it comes to returning fugitives to the US when they're accused of the most serious crimes, like murder, rape and sexual offenses against children. You qualify for two of those categories, Mark. Three, if the Chee girl turns up dead."

"Shit," Mark said. "My girlfriend thinks the same, about turning myself in to the FBI. She thinks I might have a chance of avoiding jail time if I agree to participate in the traditional Native restorative justice process. I don't believe it. We had a hell of a fight about it just before she left for work."

"Hmm. What does she know about traditional Native justice?"

"I don't know. She spent a lot of time in the library in Window Rock when she came to visit me in Arizona."

"Well, I'm not an expert in this area, but my understanding is that what we would call a misdemeanor – what the Natives label misbehavior – can be resolved through traditional Navajo justice. It's a non-judicial process where those who've been hurt and those suspected of doing the hurting get together in a room with a facilitator and talk things out. It usually ends in a group hug. But the federal criminal justice system prosecutes and punishes felonies committed in Indian Country under the provisions of the Major Crimes Act. You would fit in the latter category, Mark."

"So, what the hell can I do Jake? I'm paying you to give me answers."

"Once again, your best bet is to surrender to the authorities and we'll find a way to mount a vigorous defense. Time is of the essence. The FBI probably already suspect that you're hiding at your girlfriend's house, and it won't take long to figure out who she is and where she lives."

It didn't take long at all. Within an hour he heard an authoritative voice amplified by a loudspeaker: "Mark Snyder, this is the FBI. The house is surrounded. I'm directing you to come out through the front door with your hands over your head."

CHAPTER THIRTY-ONE

Near Navajo route 5035
January 23, 2021

Wendy wheeled the Suburban to within twenty feet of the container, catching the man by surprise. As she and Smitty jumped out, weapons drawn, he was facing the other direction brutishly shouting into his cell phone. "I don't give a good god damn what day of the week it is, Sharon, and of course I know it's Saturday afternoon. Get someone out here to pick me up. My truck's been stolen ... Yes, that's what I said, *stolen*. What part of that don't you understand. ... Get one of those lazy, security bastards out here to get me. There's a fast-moving line of squalls heading my way out of the north."

Wendy assumed the firing stance and, with both hands, gripped her Glock nine-millimeter firmly and aimed it squarely at the man's back. "That's no way to talk to your secretary, Mr. Behrendt. FBI. Put both your hands over your head, turn around, face me, then get down on your knees."

Derek Behrendt, a.k.a Meriwether, whirled around wide eyed to look straight into the business end of two powerful FBI pistols. "Shit." He dropped the phone and put his hands on his head. "I can explain. Mark Snyder put—"

"You're better off to keep your mouth shut, Mr. Behrendt. Get down on your knees."

"I didn't do anything. I'm just the camp manager. You met me before." Now eager to comply, words tumbled out of his mouth as he dropped to his knees. "Mark Snyder put that girl in the container. I was taking care of her."

"Shut up. You have a right to remain silent. Anything you say can be used against you in court. Now put your right hand behind your back. Keep your left hand on your head."

Raymond Phillips and the two other Navajo policemen joined Wendy and Smitty in forming a semi-circle around Behrendt.

"Cuff him, Smitty," Wendy said. "You also have a right to an attorney. In the remote event that you, or your company, cannot afford one, the FBI will obtain a public defender for you. Do you understand your rights?"

"Yeah." He winced as Smitty snapped a handcuff around his right hand, and then jerked his left hand down and cuffed it as well.

"That's not too tight I hope," Smitty said sarcastically.

The sky darkened as downdrafts from the approaching line of storm clouds washed over them. Raindrops stippled the ground.

"Detective Phillips, will you and your deputies entertain Mr. Behrendt here, while Smitty and I try to catch up with the pickup truck?"

"Be happy to, Agent. We can all sit in the Blazer and enjoy the thunder and lightning show. Coming soon, to a theatre near us."

"Let's go Smitty." As Wendy climbed back in her vehicle, she spoke into the open cellular circuit. "Okay, Bill. Where's that truck now? We can see where it went into the rough terrain. I'm going to follow."

"Roger. It's thumping and bumping along at about 10 MPH, a mile and a half or so south of you. Has that weather front hit you yet?"

"We're just in the leading edge. But I'll plow ahead as long as I've got some visibility." As she spoke, the rainfall, now mixed with hail, drummed on the roof of the vehicle.

Wendy put the Chevy into four-wheel drive and piloted up the low embankment and into the rough terrain. The pickup had left a conspicuous trail of broken and disturbed undergrowth that she was able to follow. She put the vehicle up to fifteen miles an hour, but its relentless pitching and juddering soon forced her to back off to around eight as the big vehicle yawed and rolled over moguls and rocks. Underbrush caught in the undercarriage, scraping the ground with a sound like rattlesnakes.

They were no more than a mile from the container site when the line of thundershowers hit them full force. Lightning cracked around them, claps of thunder exploded and visibility reduced to almost zero as the overworked windshield wipers swiped uselessly. Wendy slowed the vehicle to a crawl.

Seconds later, Bill Hartley's voice squawked through the speaker, "The drone's blind in this weather. The pilot will try to keep it on station, but the images on the monitors look like swirling black smoke." An enormous thunderclap eclipsed his voice. "... Bad news too. The HRT is still on the ground in Albuquerque. They've only just now pulled together all of their members at the airport."

"May as well hold them there for now," Wendy said. "We've taken down a bad guy at the container. And I think he's the only one in the neighborhood right now. We may still need them, though, depending on what we find when we catch up with that pickup."

•   •   •

As the truck suddenly hurtled down a steep embankment, bouncing and thudding off rocks as it plummeted, Beth took her foot off the gas pedal and frantically felt around for the brake with both bare feet. Then the vehicle miraculously rolled to a stop on comparatively level ground. Beth found the accelerator again and pressed down. Rain flecked the windshield and the sky ahead grew darker. She fumbled around and found the lever for the wipers and flipped them on as she heard the first thunder clap from the angry frontal system churning with roiling clouds.

She had been so intent on getting away from the container and Meriwether that neither a location nor a destination had occurred to her until this moment. She'd seen oil rigs and pumpjacks near the container, so she had to be somewhere on the north side of the rez, near the San Juan Basin. But where were the principal paved roads? Much of the rez in this region was criss-crossed with dirt and gravel roads. If she could find one, she'd follow it until it took her to a ranch, a hogan or a paved road. She had to find one soon. For all she knew, Meriwether was in pursuit of her.

The line of squalls engulfed the vehicle with a fierce wrath, swallowing up the landscape. The downpour and sudden loss of visibility left Beth stunned, surrounded by turbulent lightning and thunder. Ferocious rain overpowered her wipers and pounded on the roof. Unsure whether to stop or not, she continued to plow ahead, blindly.

Within seconds, the pickup passed over the edge of a steeply banked arroyo and plunged, nearly vertically, down fifteen feet, until it crashed onto the rocky bottom and stood on its crushed nose. The driver airbag deployed instantly, then deflated. Beth, who hadn't thought to put on the seatbelt when she stole the truck, fell forward against the steering column, her forehead smashing into the dashboard. Everything went black.

Minutes later, when she regained a muzzy semi-consciousness, she couldn't move. She opened her eyes but could discern only snippets of gray-like objects in dim light, like the flickering images of a dull monochrome movie. Her chest and forehead were wracked in pain. "Dear God," she moaned, and then passed out again.

• • •

The thundershowers had passed, but the sky was the color of fireplace ash when Wendy and Smitty arrived at the edge of the arroyo. Wendy jumped from the Suburban and peered over the edge of the embankment. "Oh shit," she yelled, and scrambled down the steep slope.

Smitty rushed to the back of the Suburban. "I'll bring the first aid kit."

When Wendy reached the truck, Beth was splayed around the steering column, head forward, chin on her chest. Blood trickled across her forehead. Her eyes were open but glazed over. "Beth. We're the FBI. Here to help you. Can you hear me?" She tugged on the jammed door handle, and then stumbled around the vehicle and tried the other door. Also jammed. She yelled, "Can you hear me, Beth?" No response. She shouted up to Smitty, just starting to descend the slope, "Bring my cell. Bring a handheld radio as well, in case there's no cell signal here. We're damn lucky the rain didn't trigger a flash flood in this arroyo."

Wendy returned to the driver's side window, where she hammered on the glass with the butt of her service pistol until Smitty arrived with the first aid and communications equipment. The tempered glass, if broken, would smash itself into pebble sized pieces, and be less potentially harmful to Beth than the jagged edges of ordinary window glass. "Smitty, take over here. Use your superior man-strength while I get on the horn."

She snatched the phone and said, "Bill, you still there? Have we got comms?"

"Right. I hear you Wendy. And the drone just came back on-line. We can see you've got a situation there."

"Roger that. See if you can get a medevac chopper out here and have them bring The Jaws of Life, or some kind of hydraulic rescue tool."

"Will do. Standby."

Wendy turned back to the vehicle just in time to see Smitty successfully breach the side window, which shattered with a series of pops. She reached into the vehicle and touched Beth's shoulder, then stroked her chin gently. "Beth, can you hear me? Smitty, get a cervical collar out of that kit. We don't dare try to move her without stabilizing her neck."

She put a hand in front of Beth's mouth and nose and waited for breath. "Airway's clear. She's breathing okay." She felt for a carotid pulse. "Pulse is good too. Beth, can you hear me?"

The girl moaned, "Umm hmm. Head ... hurts."

"It's okay, Beth. We're going to help you. We'll get you home. I'm just going to slip this collar around your neck."

Just as she wrapped the splint around Beth's neck, Bill Hartley's voice squawked out of the cell phone, "We've gotta medevac bird from the National Guard enroute to you. His ETA is 55 minutes."

"Okay, is he carrying equipment to extricate this girl from the vehicle?"

"Affirmative. There're actually two birds on the way. One has the Jaws of Life on board."

Wendy said gently to Beth, "You lucky girl. You're getting a helicopter ride. I want you to keep talking with me. Don't go to sleep."

"Julie? ... Okay?"

"She's fine, Beth. She's eager to see you."

CHAPTER THIRTY-TWO

January 23, 2021
Northeast of Round Rock

Two Army National Guard helicopters settled cautiously on the undulating terrain at the lip of the arroyo. The squalls an hour earlier had helped keep the dust down and on the monitor Melissa watched two firefighters in heavy bunker coats and helmets emerge from one of the choppers and from the other, two paramedics in olive drab flight suits. A third firefighter stepped from the helio. The three struggled with heavy equipment as they made their way down the steep embankment to the crashed pickup truck.

Melissa glanced at her watch; 4:30. Only about an hour of good daylight left. The responders would need to bring lighting in if they couldn't extricate Beth before nightfall. She adjusted the brightness of the monitor she was glued to and tried to make out the words passing between Wendy Burkenshaw and the firemen.

Just then her cell phone rang with a call from Elberton, Georgia, and her stomach fluttered as she excused herself from Bill Hartley and stepped out of the motorhome. The tent held several NPD police officers, but she found privacy near one of the portable toilets.

"Willie," she said. "Is that you? My heart just speeded up when I saw this call was from Elberton."

"It's me. I hope you're sitting down, Melissa. The Ancestry.com test turned around in less than a week. The report says that you and I are father and daughter with a confidence rating of extremely high. I didn't want to tell you this by e-mail."

"Oh my God." Melissa steadied herself against the side of the toilet. "This is surreal. I'm twenty-six-years-old, standing behind a porta-potty in the middle of the desert and I just learned who my father is? I think I'm thrilled, but I probably need a few moments to process this, Willie ... er, Dad."

"Of course. Me too. Why don't we meet face to face on Zoom the day after tomorrow? Will you be someplace you can talk at, say 2:30 your time?"

"I think so. I'm sort of participating in the rescue of a Native girl who was abducted. She just managed to escape, but she was in a vehicle accident. Police, firefighters and paramedics are trying to help her now. I'm watching it all by way of drone surveillance from about fifteen miles away. I think her rescue's imminent. I should be able to get back to Window Rock by 2:30, the day after tomorrow."

"Jeez. That sounds like a lot of excitement for one afternoon. Especially with my news on top of it. Okay, let's both take some time to process this. Meanwhile I'll send you a link for a Zoom telecall on Tuesday."

"Okay. I can't wait."

As she stepped back into the motorhome, Bill Hartley said, "Come watch this, Melissa. They're rolling the roof on that pickup truck back like they're opening a can of sardines."

In the fading light, with her heart still beating overtime, Melissa watched as several fire fighters worked. One held a heavy device that looked a bit like a chain saw. Instead of a bar with a bladed chain on it, the working end had a pair of eighteen-inch-long spreader arms. Two power cords ran from the rear of the device to a portable generator sitting on the ground about fifteen feet back.

Inserted into the passenger side door jamb, the arms slowly came apart, bending the door and partially opening it as well. Another firefighter, wearing heavy-duty work gloves, gripped the door as it was bent forward. The operator then moved the spreader arms to the forward edge of the door and cranked up the power, causing hydraulic pressure to spread the arms. The door popped off and the second fire fighter jerked it away from the vehicle and threw it to the ground like a wrestler throwing his opponent down.

Melissa and Bill continued to watch as the two paramedics then reached into the vehicle and gently lifted Beth out. Careful to keep her neck stable, they laid her on an orange medevac litter board, covered her with blankets and strapped her on.

"She looks so tender and frail," Melissa said. "I hope she's not seriously hurt."

Wendy's voice came through the speaker and took precedence over any response Bill might have had. "Bill, the medics say she's probably concussed, but apart from that no apparent serious injuries. As soon as they get her into the medevac chopper, they'll take her to the hospital in Fort Defiance, just north of Window Rock. Melissa, if you're there, can you call Bernice Begay and let her know that? I'll call Beth's mom, Flower, in Gallup."

"Right. I'll call Bernie right away," Melissa said.

It took another twenty minutes for the crew on the ground to get Beth into the chopper. Strapped to the litter board, they couldn't get her up the embankment to the waiting chopper, so instead, the helicopter lifted off, hovered over the arroyo and lowered a stout cable from a door-mounted davit. Struggling against the turbulent downdraft from the Blackhawk's beating rotor blades, the firefighters and medics rigged a four-point sling attachment to the litter and connected it to the cable.

"Those guys really know their stuff," observed Melissa as she watched the drama unfold on the monitor. "It's amazing to see that kind of teamwork."

The voice from Albuquerque came through a speaker. "The drone is getting low on fuel. I'll have to take it home soon. But it looks like it's done its job."

Hartley asked, "Can it loiter for about five more minutes, so we can watch that litter as it's hoisted?"

"That's about it. Five minutes," said Albuquerque.

In a stationary hover, the helicopter nonetheless rocked and yawed as Beth was winched up to the open doorway, a slow and deliberate procedure which took several minutes. A crew member swiveled the davit and she and her litter disappeared into the bosom of the bird. The chopper then touched down atop the bank of the arroyo to retrieve the paramedics who had clambered back up from the gulch.

Special Agent Bill Hartley turned to Melissa. "Wow that was more drama than I've seen in a long while. And thankfully, no shots were fired."

CHAPTER THIRTY-THREE

Seattle, Washington
January 24, 2021

The conference room had a Spartan quality. Framed prints with a Puget Sound theme hung on the cheaply paneled walls: a ferry pulling in to land at Coleman dock, Mount Rainier basking in a corona of sunrise, Snoqualmie Falls debauching into a fog of mist. The floor was vinyl laminate, hard and shiny, pretending to be expensive hardwood. Late afternoon sunlight slanted in through three windows on the west wall and lay on the floor in tall shallow rectangles.

Despite the drabness of the facility, Special Agent Sally McKnight, dressed professionally in a tailored mauve pantsuit, sensed an air of electricity in the room as the various participants took their seats and shuffled papers. On her right, Mr. G. Douglas Winchester, recently quaffed and neatly tailored in gray pinstripes, removed several file folders from his briefcase and arranged them on the polished surface of the conference table. To his right, a secretary, also from the US Attorney's office, flipped on the recording function of her iPhone then sat with a pencil in hand poised over a long yellow legal pad. To Sally's left, Special Agent Fred Wong, wearing his navy-blue suit with American flag lapel pin, leaned on his elbow and glared at the two men sitting across the table.

It would be difficult for Snyder and Gabriel, seated on the opposite side of the table, to make out the features of the law enforcement team, backlit by the sun as they were. Sally figured that Winchester had deliberately, and astutely, arranged the seating in this fashion. Conversely, she could clearly read the body language of Mark Snyder, who leaned forward in his chair, appearing penitent and eager to cooperate, if it would buy him some leniency. Mr. Jake Gabriel, on the other hand, sat relaxed and confident, the ubiquitous yellow legal pad before him.

Once everyone had settled in their chairs, Douglas Winchester threw down the opening gauntlet, "Good afternoon Gentlemen. Well, Mr. Snyder, the DNA specimen we took from you matches that found in the girl Julie Longwalker and also matches that found in the pickup truck bearing license plate **2 OIL 773.** That single piece of evidence is a clincher. Even though we don't have any evidence tying you to the murder of Guy Primeau, the DNA link to the kidnapping and rape of two Native girls is enough to put you away for a long time."

"I need a brief conference with my client," said Gabriel as he hurriedly scrawled notes on the yellow pad.

"Sure," Winchester said. "Take your time."

After four and a half minutes of whispered consultations, Jake Gabriel asked, "What are you offering?"

"Nothing at this point. We might, however be open to discussing some level of leniency in exchange for Mr. Snyder's cooperation and some additional information."

Perspiration was beading on Snyder's forehead. A slight tremor developed in his hand. He quickly grasped it with the other hand and pulled both from the table to rest in his lap.

"What cooperation? What additional information?"

"Before we get to that, let me apprise you of a couple more developments. Yesterday, the second girl abducted and raped, Ms. Beth Chee, Native American, aged seventeen, was rescued from a shipping container where she had been held captive and used as a sex slave for forty-nine days. This morning she identified your client, Mr. Mark Snyder, from a digital line-up shown her in the hospital at Fort Defiance. On top of that, our colleagues in Arizona are holding a Mr. Derek Behrendt, who has also identified Mr. Snyder as the principal perpetrator. I believe he's the site manager at the drilling operation."

Mark Snyder paled and appeared to shrivel into his chair.

Winchester shifted his gaze from Gabriel to Snyder, "Mr. Snyder, under federal statutes, Aggravated Sexual Assault is punishable by twenty-five to life and Aggravated Kidnapping can get you another twenty to life. We're prepared to recommend the max and ask that the sentences be served consecutively." He paused and waited for a reaction.

Again, the attorney exchanged whispers with his client. Sally noticed that a tic had developed under Snyder's eye.

"All right, what do you want? And what are you offering?" asked Gabriel.

"We want a statement, signed by Mark Snyder, attesting to his involvement in the abduction and rape of the two girls. We want the names of the other two men involved, apart from Snyder and Behrendt. We want the details of the murder of Guy Primeau to include the name of the one who actually offed him."

"And what are you offering in return?"

"That depends, Counselor, on the veracity of the statement. We *might* be inclined to ask for concurrent sentences instead of consecutive."

"Can you give us thirty minutes, alone?"

Sally thought this question was framed with a little less defiance than his earlier behavior.

"Sure. We'll take a coffee break," said Winchester.

"Right," Gabriel said. "And please turn off that video camera while we confer." He glanced up at the mini-cam over the doorway.

•   •   •

The video camera was back on, the iPhone was set to audio-record and the secretary was again poised to take notes. "All right, this is the 24th of January, 2021," said G. Douglas Winchester. "Present are myself, Douglas Winchester, Special Agents Sally McKnight and Fred Wong, Ms. Lillian Burink, legal assistant to the US Attorney's District of Western Washington. Also present is Mr. Jake Gabriel, attorney for Mr. Mark Snyder who is present and who's going to make a statement. Go Ahead Mr. Snyder. You may start. Please be prepared for us to interrupt you with questions at any time."

Snyder glanced sideways at his legal counsel who nodded. He cleared his throat and with a somewhat tremulous voice began.

"On Tuesday, the ... uh...5th of December, me and three other guys from the camp drove a company truck down to Window Rock for some, uhm, sightseeing. We had beer and whiskey with us in the truck and we all drank as we were driving down. The other guys were Derek Behrendt,

David O'Hara and Guy Primeau. By the time we got to Window Rock, we were drunk and decided to look for girls to, uh, pick up. It was about 7:30 I guess when we got to Window Rock. We spotted two Indian ... I mean Native ... girls walking along a residential street and tried to talk to them. But they just walked faster and moved to the right of the shoulder."

Sally asked, "Who was driving?"

"I was. I pulled the truck in front of the girls so they couldn't keep going straight. We just wanted to talk to them. But they acted really stuck up or something. Then the other three guys jumped out and wrestled the girls into the back seat of the pickup. We drove out of Window Rock and headed north with the girls in the truck."

"Were the girls still resisting as you drove north?" asked Fred Wong.

"Yeah. They really didn't want to be with us. And I could tell they were real afraid we'd hurt them."

"About an hour later, I turned off the highway and drove into the desert somewhere northeast of Round Rock. We found a spot and I stopped the truck. We ... uhm ... we did 'em then."

"By 'we did them' you mean you raped them?"

Snyder lowered his head to where his chin touched his chest. "Yes."

"All four of you?"

"No. Guy didn't want to participate. Just Derek, David and me."

Winchester asked, "Did each of the three of you rape both of the girls?"

"I don't really remember. We were really drunk. But when we finished, someone had the dumb idea that we should burn their clothes. Like burn the evidence, I guess. I think it was David. So, we piled up one girl's clothes and lit them on fire. Then we put 'em both in the truck and drove back to the highway."

"Why did you just burn one girl's clothes?" asked Sally.

"Uhm. Guy kept screaming 'C'mon, you guys. This isn't right,' or something like that. He wanted us to get going and go back to the camp. He was makin' so much racket. And we knew there were hogans nearby, so we just left. When we got back to the highway, we let one girl out and told her to go home. We kept the other girl, the naked one, in the truck."

"Why on earth would you let one out and keep the other one?" asked Sally.

"I dunno. We weren't thinking right. We were drunk. I guess we thought the naked girl would draw attention if anyone happened by on the highway."

"And it didn't occur to you that the other girl, whether she had clothes on or not would garner some attention just by the fact that she was alone and disheveled in the middle of nowhere?"

"Like I said we weren't thinkin' straight. As we headed north with the naked one, we kept asking ourselves 'What'll we do with this one?' Finally, David said, 'Let's put her in one of the storage containers for now.' This seemed like a good idea, so that's what we did. All the time, Guy was still yellin' 'This isn't right. This isn't right. We gotta let her go.'

The next morning, I woke up in the camp all hung over and stuff, but I still took my crew and drove out to the rig we were working on. It took me most of the morning to get a clear memory of what all we did the night before. When I finally realized we had locked a girl in the container, I got really worried about her. I was afraid she would die. So, after we got off work, I packed up some food and water and took it to her in the container."

"And did you force yourself on her again? Did you rape her again?" asked Winchester.

"Uh ... Yeah. I hadn't intended to. But there she was, all naked and I just couldn't help myself."

"So," said Fred Wong, "You continued to visit her, to take her food and rape her every day until you left for Christmas and came up here to Washington?"

"Not every day. No. I went every few days. I took her fresh food and water and some clothes. Once or twice I took soap and hot water so she could take a bath."

Sally asked, "What about the other three guys? Did any of them go to the container in the days between the 5th and the 24th when your shift was off for Christmas?"

"No. Not until about the 21st of December. Then I took Derek to the container and asked him to look after the girl while I was gone for Christmas break and our regular time off in January. None of us even talked about the night of the fifth until then. It was like everyone was so drunk, they'd forgotten about it. But I could tell that Guy probably remembered it. He was really quiet and hardly talked to anyone until he died."

"That's a good segue," said Winchester. "How did Guy Primeau die? At whose hand?"

"I don't know for sure. But I suspect that it was David O'Hara who killed him. David told me he'd seen Guy put a note on the windshield of an FBI woman's car in the camp on the day before Guy died. He —David— said he was afraid Guy was telling the FBI about what we done on the 5th."

"Wait a minute," said Sally. "Something's wrong with the timeline here. Didn't you just tell us none of the four of you talked about events of the 5th until you took Derek to the container on the 21st, which was the same day Guy died? But now you're telling us that David told you about Guy putting a note on the FBI car on the 20th."

"Maybe I'm a little confused. It could have been the 21st, in the morning, when David told me that."

"Didn't it worry you too?"

"Yes. But there was nothing I could do about it, except stew. At least not on that day. My crew and I were working on a drilling site, miles from where Guy had been working on an established wellhead on that day. David was the driver of the crew bus. He dropped crews off and picked them up at various times during the day. In between runs, he deadheaded the bus."

Sally lifted her head from her notes. "What does that mean? Deadheaded?"

"It just means he drove the bus one-way without passengers."

"So, you're suggesting that at some point, when he had no passengers on the bus, David could have doubled back to the wellhead where Primeau was working and killed him."

"That's my guess."

"Where does David O'Hara live when he's not in the camp? We can get that info from his personnel records of course, but it might expedite matters if you can tell us now?"

"Boise, Idaho."

Winchester pushed his chair back and stood up. "Okay, Mr. Snyder. Here are the next steps. We'll have the statement typed up and presented to you for signature and witnessing later this evening. After that, you'll be arraigned. This is Sunday. We may be able to get this case onto one of the judge's dockets within the next ten days. At the arraignment the judge will also entertain a motion for bond, which I'm sure your attorney will have in his hip pocket. In the meantime, I hope you brought your toothbrush because you're going to enjoy some jail hospitality."

"What about the bargain?" asked Jake Gabriel.

"We'll stick to my suggestion of concurrent instead of consecutive sentences provided the statement proves to be veracious."

CHAPTER THIRTY-FOUR

Window Rock, Arizona
January 25, 2021

It was 2:30 p.m. in Window Rock, 5:30 p.m. in Elberton, Georgia. The smiling face on Melissa's computer screen was that of a handsome gentleman in his early to mid-forties. Clean-shaven, save for a close-cropped black and silver moustache bristling his upper lip, his full head of hair was neatly trimmed and uniformly dark except for tinges of gray at his temples. Beneath a green pullover-sweater, he wore a pale blue shirt with faint checks, open at the neck. An impressive assortment of books and framed memorabilia lined the bookshelves behind him.

"Well, good morning, Melissa," said Willie Cole through a broad smile. "Great to see you live and direct. I've been trying to imagine what you look like. You're even prettier than I thought."

"I guess I got my looks from you." Snide, sassy, forward? She paused to drink him in and study his features. Did she have his eyes? Great books on the shelves. A reader like herself. Did he always wear a sweater? Scattered, crazy thoughts.

Finally, she responded. "Hello. Good morning to you too. Sorry, this is a bit befuddling, isn't it? Shall I call you Willie?"

"Suits me," he said, still smiling on the screen.

Melissa was suddenly conscious of how little she had prepared for this meeting. She had no agenda in mind, had not listed any exploratory questions, had not thought of what and how she would reveal herself to him. More importantly, she really had not thought through what she wanted from him. She never would have launched into a business meeting so ill-prepared.

"I'm thinking I should ask you about the weather or something to ease us into a conversation Willie, but so many things are jogging around in my head at the moment. I apologize. I was just thinking to myself that I am usually more prepared for a business meeting than I am today and yet meeting you is significantly more important. I don't know where to begin."

"I think we're both a little apprehensive," Willie conceded. "I never in my wildest imaginings thought I'd be in this scenario, and I admit I don't know anyone who's faced this same thing. I don't think I've even seen a movie about this. I have though, since our first contact and especially since the DNA results, done a bit of research online. Basically, the advice is to go cautiously and do a lot of listening so that we respect each other's intents and wishes about any relationship. So that's what I want to do."

Melissa felt a rush of gratitude, and her eyes filled. "Thank you. I really appreciate that you've given this thought and that we can proceed slowly. I'd prefer that too."

Silence hung between them now, each wondering how to move forward given their agreement to tread lightly.

Willie began tentatively. "So, Melissa, tell me about this volunteer work you're doing on the reservation. Was it your own story that drew you to the reservation, the issue of MMIW, or a combination of both?"

Melissa easily slipped into an abbreviated version of her growing interest in the vulnerability of Native Americans while she was working at the Legislature, the chance posting of the volunteer position, the nature of her work at INW and the current case of the rape of Julie and Beth. Willie listened quietly.

"I'm prattling away," Melissa said, when she stopped for a breath. "I don't want to take up all of our screen time. Tell me about you. Are you happy being a school principal? It must be grueling to face all the threats and challenges confronting the public school system these days: funding, gun violence, drugs, racial tensions. Do you get discouraged?"

"I'm the vice principal, not the principal. But yes, I do get discouraged. Still, there are rewards too. When I see a kid who entered my school disadvantaged, poor, and angry, step across the stage to get his diploma four years later I get a real sense of accomplishment for him and my staff...for me too."

Forty minutes passed quickly and it was fast approaching the time to end the Zoom call.

"I do have one serious question to ask before we end our call," stammered Melissa. "It is really important for me to know right now if I was conceived against my mother's will. I guess this is a brash question given our agreement about how we should proceed, but I hope that you understand my perspective."

"You were conceived because of teenage passion and ignorance Melissa. We were kids, fascinated by each other's physical beauty and our hormones were raging. Maybe your mother thought that she might snare herself a white guy and a ticket off the reservation, but I don't think that either of us was capable of any deep contemplation at that point, nor even a future beyond the next week. I did have a vision of university, or maybe that was just an expectation of my parents. Anyway, all that mattered on those few dates that I had with your mother was her glowing skin, raven hair, a full moon, and a thousand stars."

Melissa once again blinked back tears. "I'm relieved. Rape is a strong political issue for my generation and my current work on the reservation and my cursory involvement in this recent criminal case has me really sensitized and even more radical about women's rights. I'm struggling with my own abandonment as a baby. It's hard to be objective."

"Melissa, we'll get to know each other better. But from my perspective, at this point, I have nothing but respect for your courage in seeking the truth about your origins. The least that I can do is give you what details I can. Let's talk again in about a week. And maybe this Covid crisis will recede soon and we can manage a face to face meeting, somewhere. Maybe at my niece's house in El Paso. She has a very spacious hacienda."

"Yes. That would be cool."

• • •

She had been at work for two hours now, but she had ignored the stack of interview notes in front of her, to reflect on the Zoom call with her biological father. Her adoptive parents, Bob and Lois Cody, would share her joy, and she was about to call them when her cell rang with a call from Ronald George. Inexplicably, her heart skipped a bit. "Ronald, good morning," she said. "Nice to hear from you."

"Me too. Good to hear your voice. I've been thinking a lot about you. I think I've found a really good reason for you to come up to Shiprock so we can have another date."

"Well, I think that's reason enough. But what's new?"

"I usually do my laundry on Sunday nights at a place called the Elite Laundromat. It's close to the restaurant where we had lunch ..."

"Gosh Ronald. That's really exciting. You want me to come up to Shiprock so you can show me the Laundromat? Is that better than watching the trucks unload at the grocery store?"

"Ha ha. Smart Alec. No. Here's the thing about the laundromat. There's a forty-something Native woman who's frequently in there doing her stuff at about the same time on Sunday nights that I'm there. I've never thought much about her, other than to exchange polite 'hellos.' She usually has a nice dog with her that I play with and pet. But last night, we were both folding our clothes at a long counter and I noticed for the first time – are you ready for this? – I noticed she has a wide band tattoo of lizards circling her wrist."

Melissa felt the air leave her lungs. She couldn't have responded even if she had wanted to.

"Melissa? Did you hear me? Are you still there?"

"Sorry. Yes, I'm here. Oh my God. What a coincidence. It doesn't sound real. I only learned about the tattooed girl a month ago. Just a day after I first met you. And then you see a woman who could possibly be her? Like I said, it's hard to believe it's possible."

"Shiprock has a population of only 8,000. Familiar faces frequently pop up."

"Did you say anything to her? About the tattoo, or about me, I mean?"

"No. I was too stunned. I wouldn't have known what to say. But I think I should call Sergeant Descheene and tell him."

"You know what, Ronald? Why don't you hold off on that? How about if I drive up to Shiprock next weekend and go to the laundromat with you on Sunday evening?"

CHAPTER THIRTY-FIVE

Boise, Idaho
January 25, 2021

David O'Hara was already about ten minutes late for a gathering at Jumpin' Janet's Pub, where he planned to meet his buddies from the Class of 2015, Boise High School. He stood in front of the modest white frame house he had grown up in and stared disbelievingly at the flat on the right front tire of his Camaro. Shit. Both the street and the sidewalk were sloppy with wet snow. Did he want to fuss with changing the tire in these conditions? Or should he just call a cab, or even go back in the house and ask to use his Dad's Ford F-150?

But he hadn't seen these guys since Christmas of 2019, just over a year ago. And none of them had ever seen his pride and joy, the metallic blue Camaro. Taking the car would be his opportunity to show those dudes how successful he was. None of them was making the kind of bread that he did as an oil field worker in the Southwest. Jim was probably doing okay as a firefighter, and Roger was certainly making ends meet as the produce manager at Albertsons. But neither of them could touch the hundred grand he had pulled down last year.

They had all known each other since elementary school. They'd shared all the rites of boyhood and adolescence in a small city: Cub Scouts, Boy Scouts, fishing, camping, sand lot baseball, and pickup basketball games. Eventually, they'd even chased skirts and hacked laps around downtown Boise in their souped-up cars with the chromed, twin pipes and resonating mufflers. Three of the guys had left Boise to do military stints after high school. Gone for three or four years each, they had all returned about the time that David was leaving for his job in the oil patch. Two of them had attended the College of Western Idaho for a couple of years. All of them eventually settled into decent jobs in Boise and married hometown girls. All except David, who found the job of an oil field roughneck in the Southwest exciting and rewarding. Single life, with its challenging conquests, also appealed to him. His returns home for a month at a time had become occasions for macho, backslapping reunions with the guys.

He had just bought the Camaro from a used car lot in Farmington two months earlier and had driven it up to Boise on Christmas Eve. Best if he sucked it up and changed the tire, he decided. For him to drive up in the almost new Camaro would blow the socks off the dudes at Jumpin' Janet's.

He popped the trunk and pulled out the scissor jack and lug wrench. He positioned the jack under the frame, then took up the lug wrench and slipped its open socket over the first of the lug nuts. The long straight handle felt firm and reassuring in his hand until a fleck of dried blood on the shank near the socket momentarily unsettled him. The human body was such a fragile vessel. Life could be extinguished easily. Guy Primeau hadn't seen the tire iron as it arced downward and made contact with the back of his neck. He had crumpled quietly, as though kneeling in prayer, before falling flat on his face.

At the slushing sound of tires sluicing through the wet snow behind him, he glanced back. When the vehicle came to a stop immediately to the rear of his car, he was at first curious. Two seconds later, a feeling of dread seized him, when he realized what the black SUV with U.S. Government plates meant for him.

CHAPTER THIRTY-SIX

Shiprock Peak, New Mexico
January 31, 2021

The west face of Shiprock Peak stood dark and brooding in mystic contrast to the colored bands of dawn breaking to the east. To either side of the monolith, a layer of salmon pink bled into a band of gold just above it. Over that, a field of purple rose to star studded blackness. Ronald checked his watch. "We should see the beginning of the sun's corona just there, to the right of the peak, in about five minutes," he said.

"Thanks for bringing me to this spot again," said Melissa. "This mountain has many moods, doesn't it?"

"It's tempting to say, 'Yes, just like a woman.' But that would hardly win me any points with you."

Melissa let that go and merely sipped coffee out of her stainless-steel mug as they watched the meeting of sky and land go slowly through its sunrise metamorphosis. What a show, she thought. Far superior to the alternative of watching the grocery truck unload.

She had driven to Farmington and checked into a hotel the afternoon before and had risen at 5:00 a.m. in order to drive here and meet Ronald in time to see the sunrise. They had no plans for the day other than to show up at the laundromat in the evening. "So, if we don't go to the laundromat until 8:00 o'clock tonight, what shall we do all day after we leave here?"

"I thought we might drive to Farmington, check you out of the hotel, then return to my apartment where you can spend tonight."

Too stunned to speak, Melissa's mouth dropped open. Up until this moment she had considered Ronald the consummate gentleman.

"Oh Jeez, I didn't mean that the way it sounded. Please forgive me." Ronald touched her elbow. "What I mean is ... I mean after your experience on the highway between here and Farmington several weeks ago, maybe you shouldn't drive back after we finish at the laundromat tonight."

"Nice recovery." A rush of air escaped as Melissa relaxed.

"Of course. All I'm suggesting is that you stay at my house tonight, so that you don't have to drive that highway again after dark. I have a nice clean, modern, NHA apartment on the north side of town. You can have the bedroom. I'll sleep on the sofa. I really didn't mean to suggest anything that would create tension."

"What's NHA?"

"Navajo Housing Authority."

"Oh, tell me about that. I've been on the rez for over two months now, and every day I learn something new."

"Sure. The NHA allocates housing to nation members based on their need. I qualified at the time the apartment complex opened. But as a government employee, my income is way above average on this rez, so I'll be asked to move soon. I might just buy a house near Farmington."

"Wow. That would be cool. But ... you know what? I don't know much about your background. I mean, what kind of childhood did you have? Where did you grow up?"

"Well, I was born right here in Shiprock and grew up here. I didn't know my father very well. He and my Mom divorced shortly after I was born. But, like most Navajo women, my mother was a pillar of strength, and wisdom, and passion, right? She brought a sacredness to every space she entered, if you know what I mean. She coached me and my brothers in the ways of our people and taught us right from wrong. I really owe everything I've ever done right to my mother; may she rest in peace. She died of complications of diabetes two years ago."

"Oh, I'm so sorry Ronald."

"It's okay. Her legacy to me is my set of core values. And also, my education. Most of that, as I said, was at the kitchen table with her as the teacher. But she also insisted I enroll at Diné College when I was eighteen. She rode herd on me like a sheep dog until I graduated with an Associates of Arts degree two years later."

"So..." Melissa flashed a grin. "Were you always such a straight arrow?"

"Hmmm. Not really. There were a few years there when I got into all sorts of trouble with my friends Rebecca and Willie. We stole cigarettes and started smoking when we were about eleven."

"What else?"

"We snuck out here one day on our bicycles. We weren't supposed to be here but we came anyway. Just for an adventure. We found this baby in a gym bag."

They both laughed.

"Okay," said Melissa. "Let's go to Farmington and fetch my toothbrush."

•   •   •

Lips pursed, Melissa watched as Ronald loaded two washing machines; one with dark clothing, the other with lighter clothing and bed linens. She was amused. His mother must have taught him the intricacies of doing laundry. Surely a single man would not intuitively know about separating colors from lights. Ronald then started feeding quarters from a zip lock bag into the two washers. He marched purposefully over to a vending machine on a side wall and again extracted quarters from the bag. He fed them into the machine with a practiced hand, pulled a lever and scooped up a mini orange and blue box of Tide from the dispensing chute.

When he had started the two machines, he turned to Melissa. "I forgot to tell you the big attraction of this laundromat. Because they have front-loading machines, we can sit here and watch the clothes tumbling through the windows in front. It's almost as good as television. And no commercials."

A small bell tinkled as the front door swung open. A second later, a medium-sized ball of gray, wiry fur, snuffling and snorting, rushed towards Ronald. Excitingly wagging its club-like tail, the wire-haired terrier danced around Ronald's feet whining and yelping until the woman who had followed the dog through the door commanded harshly, "Warrior. Enough. Stop it."

"It's okay. I think we're old friends."

The woman, wearing Levis and a soiled gray sweatshirt, said curtly, and without making eye contact, "It's not okay. Warrior, over here. Lie down." She picked a machine as far away as possible from the two Ronald was using. Once the dog had settled down, she wordlessly loaded her chosen washer.

Ronald signaled with his eyes for Melissa to glance at the woman. He tapped his wrist.

Melissa noticed the tattoo at once, as the woman extended both arms into the loading port of the washer. She nodded to Ronald. Screening her voice behind the noise of the washers, Melissa whispered to Ronald, "Which car did she drive up in?"

Much to her initial horror, he responded in a voice that could be heard across the room. "Let's go out and have a smoke, Melissa."

Her eyes widened.

Sotto voce, he said, "Outside. Humor me."

Outside, they stepped away from the windows so that the woman would not see that they weren't smoking. There were three cars parked near the laundromat: Ronald's blue jeep, an older model Chevrolet Malibu, paint oxidized to a faded maroon, and a Dodge Caravan. "There," Ronald said, pointing to the Malibu.

"Any way we can find out who owns it?" Melissa asked.

"I can ask Sergeant Descheene to run the plates tomorrow morning. He's not supposed to do that for non-law-enforcement people. But, he might do me a friendly favor."

"Aha. So, you're still not a hundred percent straight arrow." She paused. "But wouldn't he do it officially anyway? He knows about the tattooed wrist. And he's reopened the child abandonment as a cold case."

"Yeah, he'd do it anyway. But he's not supposed to give me the results. Frankly, I don't know if he will."

They went back inside, causing the door-top bell to tinkle again. The woman, now seated in a folding chair, glanced at them from over the top of an old issue of People Magazine. The dog, perked up and started to rise, but the woman slapped him on the snout and said, "Warrior, stay."

Surreptitiously, Melissa drank in every detail of her—the mane of frizzy dark hair, held by a simple red elastic, like one that might encircle a bunch of broccoli or asparagus; the sunshine wrinkles fanning out from the corners of her eyes that might suggest a friendlier demeanor than she had so far shown; and the two, deep parallel lines that ran downward from the corners of her mouth, a sign that she spent as much time frowning as laughing. Slightly stout around the middle when she bent forward to briefly scratch Warrior's ears, as if in apology for her earlier slap on the snout, her legs were nevertheless thin inside the Levis, and she wore well-scuffed leather ankle boots that had seen better days.

The woman had a wide mouth, not so different from her own, Melissa noted—having finished her once-over only to start at the top again—and her jawline still had definition, despite the small pouch of flesh beneath it. Her eyelashes were short, and dark circles below the eyes added to the dour look she wore at the moment. Aside from the mouth, Melissa could see no real resemblance between herself and the woman. But still...

She rubbed damp palms against her thighs. Could this really be her birth mother?

An hour later, Ronald's laundry was dry and folded into a hamper basket. They left the Laundromat quietly, with no further exchange between them and the wide-mouthed woman.

•　•　•

When Melissa awakened at 6:30 the following morning, it took her a few moments to comprehend exactly where she was. The room, reflecting a male's taste in décor – brown striped bedspread, contrasting blue and orange carpet, two prints on the walls depicting cowboy scenes, closet door standing open to reveal an odd assortment of shirts and pants on a mish-mash of wire and wooden hangers – was definitely not her room in the Quality Inn. As though a curtain had been suddenly pulled open, her mind registered her whereabouts – Ronald's bedroom.

She pushed herself out of the bed and caught a glimpse of her reflection in the mirror over the dresser, her eyes rimmed with twin black rings of yesterday's mascara. She padded into the small ensuite bathroom where again her own visage greeted her, this time in glaring resolution under brighter lights than the bedroom. She used the toilet, and then washed her face at the basin, carefully applying light makeup for the day— a bit of color on her lips, and a smudge of blue on the lids of her brown eyes. Satisfied that the bit of color had transformed her out of plainness, she stepped back into the bedroom and listened for sounds that Ronald may have risen from his flop on the living room sofa. She heard no sounds.

For the first time, she noticed a framed certificate on a wall opposite the cowboy prints. The ornate heading on the document read **Great Southwest Council, Boy Scouts of America.** She scanned the rest of the document, which certified that Ronald George had attained the rank of **Eagle Scout** in 1999. He would have been about sixteen at that time. So, he really was a straight arrow.

She stepped over to the single pane slider, opened it and tiptoed onto the small, south-facing wooden deck. The rising sun, somewhere outside her vision, cast its golden morning light over everything she could see. The majestic silhouette of Shiprock Peak dominated the horizon ten miles away, its folds and crenellations visible as shadows in the raggéd, dust colored dome of volcanic rock. She watched as a Golden Eagle worked the thermals, soaring triumphantly through the brilliant azure sky. As she watched, a light breeze ruffled her hair.

Was she at a crucible moment in her life? She had found her biological father, was on the verge of finding her mother and sensed there was some high voltage energy between Ronald and her. The symbolism of the soaring eagle superimposed on the background image of Shiprock Peak in all its morning glory created a surge of animal-like intuition; like that of domestic cattle and sheep that instinctively bunch up and lie down together when weather systems approach. The way songbirds grow quiet then suddenly take flight. The elements had combined, and something was about to change profoundly in her life. She stood still and allowed the warmth of anticipation to creep through her.

A sharp rapping on the bedroom door behind her brought her reflections to a halt. "Melissa, are you up and about?" it was Ronald's resonate baritone. "I've just talked with Sergeant Descheene. I've got some news."

Melissa stepped in from the deck, stood at the bedroom door and said, "Just let me finish dressing. I'll be out in a minute."

Moments later, she stepped into the living room wearing jeans and a turquoise sweatshirt. "So, what's up?"

Ronald was sitting on the cheap sofa, his sleeping bag wadded up into a big ball on the opposite side. As he vigorously stirred a cup of coffee on the low table in front of him, he said, "I talked to Descheene. He goes to work very early. Oh, I don't know where my manners are this morning. You want some coffee? I think I have some yogurt in the fridge too."

"No thanks. I would love a cup of plain hot water." Then as an afterthought, "With a wedge of lemon or lime, if you have any."

"Can do the hot water part. But I don't think I've ever bought a lemon or lime in my entire life."

As he poured hot water from a kettle, he said, "Sergeant Descheene ran the plates. The car belongs to an old guy named Whitebread. He lives in a trailer, about five miles south of town off Highway 491."

"So, where does that leave us?"

"Let's jump in my car and go see Mr. Whitebread. I've got two hours before I have to be at work."

•   •   •

The silver Airstream, sitting well off the highway on a gravel lot surrounded by cacti and desert scrub, had seen better days. It's thirty-feet of curved aluminum sides and roof were dented and had long since lost their shine to become dull and oxidized. A torn blue tarpaulin sagged between the hull and two mismatched metal poles.

Several mongrel dogs lay snugged up against a row of five-gallon water cans, in the shade beneath the trailer. A portable generator sputtered a few feet to the rear of the trailer. The old Malibu, its faded maroon color the only contrast to the drab tableau, sat windows down, off to the side.

The door opened as Ronald and Melissa pulled up in the blue Jeep. "Howdy," said a wizened, toothless caricature as he stepped from the trailer, his silver ponytail bouncing and swaying, held in place with a yellow and orange ribbon.

Ronald gave him a cordial smile and got right to the point. "Good morning Mr. Whitebread. We're wondering if you could tell us who was driving your car last night."

"What for? You're not tribal cops or I'd know you."

"No sir. We're not cops. We saw the woman at the laundromat last night and noticed her tattoo. This is Melissa, who was found as an infant at Shiprock Peak. We think the woman who drove your car may be her mother."

"Heh heh," chuckled the old Native. "That'd be hard to prove. She's had more men pass through her life than an army recruiting depot. Married and divorced at least three times. Got about seven kids too. Two or three of them still living at home. The younger ones – 'bout ten and twelve – pop over here to listen to my stories 'bout twice a week."

"Still, I wonder if you could tell us her name and where she lives, Mr. Whitebread."

"Sure. No problem. Name's Carletta Tso. Lives in one of the only two houses still standing in the failed project just across the highway from here."

As Ronald and Melissa approached the small cubicle, single-story, cinder block house in the jeep, Melissa asked, "What did he mean failed project?"

"Oh, it's quite a story. The Navajo Housing Authority mismanaged a bunch of projects back in the nineties and got in hot water with the feds who'd provided the funds for several hundred houses around the rez. The former Head of the NHA was indicted for allegations he accepted bribes from the contractors. And many of the projects just stopped dead in their tracks."

"So, this was one of them?" Melissa noted the many crumbling foundations laid out in rows, now invaded by desert grasses and mesquite.

"Yup. Ninety-one houses were built here. And only two ever occupied. The rest stood vacant for a few years before they were torn down."

They pulled up to the front of the house and stepped out of the vehicle. Warrior, the wire- haired terrier came around a corner of the house and ran up to Ronald, it's tail wagging pendulously. The woman from the Laundromat, Carletta, appeared in the doorway. "Whatta ya want? Did you walk off with some of my laundry last night?"

"No sister. This is Melissa Cody. Can we talk to you for a few minutes?"

"You're here. Talk." She made no move to invite them in, but did step off the small stoop and onto the gravel driveway.

"May as well get straight to the point," Melissa said. "I believe you're my mother. I was found as an infant behind a rock over there twenty-six years ago." She pointed to the looming hulk of Shiprock peak a few miles to the Southwest.

"No fuckin' way. I got seven kids, mostly grown. And they're all accounted for." Her face was a mask of defiance.

"Does the name Willie Cole mean anything to you? He's my father. You and he dated in 1994. He met you at McDonalds."

Now Carletta's eyes widened for a flash, but then narrowed to horizontal crevices, her brows fixed and firm over the slits. "Get outa here. I don't want nuthin' to do with him. You neither."

Melissa took an involuntary step back and then doubled over as if Carletta had physically kicked her in the stomach. Her eyes filled, and a rush of anger quickly followed. She blinked away the irrational tears. How stupid to respond like this. She didn't know Carletta, and from what she'd seen so far, she had no interest in claiming her and her seven kids as relatives. She had her own parents, thank you very much, kind, good ones, who had saved her from a misbegotten life with this crude, rough woman. Ronald's hand on her arm gently steadied her as she straightened and locked dry eyes with Carletta. "I'm sorry I disturbed you," she said, her voice unnaturally terse. "We'll be off. And I won't bother you again."

CHAPTER THIRTY-SEVEN

Window Rock, Arizona
February 1, 2021

"Willie. It's Melissa. How are you?" It was just past 5:00 p.m. in the East, so Melissa knew he would be through with work at the high school for the day.

"I couldn't be better now that I'm talking to you. What's up with you?"

"I think I may have found my birth mother. Does the name Carletta Tso mean anything to you?"

There was only the briefest of a pause, then, "Carletta. Of course. That was her name. But it wasn't Tso. It was something like Ryebread. No, wait. It was Whitebread."

"Good heavens. I met an old guy named Whitebread yesterday. He lives just across the street from this Carletta. Jesus, probably my grandfather. Anyway we – my friend Ronald and I – briefly met Carletta. She refused to acknowledge that she could be my mother. When I told her your name, she remembered you. It was written all over her face. But she told us to leave. Said she didn't want anything to do with either you or me. I'm sure she's my mother. Do you remember if she had a tattoo?"

"Now that you mention it, yes. Around her wrist. It was a Navajo design. Lizards, I think. Do you think anyone can persuade her to have a DNA test?"

"No way. She made it clear she doesn't want to pursue the question of me being her daughter."

"Oh. I'm so sorry. How are you?"

Melissa tried to keep her voice under control. "My feelings are pretty mixed up about her right now. I want to forgive her for abandoning me. I want to see if we can have a relationship. But I'm very angry and hurt that she doesn't want to acknowledge either me or you."

"If it's what you want, you deserve to have both of us in your life. We all have a lot to catch up on. I'm genuinely sorry Carletta's not open to that. I think she'd be amazed and pleased at what a gem you've turned out to be."

"Oh thanks, Willie."

"Of course. By the way, I've been thinking I'd like to give your adoptive parents a call. Would you object to that?"

"I think they'd love to hear from you. What do you want to talk with them about?"

"I want to thank them for raising you to be such a great person. And I want to assure them that I respect that they are your parents."

"Oh my. You're such a gentleman."

• • •

Lois Cody's smile on the Zoom screen was broad. "Oh Melissa, we've missed you. Our Christmas visit seems a long time ago. We worry about you."

"Hi, Mom. You're right. It seems ages since we've had a long talk. How are you and Dad? You look great. Retirement suits you."

"Yes, we're enjoying our retirement, as much as we can with COVID restrictions limiting our activities. I never considered us to be social butterflies, but I miss my exercise groups and the occasional dinner party. Your Dad, though, has been to a lot of meetings at the golf club. I think maybe the clerk in the pro-shop has a crush on him. He and the other members are eager for the snow to be gone so they can get on the course again. But you must be brimming with news. Where should we start?"

"I hope you have a bit of time because I have so much to tell you." Melissa didn't know where to begin. Some of the details of the last month were unsettling—cases of rape and abduction on the reservation, rides in police cars, witnessing arrests, comforting victims and their mothers. Then there was the handsome and kind mailman, fast becoming a friend, and just having been offered a full-time job at IWN, and the most startling news of all, connecting with her birth parents. She decided to go with the big news first.

"First let me update you on my search for my birth parents. Your blessings gave me the courage to pursue this, even when I had second thoughts, but I went into it a little cavalierly. I hadn't really thought through the implications of ... what if my parents are unsavory, ne'er-do-wells? What if my father was an abuser of women? Also, until I began working at IWN I didn't realize the chasm in the cultures between Natives and Whites. It is one thing to study the culture and quite another to live it."

"Did you find them?" Lois interrupted, unable to help herself.

"I did, Mom. My father is white, a high school vice principal in Elberton, Georgia, very laid back and once over the shock of hearing from me, very interested in pursuing a relationship. He's really a gentleman and plans to give you a call to assure you that he respects your right to call yourselves my mom and dad. My mother is a Native, living outside of Shiprock with three of her children and sometimes a husband and wants nothing to do with me. I don't think I'll be able to communicate with her, even about medical histories. The best news is that she and my dad dated as teenagers and I am the result of young passion. Phew."

It took nearly an hour for Lois to get all of her questions out and for Melissa to answer in detail about the ins and outs of her search. Throughout, she avoided referring to Ronald too often because she knew her mother, or father if he came in from the golf club, would want to know how Melissa felt about him, and she really didn't know.

The story of the rapes of Julie and Beth, Beth's abduction and imprisonment, the murder of Guy Primeau, the police work, the rescue of Beth and Julie was a long story indeed. Lois had many curious and compassionate questions. The fact that her daughter had witnessed these grim realities left her heartsick.

In a painful silence Melissa whispered, "Oh Mom, I don't want to overwhelm you. When I tell you these things in a rush, it sounds horrific, but I'm fine and I've been able to absorb and learn so much about Navajo culture, the greed of men, both white and brown, and I've also learned a ton about myself. Let's talk about some good news."

"How can there be good news? This is all so overwhelming. It is not easy hearing about the gross injustices that occur in our own country. As a woman, as a mother, your mother, hearing that you are in the thick of things makes my fingers tingle. I want to lash out, I want to come right up there and throttle someone."

"Maybe you won't hear this as good news then, but I'm sure excited. IWN has offered me a full-time permanent job!"

"Remind me, what does IWN stand for?"

"Indigenous Women's Network of Arizona and New Mexico, the group I'm working with now. Some grant funds have come through and Bernie, my boss, would like me to stay on. I'm thrilled that she feels I've been making a contribution and can perhaps grow into the position of counselor. She's applying for more funds so that I can take a course in counseling psychology." Melissa hadn't realized, until she started describing this opportunity, how much she was looking forward to the challenge. A new career, with purpose, one that embraced her newfound status as half Navajo. She watched her mother's face wince with pain, her stare at the computer screen slowly crumbling.

"Oh Mom, please don't cry!"

"It's a lot to take in Dear. I'm happy to hear the excitement in your voice. Maybe you've found your "calling." And finding your birth parents must be a relief. But the danger for women on the reservation makes my heart race and the heartache of working with victimized and injured women makes me weep."

"I know. Part of me is terrified, but I've given this a lot of thought and I can't deny that the opportunity to support women really strikes a chord with me. I'll have to come home and sort through my stuff and get organized about furnishing my own place....no more hotel thank god. I'm sure that Bernie'll give me some time off. We can sit and have tea and go for long hikes. We'll talk.

"In the meantime, though, and this is a different subject, can you send me the old scrapbook I put together during the summer between high school and university? I think it's gathering dust in a box in your attic."

"I'll ask your Dad to find it. Why do you want it? Are you bringing it up to date?"

"Maybe. I thought if I get a chance to meet my birth dad face to face, after Covid, he'll probably be thrilled to see all the pictures and mementos of my childhood."

"Good thought. We'll get it off to you."

Just as she was preparing to leave the IWN office for the day, Melissa's cell phone sounded with its ubiquitous marimba tone.

"Melissa, it's Wendy Burkenshaw, your favorite FBI agent."

"Sounds like you're in your car. Where are you?"

"Just passed Yah-Ta-Hey, on my way to Window Rock, so about twenty minutes away. I need to talk with you. You wanna grab an early supper at the Diné Restaurant in the Quality Inn tonight?"

"Sure. It'll be fun to get caught up. I can tell you how Beth's doing. She's still in the hospital, but she should be released in a day or two."

"I'd like to hear about that, but the purpose for the visit is official. I need to talk to you about your birth mother."

"Oh. Okay. Word gets around fast."

Only three tables at the Diné Restaurant were occupied. Melissa and Wendy sat at a window table from which they had a commanding view of the near-empty parking lot, the highway and the open desert. In the late afternoon light, long shadows made the desert look like abstract art, a canvas blotched in black and brown.

Wendy opened a file folder as they waited for their entrees. "The Navajo Nation Police, specifically a Sergeant Descheene in the Shiprock District, has handed the case of your suspected birth mother, a Carletta Tso, to the FBI. It's my job to investigate. To see if there's sufficient evidence to prosecute her for aggravated child endangerment. How do you feel about that?"

"I have mixed feelings. I've seen her and spoken briefly with her. She refuses to acknowledge our biological connection. Says she doesn't want anything to do with me.

That hurts and angers me. On the other hand, I hold out hope that, somehow, I might get to know her and vice versa."

"We have enough circumstantial evidence to make a recommendation to the US Attorney for the District of New Mexico now. There's the tattoo and the yellowing piece of paper describing the girl —the one who had the tattoo who visited you in the nursery for a few days after you were born. And there's your birth dad's assertion that he dated a Native girl named

Carletta Whitebread, who had a lizard tattoo, and was intimate with her at about the time that you would have been conceived. The clincher would be ..."

"Wait a minute, Wendy. How did you know, or how did the FBI know, about my birth father?"

In a teasing tone, Wendy said, "We're the FBI." She skipped a beat and then added, "You may also recall that you spoke to him on the phone from our command post while I was busy sorting out Beth Chee's evacuation from the wrecked pickup truck. That's when you learned of his DNA test and that he's your father. You told me all of that when I got back to the CP. You were really excited and needed to tell someone. You told me his name too. Willie Cole of Elberton, Georgia."

"And you've spoken to him?"

"About an hour and a half ago. He's thrilled that you two have found each other. I asked him if he'd mind being deposed as a material witness, if your birth mother is prosecuted. His response was a qualified yes. He'll only give a deposition if it's what you want. He'll definitely act only in your best interests." Wendy paused to let that sink in. "Melissa, I'm here to ask you if you want to make an official complaint against your probable biological mother, Ms. Carletta Tso. You don't have to decide right now. I'm on my way up to Shiprock tomorrow morning. You can call me with your decision."

"I'm really confused. Like I said, I'm angry and hurt, but I'd like to leave a chance that we can get to know each other. I'm too emotional to make that decision right now. But I think what I'd like is for she and I, my mother and I, to participate in a traditional Navajo Restorative Justice session. I don't think she'd voluntarily do that. But that's probably the best shot at a satisfactory outcome."

Wendy reached across the table and patted Melissa's hand. "Take your time. If you decide that's what you'd like, I'll discuss it with the US Attorney and recommend he coordinate with the Navajo Nation Judiciary for that to happen. I'm pretty sure, if they're convinced it's in everyone's best interest, they can compel it."

CHAPTER THIRTY-EIGHT

Shiprock, New Mexico
March 15, 2021

Melissa's throat was dry as she entered the meeting room in the Shiprock Chapter House. She was sweating lightly and could almost hear the accelerated beat of her pulse. She had studied Native Restorative Justice at the University of New Mexico, and although she was familiar with the theory and the constructs, and had read case studies of *Peacemaking*, as the Navajos called it, she had never seen or experienced a session, other than in a moot session in one of her seminars. While the process was taken seriously, most of the student participants had seen the actual role-play as kind of a lark.

This, however, was the real thing. The circle of empty chairs, spaced well apart for social distancing in the center of the room, intimidated her. Her understanding of the Navajo tradition of *talking things out* or *story-telling*, as a non-judicial means of dispute resolution had seemed non-threatening when she learned about it at UNM. But now, about to participate in the process, as ordered by District Court 5 of the Navajo Judicial Branch, Melissa could barely swallow over the lump in her throat.

About ten people milled about the room, helping themselves to coffee on a side bar as they made light conversation and awaited the start of the process. Everyone seemed to be studiously avoiding taking their places in the circle of chairs. Melissa made directly for the only two people she knew apart from Carletta Tso and her father, Mr. Whitebread.

Ronald George and Bernie Begay had apparently introduced themselves to each other and stood bantering at one of the windows when Melissa stepped up and said, "I'm glad you could both come. I'm going to need lots of moral support."

They'd only had time to say a brief hello when a middle-aged Navajo woman, smartly attired in a black dress with a wide silver and turquoise belt, stepped into the center of the circle of chairs. "Will everyone please take a seat? Just pick any of the chairs. We have no particular order or seating protocol."

A minute of shuffling and bumbling about occurred, and then, when everyone had settled into the chairs, the well-dressed woman, now also seated in a chair nearest the windows, took off her mask. She smiled graciously and said, "Welcome everyone. Some of you know me, I'm Susan Redfeather-Newman. I'm a *naat aanii*, or peacemaker in English, with the Peacemaker Division of the Navajo Nation Judiciary Branch. That means I act as a facilitator for group sessions such as this one. In just a few minutes, I'll start by explaining the process to you. But first, it is good that both the disputants have friends and relatives here. Their support and also their stories, as we hear from them as well as the disputants, is an important part of this process. So, let's just go around the circle and briefly introduce ourselves. Feel free to remove your mask while speaking, but let's the rest of us remain masked. Can we start with you, Melissa?"

Melissa swallowed hard, and then she removed her mask and cleared her throat. "My name is Melissa Cody and I'm pretty nervous about this process." Her voice was sturdy but slightly tremulous. She went on to briefly describe the circumstances of her being found as an infant, her childhood in Santa Fe and her UNM experience. "Since age ten or so, I've sought to know who my birth parents are. Recently I located my birth father and have established a warm relationship with him." She paused. She felt as if she had left the room and was spinning backward over the years. She wore a stoical grin-and-bear-it smile, but an expression of deep misery overlaid that effort. "I found my birth mother about a month and a half ago." She looked directly at Carletta Tso, who scowled into her own lap. "Regrettably, she won't accept that fact and doesn't want anything to do with me." She looked toward Susan, the peacemaker, and nodded to signify that she was finished.

"And what is your desired outcome from this process?" Susan Redfeather-Newman asked.

Another long moment of silence ensued as Melissa considered the question. The other people in the circle of chairs remained still and voiceless. Then, her voice low, she said, "I want Carletta to acknowledge that we are mother and daughter. Beyond that I would like she and I to get to know each other."

Across the circle, directly across from Melissa, Carletta Tso looked up from her lap briefly to stare at Melissa then dropped her gaze again.

It took less than ten minutes for the remainder of the self-introductions to be made. Each person spoke briefly, stating only their names, where they lived and in some cases which of the disputants they supported.

Susan then said, "Okay, this is the way this works. We're going to open with a prayer. We can pray either to traditional Navajo deities or to a Christian god. By praying, we are summoning the gods to take part in our process and to help with the outcome. If you'd prefer a more secular view, it also helps participants to focus their perceptions and attitudes and to commit to the process.

The next stage is talking things out. We'll start there by asking Melissa, whom in authorizing this process the court views as the victim, to share her story ... her perceptions, her views and, very importantly, her feelings. Then Carletta can respond, sharing her perceptions and feelings as well. Anyone can speak after that, but only one person at a time. The idea is to continue sharing perceptions, interpretations and feelings in an attempt to find aspects of the situation on which we can all agree. Eventually we'll reach the final phase, which is 'reconciliation.' Everyone will have vented their feelings, talked out the problem and relationships, and with my guidance, should reach consensus as to how to resolve the problem. The primary element of consensus is about relationships – where people stand, particularly the two disputants, with each other at the end of the process. In the event we cannot reach consensus, the case can revert to the adjudication process in federal court and Ms. Tso would be the defendant in a felony case. But let's all pray for a consensual resolution here in this circle."

After the prayer, which Susan said in both Navajo and English, she recognized Melissa as the first speaker. "Please tell us your story and let us know your feelings, Melissa."

Melissa's eyebrows bent as if in surprise. She gazed at the floor between her feet for a moment, then raised her head and began speaking. "As a day-old infant, I was found abandoned in a sports bag at the foot of

Shiprock Peak. If you look out the window behind Susan, you can see it. When I look at it now, I have mixed feelings. I feel like that mountain gave me life ... but it could have given me death. I was found by three ten and eleven-year-old kids. They took me to the hospital. One of them, Ronald George, is here today." She looked to her right and gave Ronald a slight smile.

Melissa reached under her chair and lifted a brown leather photo album. "This is a scrapbook I kept as a child. I recently updated it with some pictures and mementos of the last few years. I'd like to ask Carletta to thumb through this scrapbook as I describe the milestones and highlights of my life. I hope she will see who I was in my formative years. And who I've become as an adult." Melissa glanced at Susan, who nodded.

Carletta accepted the scrapbook and laid it in her lap. She hesitated to open it until Melissa again spoke.

A cool prickle ran across the back of Melissa's neck as she began describing her life. She started with her first conscious memory, that of cowering in the corner of her tiny alcove bedroom, in the doublewide trailer, crying herself to sleep as her foster parents quarreled loudly and drunkenly in the kitchen. She went on to her happy childhood with the Cody's, hitting the highlights of birthday parties, school, sports and family activities, asking Carletta to turn pages and look at the pictures as she described the events.

As she spoke, Melissa's gaze moved around the circle, trying to make eye contact with each person in the room. She noted that Carletta's head stayed down most of the time, staring at the scrapbook with an intensity that suggested she was captivated by the pictures, newspaper clippings and mementos.

She continued with an account of her teen years; her first date, her sports achievements, her prom attendance, referring to pictures and items like award certificates and dance cards in the scrapbook. She interjected her childhood curiosity and concern over who her birth parents were into the chronology of growing up. "Many times during those periods of questioning and reflecting about my heredity, I shut down emotionally. The place in my heart that felt things like love seemed to die. It just quit feeling." She paused, a dark thought passing like a shadow across her face.

"But by the time I entered UNM at age eighteen, the brooding had subsided. Don't get me wrong here. I was no less concerned about who my parents were and how much I had inherited from their genetic history. I just learned to be reasonable, grateful for my good fortune and reasoned that I was strong enough to handle anything. But I wanted to learn where I belonged. Who my people were, who my clan was. I wish no harm to Carletta."

After about twenty minutes, when Melissa finished her story with the discovery of her birth father and their growing relationship, and the joy they had shared on the phone and during Zoom conversations, Carletta looked up from the album for the first time. Her eyes were wet, her face streaked with tears.

Susan allowed the silence to settle on the room for a few minutes. Melissa watched the non-verbal behavior of the others in the room and realized that Susan was deliberately using silence as a tool. Everyone squirmed in the uncomfortable void. Finally, after three full minutes, Susan said, "Carletta, would you like to respond before anyone else speaks?"

Carletta remained silent for a few moments as she searched for ways to put words to her feelings. Finally, she mumbled, "Yes I am your birth mother and I am truly sorry for how your life started." She paused to dab at her eyes with a facial tissue. Her voice became a little stronger. "When Willie left Farmington, I think I was in such denial about everything that I truly believed I wasn't pregnant until the morning I went into labor. It was the scariest thing to go through ... not knowin' what's going on and being all alone. My parents was both out of the trailer we lived in. And they didn't know I was pregnant." She glanced at Mr. Whitebread, then at Melissa. "I remember having you and cleaning you up and dressing you so you wouldn't be cold. I went to the bathroom and cleaned myself up and the mess and came back and laid on the bed with you crying, shaking. I didn't know what to do.

"My Mom called me and told me to go pick up my little brother from school and I panicked. I put you in a sports bag and ran out to my Dad's pickup truck. I don't remember much of anything else that day. I remember driving and then the next thing I remember is waking up and being in my bed at home. I don't know if I was in shock or I just blacked out. I really don't remember anything after getting into the truck."

Carletta plucked another tissue from a box, swiped at her face then sobbed, "I really didn't mean to hurt you. I'm truly sorry. I'm not a horrible person."

Another long silence fell over the room, until Susan suggested a short break.

After the stretch break, Susan asked each of the other participants to speak. "Now is the chance for you to tell your stories relative to Melissa and Carletta and to share your feelings, not only about the two of them, but about the matter we're here to deal with. Let's see if we can find some common ground."

It took nearly two hours for the stories to emerge, emotional and heartfelt accounts of the qualities possessed by the two disputants. Some were, not surprisingly, polarized, but a surprising number were focussed on the tragedy of what had passed between Melissa and Carletta. Several boxes of tissues made their way around the circle of chairs as the accounts unfolded.

Susan allowed another period of silence to grip the room after everyone had spoken. Finally, she said, softly, "Are there any common themes here?"

Ronald George waggled a finger. "Yes. I think the dominant theme is the heartbreak and sorrow, felt by most of us, that these two women – mother and daughter – have missed so much by living their lives apart."

"Anyone else feel that way?" Susan asked.

There were several nods and even grizzled old Mr. Whitebread had wet and rheumy eyes.

The room grew quiet again, until Carletta Tso raised her teary face and said, "Can we find some way for Melissa and me to move forward in a way that makes us both happy?"

EPILOGUE

Window Rock, Arizona
March 20, 2021

Bernie could not resist. She glanced out her kitchen window to check up on the girls. Not one of them would be happy to be called "the girls," especially Melissa, who was almost 27, but they were young and Bernie knew that she did tend to mother them. Tonight, they sat not fifty feet away from her in the backyard, huddled around the homemade fire pit, wrapped in blankets, She could see their slim forms, so small against the dark margins of a diamond studded sky. Beth's skinny shoulders poked mounds in her sweatshirt. She was able to eat a full meal now, but it had been painfully slow watching her struggle with fresh fruits and vegetables after her incarceration in the trailer.

Would any of them ever feel safe again? Melissa chased and harassed on the road from Shiprock to Farmington, Julie raped, Beth raped and imprisoned. Bernie knew that perps would not come into her backyard, but ugly memories still haunted her, as she knew they did her three young charges. She was a bear sow guarding her cubs.

Bernie looked down at the few dishes resting in her sink and automatically rinsed them as she stared out at the three figures bent by the fire. It had been almost 20 years since she joined IWN, but until her own daughter Julie had disappeared, she had not really appreciated the depth of the pain that so many women had suffered. Would Melissa relate any better? Probably not; she had not been raped, she had no daughter she loved more than life itself, who had been violated. Still, there was something special about Melissa. She was clearly on a journey to embrace her Native self. Bernie had sensed it, and actually seen it, during Beth's Healing Way ritual.

Beth had been found dehydrated, malnourished, thin, weak and anxious after her ordeal in the container. She had been taken to hospital and released a week after her admission. True healing had begun when she moved in with Bernie and Julie. Everyone – the medical staff, Beth's mother, Beth herself, Julie and Bernie – all agreed that a stable environment, regular meals and constant companionship would be better than her living on her own while her mother worked in Gallup. Slowly Beth's skinny limbs rounded with flesh. Water, cup after cup of tea, and hearty breakfast smoothies brought color to her cheeks.

Deep healing began in the circle. Many women had gathered at the Saint Michaels Chapter House, three miles west of Window Rock, for the ceremony. Women dressed for comfort, wearing everything from blue jeans and sweatshirts to long skirts and sweaters. Older women wore traditional clothing of flowing skirts and embroidered shawls and colorful strands of beads. They had travelled by bus to the chapter house, where outside, under the skies, the rituals were believed to be more powerful, enticing the spirits and wafting the women's prayers and chants to the open sky.

When darkness fell on the group seated outside, and the smudge of sage, cedar and sweet grass permeated the air and cleansed the participants, and the resonance of their chanting rose into the sky and reached the spirits, with her voice above the others, Beth wailed, *"Asdzáá Naadleehi, hear my voice, feel my pain."*

Melissa, seated next to Beth, had grasped her hand and into it placed a single turquoise stone, thought by the Navajo to represent spirit communication, healing and good fortune. At the same moment she spoke into Beth's ear, *"Shideezi, ayóó' áníínishní."*

Bernie again looked out the window to the fire where the three young women now sat in the gathering darkness. Bernie opened the window a crack and heard them chanting, Melissa's voice above the others, not unlike a diva performing an aria backed up by the chorus. During Beth's *Healing Way* when Melissa had uttered *"Shideezi, ayóó' áníínishní"*, the words had not gone unnoticed by Bernie. "Little Sister, I love you." Melissa had proven that she had begun to understand the deep meaning and nuances of *K'é* and the Navajo ways.

ABOUT THE WRITING OF SHIPROCK BABY:

An interview between the author and Lydia Dean, author and founding director of Go Philanthropic Foundation.

Lydia Dean is a successful business woman and an inveterate global traveler with an intense focus on areas lacking access to education and opportunity. Motivated by the simple ideal that small personal actions can make a difference, she launched Go Philanthropic Travel – a social enterprise that engages travelers with the lesser-known humanitarians of the world. In 2011 she co-founded Go Philanthropic Foundation and in 2015 she published "Jumping the Picket Fence," an inspirational mixture of travel memoir, soul searching, and non-profit building. Her latest book, "Light through the Cracks," released in 2021, explores how personal healing directly relates to one's ability to make a difference in the world at large. Lydia currently resides in Provence, France. She conducted the following interview with R. Bruce Logan in June of 2021.

Lydia - I think I understand why you chose the issue of Missing and Murdered Indigenous Women for this story. You've established a pattern of writing novels that not only entertain, but promote awareness of social problems, and the MMIW issue is very topical. But how did you come up with the subplot of Melissa trying to find her birth parents?

Bruce - I can't take credit for this being an original idea. In early 2020, I saw an article in the Victoria Times Columnist, a daily in Victoria BC, Canada, which detailed the saga of a thirty-two-year-old woman who, as an infant, was found in a ditch. She eventually found both parents through Ancestry.com and ended up having a good relationship with her father, but her mother was in denial. I found the article compelling, and I thought it would make a good subplot for my next novel.

Lydia - You had a long career as a U.S. Army officer, including two years in combat in Vietnam and three years in Germany during the perilous years of the Cold War. In retirement, you started doing humanitarian work to assist marginalized people. To some, these are contrasting focuses. What motivated you to get involved in education and human rights in marginalized regions and subsequently to write novels highlighting problems like human trafficking and violence against women?

Bruce - It's true that as a soldier, and particularly during my combat experience in Vietnam, I was not very sensitive to the needs or plights of unfortunate souls. I was too busy trying to project the image of a hard-as-nails professional soldier, hell bent on achieving the mission. But when, in my early sixties, I went back to Vietnam on a tour of reconciliation, I saw the Vietnamese people as human beings for the first time. I was tremendously moved by their love of family, their culture, their work ethic and their welcoming nature. But both my wife, Elaine, and I were also moved by the rampant poverty and social problems in the countryside of rural Vietnam. We determined we had skills that could be useful to some of the NGO's working to improve lives in Vietnam and we became involved, returning to live and work in Vietnam for two or three months a year. I discovered that I had a soft side, and frankly, I like myself a lot better for that soft side. I was particularly disturbed by what I had learned about child trafficking and decided I wanted to add my voice to the outcry by writing. That started me on the path of creating fictional accounts of human suffering.

Lydia - Your previous novels focus on child trafficking and the real danger to young girls and women in SE Asia and Mexico. What influenced you to now write about the North American issue of MMIW?

Bruce - As you know, Lydia, I serve on the Board of Directors of the Go Philanthropic Foundation, a small NGO with a global reach. During its ten-year history, Go Phil has focused on education, health care and human rights in Asia, South America and Africa. Recently, the leadership of this organization has embarked on an exploration of how it might get involved in community-based philanthropy closer to home, in North America. They are beginning by educating themselves before taking any steps. This inspired me to take a look at problems among indigenous people of North America and the MMIW issue jumped out, as did life on the Navajo Reservation.

Lydia - In your novels, there is usually a strong emphasis on the work of the networks and individuals, especially police organizations, that work to rescue women and improve their protection. Details of police interventions are meticulously portrayed. Why the concentrated descriptions of police work?

Bruce - Good question. I think there are two reasons. First, in some respects the military and police agencies have much in common. My long experience in the military has spawned a familiarity and interest with the way both military and law enforcement operations are planned and executed. Secondly, police procedures and jargon are very easy, and to me, fun to research.

Lydia - I'm going to embark on a tough question, Bruce. Can you share how you came to write from a female voice and one, that some might argue, you could not truly understand or represent being a white male? And how do you write from a perspective and voice that is not your own?

Bruce - Obviously, as an older male, it's difficult to really convey the feelings and emotions that might be experienced by a young woman. And as a white person, hard to identify with the norms of Native Americans. To be really honest, my wife Elaine is my first reader and often takes it upon herself to rewrite some passages and chapters to work in some feminine authenticity and female emotions. But with respect to *Native American* females, I confess to being on thin ice here. Despite exhaustive research, I may have missed some important nuances or misrepresented some important aspects of Navajo life.

I would add, however, that I have deep and personal experience with feeling the pain of a daughter whose life went off the rails, was in great personal danger, and was exploited, a good part of her young adulthood.

Five years ago, I lost my youngest daughter to the unholy trinity of substance abuse, homelessness and mental illness. Only one who's suffered a similar loss can really know the depth of emotional pain that is visited upon someone going through that process. For this reason, I feel that I am sensitive to the plight of young women who are troubled and/or exploited.

Lydia – What do you think the potential benefits or pitfalls might be that could come from embarking on this courageous / risky journey of writing from this perspective?

Bruce –The principal benefit is that I am adding my voice to the chorus of people horrified by the scourge of MMIW. I think the main pitfall is that I may not have represented the issue as well as a Navajo woman might. However, having been unsuccessful at finding a female Navajo with whom I could collaborate on this book, I opted to risk that criticism in order to shine another light on the dark world of MMIW.

Lydia - Tell me about your writing "habits." Are you an early morning, disciplined-for-three-hours kind of writer or a middle-of-the-night-scotch-in-hand writer?

Bruce - There is no pattern to when, or how, I sit down to write. When I'm working on a novel, I probably average ten or twelve hours per week of actual writing, and that can be at any time of the day or night. I suffer from insomnia from about 1:00 to 4:00 in the morning and often that is when I attempt to create narrative. Writers are often characterized as either "plotters" or "plodders." I probably lean more toward the plodding side. When I start a novel, I know what the defining incident is and roughly how I want the novel to end. So, I usually start with an idea of what "Act I "and "Act III" will look like. Then I make up "Act II," the middle, as I go along. But I'm always conscious of the need to have a narrative arc wherein each scene and chapter do something to move the story along.

Lydia - What is the most challenging part of getting the words down on paper for you?

Bruce - I think it would be taking an idea for a scene, event or incident and crafting it in such a way that the reader can picture it in his or her mind. I want to transport my readers into a space where they feel like they are part of the scene or can relate to one or more of the characters. The challenge for me then is adhering to the axiom "show don't tell."

Lydia- I hope that "Shiprock Baby" finds its way into many readers' hands, Bruce, and that we will find a way, through Go Philanthropic, and other organizations devoted to social justice, to become more than witnesses to the issue of MMIW.

ACKNOWLEDGEMENTS:

Writing a novel is a formidable task. One which requires understanding of the craft of fiction writing, a fluid imagination, meticulous research, fact verification and, above all else, advice and ideas from others.

Among the people who have contributed to the form and substance of this novel are:

- My wife, **Elaine Head**, who is always my first reader, confidante and constructive critic.
- **Pearl Luke**, my content editor, who advises me on narrative construction, plot and story line flow.
- **Dr. Karl Nicholas,** who served as my medical jargon policeman and helped me ensure the accuracy and credibility of clinical language.
- **Michele Belanger-McNair,** a fellow frequent traveler to Vietnam and semi-retired attorney, who contributed materially to those portions of the narrative that describe criminal prosecutorial and judicial proceedings.
- **Bruce Eggertson,** a retired petroleum geologist, who assisted me with language and descriptions of oil field work.
- **Matt Payne,** of Matt Payne Photography who generously gave me permission to use his stunning photo of Shiprock Peak on the cover.
- **Ken Harris,** a retired FBI agent who was kind enough to read the manuscript and comment on the authenticity of the FBI scenes.
- **Dave King,** of Black Rose Writing, who designed the layout and the cover, using Matt's photo.
- The following persons who served as **beta readers,** and waded through the manuscript in installments, offering constructive suggestions:

Debby Bardavid, a retired social worker.

Linda DeWolf, humanitarian and philanthropist, co-founder of Go Philanthropic Foundation.

Irene Frances Olson, author of two successful novels.

The above listed folks constitute, in my mind, a community of people who are passionate about social issues, who admire good writing, and love turning the pages of a suspenseful read. My profound gratitude to all of you for participating in this project.

Other books by R. Bruce Logan:

- **Back to Vietnam: Tours of the Heart,** 2013
- **Finding Lien,** 2016
- **As the Lotus Blooms,** 2018
- **The Road from Tenancingo,** 2020

Check out my website at: www.rbrucelogan.com

ABOUT THE AUTHOR

R. Bruce Logan has retired from two satisfying careers. He was a U.S. Army officer for twenty-five years and a management consultant for twenty years. He has devoted his retirement years to humanitarian work and philanthropy, largely in Southeast Asia. He proudly serves on the board of directors of GoPhilanthropic Foundation, a small humanitarian NGO with a global reach. In 2012, he and his wife, Elaine, wrote the memoir, *Back to Vietnam: Tours of the Heart.* He has subsequently written four novels dealing with social problems; *Finding Lien, As The Lotus Blooms, The Road From Tenancingo*, and this one. When not traveling, Bruce and Elaine live on Salt Spring Island in British Columbia.

NOTE FROM THE AUTHOR

Word-of-mouth is crucial for any author to succeed. If you enjoyed *Shiprock Baby*, please leave a review online—anywhere you are able. Even if it's just a sentence or two. It would make all the difference and would be very much appreciated.

Thanks!
R. Bruce Logan

We hope you enjoyed reading this title from:

BLACK ROSE
writing™

www.blackrosewriting.com

Subscribe to our mailing list – *The Rosevine* – and receive **FREE** books, daily deals, and stay current with news about upcoming releases and our hottest authors. Scan the QR code below to sign up.

Already a subscriber? Please accept a sincere thank you for being a fan of Black Rose Writing authors.

View other Black Rose Writing titles at www.blackrosewriting.com/books and use promo code **PRINT** to receive a **20% discount** when purchasing.

www.ingramcontent.com/pod-product-compliance
Lightning Source LLC
Chambersburg PA
CBHW010735100726

47899CB00009B/3064